CLAIMING THE WARDENS

DIA COLE

SUMMARY

They imprisoned me. They tormented me. Now they need me to save them...

I don't know what strange compulsion made me stalk the halls of the Elemental Academy until I found the handsome warlock. All I knew is I'd die if I didn't taste him. I never meant to steal his power. I never meant to nearly kill him.

For my crime, I'm sentenced to eternal life in the darkest pit of the Lost Soul's Penitentiary. Or at least I was until the warlock interrupts my stasis. He's a warden now and he wants me to pay for destroying his life. He's enlisted the help of the other wardens and together they torment my days with pain and my nights with pleasure.

They promise to stop my punishment if I return what I stole, but how can I when I don't understand how to wield my deadly power?

Just when I've resigned myself to this nightmarish fate, the magical wards protecting the prison fail. Suddenly, the wardens need me to save them.

Turnabout is a fair play and, after what they've put me through, the price for my help will be nothing less than their bodies and souls...

For my miracles...

❦ I ❦

SYDNEY

"**S**yd, why is the temple always so freaking cold? My balls are turning into ice cubes over here." The handsome blond warlock shifted closer to me on the hard, stone pew.

My choked laugh drew the attention of the frizzy-haired witch seated in front of us.

Andrea spun around and glared at me. "Hush, freak."

I flinched at the vitriol in my roommate's tone. I wish I knew why she, and all the other students, disliked me so much. Maybe it was my purple hair and eyes so different from all the other students at the academy. Or maybe it was the ragged hand-me-down uniforms I wore. There really wasn't much I could do about that though. Being abandoned at birth left me dependent on the charity of the academy—the only home I'd ever known.

Jasen pushed his shaggy blond hair out of his face and gave Andrea the finger. "Lick my snowballs, fugly."

Andrea's over plucked eyebrows came together as she eyed Jasen the same way she might an exotic bird that had just crapped on her face. She, like the rest of the students, didn't quite know what to make of the half-human warlock.

Unlike her, I'd spent enough time with my cocky jokester of a best friend to know he'd just insulted her.

"Apologize," I whispered into his ear.

He gave me a sour look, which earned him my elbow in his six-pack abs. "Ugh. Okay." He turned back to the witch and gave her a dazzling smile. "Sorry. Now if I throw a stick will you leave?"

Andrea, who was a twelfth year like us, stared at Jasen with a slack-jawed expression. Her gaze traveled from his stunning blue-rimmed irises, to the cleft in his firm square jaw still visible under his scruffy facial hair, and then back to his sensuous lips. "I'll do anything you want."

Jealousy jackknifed through me, but I immediately slapped it away. Jasen was my friend and despite the forbidden feelings I'd developed for him, he could be nothing more.

As Jasen and Andrea bantered back and forth, I turned my attention to our surroundings.

The academy temple, like all elemental temples, looked like an underground, dome-shaped amphitheater. The rows of tiered pews circled an arena-like space containing a long stone altar. On the floor next to the altar was a massive five-point pentagram with incandescent energy swirling in the center. That glowing pool of energy was the portal to the hidden realms and the font of our power.

The academy professors, dressed in formal brown robes, sat in gilded chairs behind the portal along with several distinguished members of the Arcane Assembly who had traveled through the portal to assess students today.

My palms grew sweaty at the thought of being tested in front of the most powerful members of our kind. To ease my growing anxiety, I focused on the four-foot-tall stone pedestals fixed at each point on the pentagram.

Four of the pedestals contained affinity symbols. There was the candle with the ever-burning flame. A dish containing water that rippled hypnotically. A mound of rich soil out of which grew flowers. And a wind chime tethered to a wood frame that continuously tinkled a pleasing glissando.

Although each symbol was enchanting in their own way, my attention was drawn to the empty pedestal sitting at the highest point of the pentagram. The runes on that charred pedestal had been chipped and burned away beyond all recognition giving no clue as to what affinity symbol it might have once held.

Why do we set out five pedestals when we only recognized four elements? It was a question my caregiver, the closest thing I'd ever had to a mother, couldn't or wouldn't answer for me.

My gaze sought out Novah's round, softly lined face among the academy faculty.

She was seated in the back with the other caregivers dressed in their light pink robes. I tried to catch her null-brown eyes, but her attention was focused on the altar where the headmistress, a tall, thin, silver-haired witch, was testing a student.

Poor Shiloh. The short, dark-haired student held her trembling hand over the four egg-sized testing stones on the altar. Fat tears rolled down her cheeks as the testing stones remained dormant.

My heart ached for her. I knew from experience how devastating it was not to have developed an elemental affinity. Being forced to demonstrate that lack of power in front of everyone only added insult to injury.

"Null," the headmistress announced in a frosty voice.

Shiloh let out a muffled sob.

The headmistress's pale, blue-rimmed eyes narrowed. "Go

sit with them." She motioned the witch to join the handful of other nulls seated on a pew closest to the altar.

They, like me, would be formally given their assignments after the testing ceremony was over. There was no need to waste the valuable time of the Assembly deciding our insignificant fates.

I bit back a sad sigh.

Ever sensitive to my mood, Jasen twined his fingers through mine. "Are you okay, Violet Eyes?"

Hearing his nickname for me always made me smile. "Of course." *How can I be sad when he's by my side?*

"Jasen Carlow," the headmistress called out, twisting an invisible knife into my stomach.

No! I wanted to hold him next to me, but that was impossible.

"My turn to touch the rocks," Jasen said with his signature grin. Even though his demeanor was laid-back, I could tell he was nervous.

I squeezed his hand. "You'll get the best assignment."

"I won't go anywhere without you," he promised, bringing my hand to his mouth.

The feeling of his soft lips on my knuckles sent shock waves through me. How I longed to reach up and bring his mouth down on mine, but I didn't dare. It was forbidden as I was sworn to another. Besides, Jasen's words, although sweet, were just words.

He will leave.

I will stay.

The headmistress already informed me I'd be assigned to care for the orphaned nurslings at the academy. I hadn't told Jasen yet because I didn't want his sorrow added to my own.

My chest tightened as I watched him move to the end of the pew. He had to stop a few times and slap the hands of other students wanting to preemptively congratulate him.

When he'd arrived two years ago, he'd taught us all to high five. His knowledge of all things human combined with his wisecracking nature made him one of the most popular students at the academy.

It was a mystery that he spent all his time with me, the school pariah. Maybe it was because he'd transferred into the academy late—long after the other students had shunned me. Or maybe it was because he'd been raised among humans and his tolerance for strange and unusual things was higher than the elementals I'd known since toddlerhood. Whatever the case, I was incredibly grateful for his companionship.

But it's over.

He'll leave.

I'll stay.

The moss-covered walls of the academy would continue being my prison. My stomach curdled and a bitter taste filled my mouth.

"Warlock Carlow," the headmistress said again, her tone even frostier than usual.

Picking up his pace, Jasen jogged to the altar and stuck his hand over the testing stones. Immediately, the water stone glowed a brilliant blue.

"Water affinity level seven," the headmistress announced.

Shocked murmurs and exclamations filled the temple.

"Wow, he's the highest of everyone," said a student next to me.

I blinked trying hard not to feel betrayed. I'd always known Jasen had a strong affinity for water, but I didn't think he was that high a level. *Goddess.* If he were two levels higher, he'd be in range of the Arcane Assembly members up there.

The representatives from that distinguished ruling body looked as impressed as I felt. They convened for only a second before flashing the headmistress a hand signal.

"Warlock Carlow will be a Guardian," the headmistress announced, placing her hand on Jasen's shoulder.

The room broke out in whoops and applause, before the headmistress leveled the students with a chilling glare. "Silence."

Jasen wagged his eyebrows in my direction.

"Congratulations," I mouthed. Jasen and I had been dreaming of a Guardianship for years. One of our favorite games had been fantasizing where our placement would be and the kinds of jobs we'd assume to blend into human society.

Jasen wanted to become a beach bum near the ocean, no surprise. I'd settle for anything that got me far away from this place.

I'll never see him again.

The realization was a bear trap snapping around my heart. I blinked rapidly to keep my tears from spilling over, and then took a deep breath. *We can scry each other.* It wouldn't be the same, but it was something. Forcing a smile, I waved at him.

Jasen grinned back, and then turned to receive a new robe denoting his assignment and affinity. Normally, a family member would present the gold robe embroidered in blue, but since Jasen wasn't allowed contact with his human family, one of the professors did the honors.

My heart skipped a beat when Professor Razell stepped forward. The dark-haired, bronze-skinned teacher looked sinfully gorgeous in his chocolate robes accented in the deep red of his fire element.

As a second-year professor at the academy, Professor Razell was only a few years our senior, but it wasn't his youth that made every witch in the school pant after him. It wasn't even his incredible looks although his high cheek-bones, aristocratic nose, and smoldering crimson-rimmed eyes would make even the frigid headmistress look twice.

No. It was the magnetic energy that thrummed around the warlock.

There was no doubt Professor Razell was a high-level fire elemental. But despite his enviable, nearly arcane level of power, the professor was incredibly kind. He had never berated me in front of other students and he actually tried to stop them from bullying me. Not that he'd been successful.

Seeming to feel my stare, the professor turned and looked straight at me.

Wow. I felt the impact of those thickly lashed eyes straight to my soul. *Does he know the fantasies I have about him?* My breath came faster.

Jasen reached for the robes in the professor's hands.

Professor Razell turned his attention to him. "Congratulations on your new assignment, Mr. Carlow."

"Thanks, bro." Jasen's irreverent reply garnered him an amused look from the professor.

Seeing the two of them standing together reminded me of the dream I'd had last night. My cheeks warmed as I remembered in vivid detail what the two warlocks had been doing to me. *Oh, Goddess.* I really needed to stop reading the erotic paperback romances Andrea smuggled into the dorm.

So lost in thought, I almost missed the headmistress calling my name.

A student behind me kicked me in the small of my back. "That's you, freak."

"Sydney Castaway," the headmistress called out again.

I froze. I wasn't supposed to go up there. Novah said she'd asked the headmistress to skip my testing.

There was no point to it. We all knew I had no affinity. Every year the headmistress marched me into her office and demanded I place my hands on the stones. Every year the results were the same.

Her laser-like gaze zeroed in on me. "Come now, child."

I was nineteen, far from a child. Not that the head-mistress would ever see me as anything other than the abandoned baby brought to her so many years ago.

Far behind her, my caregiver wrung her hands and gave me a look of deepest sympathy.

The headmistress had clearly ignored her request. *Why would she want to shame me in front of everyone?*

Sucking in a deep breath, I stood and navigated my way toward the end of the pew.

The witches and warlocks I stepped around recoiled.

I didn't understand why I inspired such revulsion in my schoolmates, but it'd been that way for so long, I didn't even react to it. Instead, I focused on planting one foot in front of the other and following the pale blue carpet leading to the altar.

The headmistress motioned me to lay my hand over the stones.

Sucking in a deep breath, I held my right palm out over them and... nothing. Not a single stone reacted. Even though I'd known what would happen, the pitying looks from the professors and the Assembly members felt awful.

Maybe if I concentrate harder.

I closed my eyes and tried to picture the elements. For some reason, the only thing I could see in my mind's eye was the empty pedestal.

One archwarlock from the Assembly cleared his throat with barely veiled impatience.

I gritted my teeth in frustration. I didn't want to be powerless. I didn't want to be ineligible for a Guardianship. I didn't want to lose my only friend.

Please wise and benevolent Goddess, grant me an affinity and I will use it to serve you all my days.

That cursed archwarlock cleared his throat again.

Please Goddess.

I knew tears were streaking down my face, but I didn't wipe them away. *Please. Please. Please.*

A delicate clinking noise had me opening my eyes. My desperate hope that one stone was glowing evaporated when I saw that a small gemstone had fallen out of the star pendant I'd always worn around my neck.

It winked up at me from atop one of the sacrosanct testing stones.

The headmistress gave me a horrified look.

The giggles and scoffs of the students in the pews made it clear my faux pas hadn't gone unnoticed.

My face heated, and I wanted the portal to swallow me whole.

As I debated retrieving my lost gemstone, a wave of vertigo hit me. My vision blurred and my knees gave out. I tried to grab the edge of the altar to stop myself from falling and missed.

The last thing I heard before my head slammed against that damned empty pedestal was Jasen shouting my name.

2

SYDNEY

A violent storm swept me away. Desperate to escape, I clawed toward the light just as a giant wave crashed down and the undertow dragged me back into the darkness. As I rose and fell in the turbulent seas of my unconsciousness, I was dimly aware of voices—the soft lilting tone of my caregiver and Jasen's deeper voice. Both pleaded with me to wake.

If only I could.

No matter how I fought, I couldn't free myself from the merciless abyss that held me hostage. Even more terrifying were the frequent glimpses of a shadowy presence in the darkness with me and the sense that I was changing—transforming. Into what, I didn't know.

Slowly, ever so slowly, the undertow released its grip and I began to surface.

"Novah? Jasen?" I called out through parched lips. Neither answered.

An antiseptic scent burned my nostrils as I peeled my eyes open to look around.

I was in the academy infirmary. And I was alone.

Chiming bells sounded through the open window across from the cot where I lay. That explained why I was alone. *Everyone's at morning temple.*

My head spun as I rolled out of the cot. I rubbed the side of my head surprised to find neither a bandage nor a lump there. *How long have I been unconscious?*

I pushed myself to standing on shaking legs relieved to still be wearing my academy uniform. If they hadn't bothered to change me out of my white button-down shirt and plaid skirt, it couldn't have been too long.

Needing to find someone with answers, I shuffled toward the healer's desk. As I moved, an all-consuming hunger swelled inside me. I swayed in place a moment as a painful ache throbbed in the center of my chest.

Must feed.

I staggered past the empty desk and pushed through the double doors out into the deserted hallway. The rows of class-room doors were closed. There was no one around.

An anguished cry escaped my lips. The gnawing ache grew more painful. *Find someone. Anyone.*

I sensed a presence near my homeroom. *Yes!*

Desperation had me stumbling faster down the hallway.

The classroom door swung open and Professor Razell stepped out. He let out a gasp of surprise as he crashed into me. "Miss Castaway?"

A strange wild craving had me throwing myself at him.

The gorgeous professor stepped back into the doorway, catching me. "Are you okay?"

I wrapped my arms around his neck and dragged his lips down to meet mine. All at once, I was tasting the spearmint flavor of his mouth and inhaling the smoky scent of his skin.

He seemed frozen in shock for a moment, then his lips and tongue moved against mine in a kiss that heated my blood.

"Sydney," he gasped, as if he didn't quite understand what was happening.

The darkness urged me to deepen the kiss. "More." I nibbled his bottom lip.

With a curse, he carried me into the classroom and set me down on the edge of his desk.

Desire pulsed through me as he stepped between my legs and kissed me again. I brought my knees around his hips feeling the sharp point of his desire pressing through the fabric of his brown robe. A wave of lust had me rocking against him.

Professor Razell tore his mouth from mine. "We can't do this." His broad chest heaved with his panting gasps. "As much as I want to."

I licked my swollen lips savoring his taste. "Why not?" Everyone was at morning temple. There were no other teachers or students to catch us.

"Because I'm your teacher," he said, running a shaky hand through his tousled collar-length black hair.

"So. Teach me." I sat back on his desk and hiked my plaid skirt higher up my thighs. At any other time in my life, I would have been scandalized by my actions. But the desperate ache inside me didn't allow for self-reflection.

Professor Razell inhaled sharply as if scenting my desire. Then he pulled away. If I hadn't already known he had an affinity for fire, the glowing crimson ring around his irises would have been a dead giveaway. That and the fact that the temperature inside the classroom had just jumped ten degrees. Good thing I loved heat and the smoky campfire scent that clung to his skin.

When he didn't move, I snared his gaze and slowly opened the buttons of my white uniform shirt. "Please."

His Adam's apple jumped, but he still didn't move. "I-I'm sworn," he confessed in a hoarse voice.

That made two of us, not that the warlock I'd been arranged to marry since childhood wanted anything to do with me. "But I ache for you." That wasn't a lie. Every inch of my skin yearned for his touch. I needed his bronze flesh pressed against me more than I needed oxygen.

I couldn't believe what had come over me. In my nineteen years of life, I'd never so much as made out with a warlock, and now I was practically begging my teacher to bone me right here and now. It made no sense, but the feverish craving wouldn't be denied. I needed this. I needed him.

Professor Razell took a step forward, and then stopped. He clenched his hands, warring expressions crossing his gorgeous face. If only he'd keep kissing me... touching me... tasting me...

How do I persuade him? It wasn't as if I'd had any experience to draw from. All I knew from romance came from Andrea's erotic novels. Now that I'd thought of it, none of the characters in those books had been shy in expressing their affections for their romantic partners. I needed to be bolder.

Tossing back my purple hair, I whipped off my button-down shirt and pulled up my white camisole, baring myself to his feverish gaze. "Please, touch me." I didn't have huge breasts like Andrea, but he didn't seem to mind.

He stared at them like a starving man would a bountiful feast and then his hot wet mouth was crushing down on mine.

I moaned against his lips and wrapped my arms tightly around his neck.

He pressed me back onto his desk. "I can't resist you. I can't stop myself." His words almost sounded like a plea for help, but the burning inside my chest and between my thighs demanded we keep going.

As our tongues danced, the most incredible feeling came

over me. Waves of heat flowed over my skin. My head spun like the time I'd drunk too much temple wine and my blood hummed.

Suddenly, he let out a garbled cry and tried to pull away.

Not allowing him to reconsider our forbidden liaison, I locked my ankles around his hips. Euphoria swept over me. "Yes," I moaned against his lips. His cracking, papery lips.

Startled, I opened my eyes to see the desiccated face of a mummy staring down at me. I screamed.

Professor Razell's eyes, sunken into his hallowed cheek-bones, rolled white and his emaciated body collapsed over mine.

What's happening? My heart pounded as I slid out from underneath him.

The professor was hardly recognizable. The bones of his face were stark against his parchment-like skin. His skeletal chest rattled as he labored for breath.

Oh, Goddess, what have I done? I brought one hand to my mouth to hold back my scream only to find bluish-orange flames dancing on the tips of my fingers.

"Ahh!" I shook my hand and a bolt of fire shot straight into the blackboard which burst into flames.

The smell of burning wood only increased my terror. *Have I finally come into my power?* I looked down at my flaming fingers with wonder and dread.

Professor Razell made a wheezing sound.

Fear choked me. *Or did I steal his affinity?* I reached for the warlock but stopped when my fingertip flames grew. *Curse it.* Although they didn't hurt, I shook my hand trying to put them out. Fire spewed from my fingertips. In under a second, crackling flames covered the desks, chairs, and posters hanging on the walls.

A loud alarm rang in my ears as the sprinklers in the ceiling went off. The cold water extinguished the mini fires in the classroom, but not the ones on my fingertips. Panic tightened my throat. *Why won't they go out?*

The door burst open, and the headmistress rushed into the room. The silver-haired witch stopped in the middle of the classroom. She waved her hand and the sprinklers went off. Her eyes widened as she glimpsed my half-naked body. "Sydney, what is the meaning of this?"

As she looked from me to Professor Razell sprawled over his desk, I tugged down my camisole. A grim expression crossed her face. "Did he attack you?"

"N-no," I gasped. "I-I think I hurt him. I didn't mean to hurt him. Why won't the flames go out?" I held my burning hand up.

She took a step back, horror reflected in her pale, blue-rimmed eyes.

"I'm sorry. I'm so sorry."

As if in a daze, she walked over to the desk and stared down at Professor Razell's body.

"Is he alive?" I needed him to be alive.

"Yes." She pressed her thin lips together. "His body can be healed, but he's been completely drained of power. Did you take it, child?"

I trembled. "I don't know." I needed to tell her about the insatiable hunger and how it compelled me to seduce him, but I couldn't form the words.

She laid her hands on him.

I dared not breathe as an otherworldly blue light lit the tips of her fingers and seeped into the professor's skin

Slowly, the professor's face and body filled out. His skin smoothed and his breathing went from labored to steady.

When the headmistress pulled her hands back, I could only gape at her. Only arcane water elementals could bring someone back from the brink of death like that.

My head spun as everything I'd believed about the head-mistress was called into question. *Who is she really?*

The headmistress moved to my side. She held her hands over mine and snuffed out the flame on my fingers. "Where is your pendant, child? You are never supposed to take off your pendant."

Flinching at the admonishment in her voice, I reached for my necklace, but it was missing. "I don't know where it is. What's happening to me?"

Instead of answering my question, the headmistress swung her frosty gaze around the room. "The Adjudicators will come."

My breath froze. The Adjudicators hunted down elementals that violated our laws—the most sacred being never use elemental power to harm another.

I didn't know how or why, but I'd just broken that law.

She grimaced. "They'll put you to death."

My breath came in jagged gasps as terror gripped me. *I don't want to die.*

Footsteps thundered down the hall.

"I'm sorry, child." The headmistress put her cold hand on my face, and everything went dark.

I woke shivering, colder than I'd ever been in my life. I gulped in a breath of damp, musky air through my chattering teeth. *Where am I?*

Unable to recall anything from the last few hours, I slowly opened my eyes and found myself positioned upright against a rocky wall in near total darkness. The absence of light sent my heart racing. My senses told me I was alone and deep underground. *How did I get here?*

As my eyes adjusted, I made out the faint pulsing glow of lights all around me. *What are those? Why can't I remember anything?* The last thing I recalled was passing out during the testing ceremony at the temple. But surely the headmistress would have had me brought to the infirmary, not some cave.

My hair was damp and when I moved, a cold, wet tendril fell over my face. I tried to push it back but couldn't. My arms were trapped. With a cry, I realized my entire body from the neck down was entombed in ice.

Oh, Goddess. What is this?

Panic had me trying to thrash my way free. The thick ice didn't give an inch. After trying to escape for twenty minutes, I was exhausted and so very cold. The urge to sleep had me dropping the back of my head against the craggy wall.

"Don't give up, cupcake," a husky voice whispered inside my mind.

I started. "Who's that? Who's there?" My voice echoed around me as if I were in a deep well. I scanned the darkness sensing no living creature.

"You can hear me?" the voice shouted excitedly.

"Yes," I said, relieved not to be alone.

"Bless the motherfucking Goddess! It's been ages since I've been able to talk to anyone."

"Who are you?"

"Just someone who wants to help. Use your power to free yourself."

"I don't have any power," I confessed, my throat going tight. The testing ceremony had confirmed it.

The voice let out a honeyed laugh. *"I call bullshit. The Assembly wouldn't have locked you in here with us if you weren't powerful."*

Her use of "us" sent me into a mental tailspin. *"How many others are in here?"*

"Legions," she said, her tone darkening. *"For eons, this has been the resting ground for spirit elementals."*

Spirit elementals hadn't existed for over a thousand years. According to my teachings at the academy, they'd been considered monsters before they'd died out.

The worst of them were the Quagos, an infamous family of exceptionally powerful spirit elementals. Their ability to consume the souls of their enemies gave them a starring role in most of my childhood nightmares. "A-are you a spirit elemental?" I dared to ask.

"How else would I be talking to you right now?"

My body temperature dropped to the single digits. *I'm*

trapped in a cave with monsters. I'm talking to a monster. Terror brought tears to my eyes.

"Oh, stop with the waterworks. I won't hurt you. Besides, I can sense you have both spirit and fire affinity."

I shook my head in denial, but suddenly the memory of my encounter with Professor Razell bombarded me. *Oh, Goddess.* I'd attacked him. Then I'd made fire.

"Why don't you release some of your inner Ghost Rider and blow a hole in your ice coffin?"

Her strange lingo reminded me of the way Jasen talked. I found it oddly comforting. "What's your name?"

"You can call me Al.... Call me Al. Na na na na, na na na-na na-na."

It seemed Al had lost some of her marbles. Although if I were trapped here any longer, I might lose what was left of my sanity too. Deciding to take her up on her suggestion, I took a deep breath and tried to summon fire.

Nothing happened.

"Curse it."

"What's up, buttercup?"

"I-I don't know how to use the power I stole."

She gave a low whistle. *"Did you say stole, sweetheart?"*

I hung my head in shame. "Yes."

"Aren't you the hostess with the mostest?"

I wet my lips not knowing how to respond. "Uh, I don't think—"

"But you do think. And that's your problem, my little Padawan. You're thinking too much. If you want the fire, feel the burn."

"I'm not following."

She made a sound of exasperation. *"I'm talking about feeling the heat between your legs, honey bun. Imagine the last male you rode to paradise. Picture his sweat-soaked skin, the color of his eyes as you blew his mind, the feel of his cock sliding deep—"*

I gasped.

"Oh, screw me sideways, you're not a virgin, are you?"

I lifted my chin. "I'm saving myself for my sworn." Even though Logan had tried to break our engagement a million times, the arrangement still stood. As such, it was understood that we both would arrive at our consort ceremony virgins. It made what happened with Professor Razell that much worse.

Al started laughing again. *"You're cracking me up, girlfriend."*

"What's so funny?"

She sighed. *"No spirit elemental can remain chaste once their power manifests. You'll totally get sweaty with the next male you see."*

"I will not," I said, slightly offended.

"Or female," she added. *"I was never very particular about who I fed from. As long as they're attractive and willing, why not?"*

"What do you mean, fed from?"

"I'm really going to have to break it all down for you, aren't I?"

"Please," I said, feeling completely out of my depth.

"You know all elementals need to feed their power, right?"

I nodded, which was ridiculous because it was pitch-black, and Al's voice was in my head. "We replenish our power by visiting the temples." The elementals in our realm needed the connection with the hidden realms to fuel our power and life force. It's why all covens and academies were in close proximity to the many underground temples scattered around our realm.

"Not that. I'm talking about how fire elementals need to be around fire to absorb some of its energy, water elementals need to immerse themselves in water, and earth elementals need to—"

"I get the picture," I said dryly. We'd learned early in the academy that once our powers manifested, we should carry a symbol of our element with us. I'd never connected that with energy absorption, but then again, I'd never developed an affinity, so it hadn't really been relevant. "But I don't get why spirit elementals need to..." I couldn't even say it.

"Get it on. Hit the skins. Bury the weasel. Tickle the kitty."

I made a face. "Please stop."

She let out a gleeful giggle which made me wonder about her age. *"What better way to absorb some spirit than bumping and grinding, sugar cakes. You get yours while your partner gets theirs."*

I looked down at my entombed hands. "But what if I hurt my partner?" I cringed, remembering the expression of anguish on the professor's mummified face.

"That means you drank too deep. Spirit elemental rule number one, never get to the point of starvation. Bad things happen if you do that..."

The warning in her voice sent a shiver down my spine. "Bad things like what?"

"Best you don't wander down that path, dove. Just remember to feed and feed often. If you skim a little life force off the top of your partner during sexy time, they'll never know."

That didn't sound too bad. "Do you always have to... you know... in order to feed?" I could feel my face heat.

"No. You can tear a hole in their skin and suck up their life force." She made a slurping sound. *"But where is the fun in that?"*

I gagged. *Goddess. Sucking up life forces? That sounds monstrous. I can't do that.* But I had. The memory of kissing the professor jolted me. When I'd put my mouth to his, it'd felt amazing. I must have been feeding from him and hadn't even known.

She lowered her voice. *"Of course, the Quagos can feed from a distance."*

My heart jumped. "There aren't any Soul Eaters in here, are there?" My breathing stalled as I frantically surveyed the darkness.

The sound of stone scraping against stone interrupted her throaty laugh.

My heart pounded. "What's that?"

"Who is that, is the better question. It's that warden who's been

trying to free you from your ice coffin. Aren't you lucky? I'd tap that sexy hunk of male in a heartbeat if I could."

I blinked. "Warden? Does that mean we are in a prison?"

"The Lost Soul's Penitentiary."

My stomach dropped to my feet. "Oh, Goddess. No." The super max prison held the worst elemental criminal offenders in our realm.

"The Goddess has nothing to do with this," Al said in a bitter voice.

A beam of light appeared in what looked like an enormous arched doorway. Although I couldn't make out the features of the approaching figure, for the first time, I glimpsed my surroundings.

As I'd suspected, I was in a vast underground cave. Overhead, stalagmites jutted from the domed ceiling like vicious fangs. Around the walls, limestone and calcium deposits glittered like sugar around strange etched symbols. Also glittering were the crystals affixed to the rows and rows of sarcophagus filling the cavernous space. It was the crystals on the stone coffins that pulsed with otherworldly light.

A scream caught in my throat. There were thousands of coffins. They lined every inch of the cave floor as far back as I could see along with sculptures, scrolls, books, and ancient looking tapestries. *I'm in a burial chamber.*

"Al?" I shouted.

The beam of light swung over my face.

Temporarily blinded, I was forced to close my eyes. My breathing came in panting breaths.

"Chill out, peaches. Your rescuer approaches."

"He does?"

"Keep it down. He'll think you're cray-cray if you keep talking to yourself," she admonished.

A deep male voice called out, "You're finally awake. Good."

I opened my eyes. "Who are you?" When he didn't answer, I telepathically asked Al. *"What does he want with me?"*

"Maybe he wants to free you so he can have his wicked way with you." She sighed wistfully.

My shivers turned into convulsions.

The figure holding the light stepped carefully around the coffins with practiced ease. He'd obviously been here many times before. When he was a few feet away, he wedged the torch he was holding between two of the coffins and came to stand in front of me. "Hello, Miss Castaway."

I blinked in confusion at his familiar tone. My gaze first went to his eyes. They were a deep brown, with no hint of elemental affinity. *He's a null.* Where would I have run into a male null? *Maybe he was one of the older students at the academy?*

I immediately rejected the idea. If I'd ever seen him in the hallways, he would have been branded into my mind for all time. He was easily nine inches taller than me and looked to be in his mid-twenties. The rippling muscles of his broad chest pressed against his tight black uniform-shirt making it clear he was no stranger to heavy lifting.

His shoulder-length hair was pulled back in a ponytail. It was ink black except for a startling streak of silvery white that ran down his temple.

I couldn't stop my gaze from dropping to his full, very kissable lips. They were framed by a dark goatee that gave him a rakish appearance. All in all, the male was sexy as sin.

Despite my ice prison, my skin seemed to warm. "Do I know you?" *Because I'd really like to know you.*

Al hummed her approval in my mind.

He let out a cold laugh. "Classic. You don't even recognize me." He stepped closer, so our faces were only a foot apart. "Look harder." His warm, spearmint scented breath washed across my face.

"Professor Razell?" My jaw dropped as I suddenly recognized the aristocratic nose and high cheekbones. My clean shaven, scholarly instructor whose passion for understanding ancient mysteries looked completely different. There was nothing scholarly about him now.

"If this is what teachers look like in this age, sign me up for school," Al chortled.

"I go by Raze now," he spat.

"Oh! This one's sassy," Al purred.

He balled his hands into fists, the energy around him thrumming with barely repressed rage.

Hoping against hope that his menace wasn't directed at me, I said, "Are you here to rescue me?"

The corner of his lip curled in a sneer. "No. In fact, in the twenty months since you attacked me, I've imagined a million different ways I'd punish you for destroying my life."

The venom in his words sent my hope plummeting down to my frozen toes. *Twenty months? "Have I been here that long?"*

"Afraid so," Al answered. *"I'm starting to suspect that you stole this guys' power. Am I right?"*

I nodded my head forgetting we were having a telepathic conversation.

She made a sympathetic noise. *"That sucks. Based on how he's looking at you, he'd sooner kill you than fuck you and that's never a good thing."*

"Tell me something I don't know," I replied, trying not to give in to the anxiety clawing up my insides.

Raze's fury-filled gaze bore into mine. "I'm here for one reason and one reason only. To take back what you stole from me."

❆ 4 ❆

RAZE

Sydney wilted under my scowl.

I refused to let it affect me. She was the one who'd hurt me. She was the one who'd taken everything from me.

Before the purple-haired succubus drained me of my power I'd been well on the way to a successful scholarly career.

Unlike others with fire affinity, I didn't thirst for danger or adventure. I enjoyed long afternoons exploring ancient scrolls and translating long forgotten spells. Therefore, when I'd been awarded a faculty position at the most prestigious academy in the human realm, I'd been euphoric.

Everything had been going so well. The headmistress appeared to have a high regard for me, and the students seemed to enjoy my classes. I even had enough time for my research on the fourth dynasty of the hidden realms and for visits to my sworn, Jessalyn. Although she didn't get my blood pumping the same way aged-parchment and ink did, she was sweet and accepting of my intellectual pursuits. Best of all, my father approved of our match and seemed to eagerly await our consort ceremony.

And then Sydney crashed into me in the hallway.

The minute she put her lips on mine, I should have pushed her away. *Why didn't I?* An all too familiar surge of anguish and bitter despair tightened like a noose around my neck.

Curse the Elders. Sydney's mouth had carried the sweetest, most intoxicating flavor. One taste and everything but her fled from my mind. And when she'd bared herself to me every shred of self-control had gone up in smoke.

I hadn't cared that she was my student. I hadn't cared that I was sworn to Jessalyn. I hadn't cared about anything other than the overwhelming need to thrust so deeply inside her, we'd become indistinguishable from one another.

Now I knew my inability to resist her was due to her dark affinity. Just like the ancient tales of other spirit elementals, she was a succubus. She lured her victims close to feed off them. Like a fool, I'd allowed her to drain nearly all of my life force and take my power. Because of her, I'd lost everything.... *Everything.*

My hands shook with rage as I stared at Sydney. "Give me back my fire affinity." My shout reverberated off the ceiling of the subterranean chamber. A burial chamber that, just two years ago, would've thrilled me to see. Now I didn't give a damn that some coffins were from the third and fourth dynasties. Now I only cared about one thing—getting my life back.

Tears welled in Sydney's eyes and her lips, tinted blue with cold, trembled. "I don't know how."

"You lie!" During the weeks I'd spent in recovery, I'd searched for information on spirit elementals, not that there was much to find. Someone had gone to a lot of trouble to wipe all record of them from our history. However, I did come across a passage from a noted fourth century scholar who called them the scourges of all the realms and warned never to trust one. I would heed his words.

Moving closer, I gripped the back of her wet head and forced her face closer to mine. "Give me my power!"

Tears streamed down her cheeks. "I swear, Professor Razell, I don't know how." She let out a sob. "Don't you think if I had your power, I would have used it to get out of this?" She glanced down at the ice surrounding her.

"You have my power." Just because I couldn't see any sign of it in her fascinating purple eyes didn't mean it wasn't there. *It has to be there.*

She licked her lips, lips that were just a fraction away from mine.

Suddenly, I couldn't focus on anything but their proximity. *Does she taste as good as I remember?* I swayed toward her.

"Tell me how to summon your fire, Professor. Maybe then I can give it to you."

Getting a hold of myself, I reared back. "Or maybe then you can attack me with my own element. I will not let you finish the job of killing me."

She blinked as if I'd slapped her. "I'd never do that. I don't know what came over me this morning."

It took me a second to realize the events in the classroom that seemed a lifetime away for me, seemingly just occurred to her.

She gave me a sad look. "I never meant to hurt you."

"Hurt me? You nearly killed me." I shook with emotion as I remembered those initial pain-riddled weeks when the healers weren't sure I'd ever make a full recovery.

"And more than that, when you stole my power you stole my future. I lost my faculty position." The headmistress had been most apologetic, but the academy forbid nulls from teaching. "I also lost my sworn." I sucked in a breath, remembering the sad scry I'd received from Jessalyn. Her family had ended our engagement because of my loss of power.

Sydney's face whitened. "Oh, Goddess. I'm sorry."

"I don't want your apologies. I want you to give me back my affinity."

"I can't," she said in a whisper-soft voice.

She wants to keep my power for herself. I stiffened. "If you don't, I'll leave you here to die."

"No, please."

"Then give it back." How I longed to feel the flames once again.

Sydney sobbed. "I told you. I don't know how."

Refusing to be swayed by her theatrics, I turned and strode back over to the torch. "Fine. You've made your decision." *Another night in here might compel her to see things my way.*

As I ripped the torch free, I heard a crunching noise. I looked down to see that I'd accidentally stepped on one of the soul markers embedded in the lid of a plain black sarcophagus.

I froze, petrified that I had somehow shattered the crystal and released the imprisoned soul inside. However, when I looked down, I found the crystal slightly fractured, but intact. *Thank the Elders.*

"Please don't go," Sydney wailed.

Ignoring her pleas, I navigated around the coffins until I got to the arched doorway. "Enjoy what's left of your life." I didn't turn around. I needed her to believe I wasn't coming back.

"Nooo!" she howled.

I stepped across the threshold and felt an immediate sense of relief. I hadn't realized how suffocating the musty air inside had been. More than that, my skin had crawled, and my senses had screamed with the wrongness of that chamber.

"Any luck?" My six-and-a-half-foot tall friend, Terran,

asked. Although he'd pulled a lot of strings to get me this warden position and he'd helped me find Sydney, he'd drawn the line at entering the burial chamber.

"She's awake, but not cooperative."

"I can hear that."

"We'll come back tomorrow. She'll be more compliant then," I said more to myself than to him.

Sydney's wails hit a hysterical pitch.

Victor, another warden who'd been keeping watch a few yards away, looked back at us. "She sounds pitiful. Let me talk to her."

I scowled at the brown-eyed null. Something about him set my teeth on edge. "She'll eat you for breakfast."

"I'd like to see that." Victor flashed a set of blackened teeth. "Does she have nice tits? I'll go in the crypt for a pair of nice tits."

Terran scowled at him. "Fuck off, Victor."

Victor pursed his fleshy lips together. "But it's been ages since I've gotten any play. Let me see her."

"No," Terran and I said in unison.

"Watch the lift," Terran ordered.

"Watch the lift," Victor mimicked in an unflattering impression of Terran's voice.

"I really don't like him," I whispered to Terran.

Terran shrugged his massive shoulders. "He caught us going down here. Do you want him ratting us out to the Head Warden?"

"No. But maybe we could have just threatened him instead of letting him come with us," I muttered.

Victor turned his head and glared at us. "I can hear you, assholes."

I gritted my teeth, wishing I had some of my power. A zap with a fireball might make the null more respectful. As a high-level fire elemental, I'd always been treated with deference. The disdain and prejudice I'd experienced since losing my affinity was yet another bitter pill to swallow.

Terran clamped his textbook-sized hand on my shoulder. "Ignore him. Do you think you can convince the witch to give you back your power?"

I looked back into the chamber. "She has to…" The alternative was untenable. The only thing that kept me going all these months was hope that I could regain my power and get my life back on track. My family's mantra, 'power is everything' rolled through my mind. If power was everything, then I had nothing. I was nothing.

Terran nodded. "We'll make it happen or die trying." His unwavering loyalty was one reason we'd stayed close after being roommates at school. Not only was Terran a high-level earth elemental, when he set his mind to something, he was unstoppable.

"Thank you, old friend," I said, overcome with gratitude.

"Let me out!" Sydney shrieked through breathless sobs. She sounded as desperate to get free as I was to get my power.

Victor suddenly appeared behind me. "She sounds pretty. I need to see her."

"The hell you do." I motioned at the twenty-foot stone door. "Close it, Terran." When we came back tomorrow, I'd bring food and water to bribe her. By then, she'd be starving if she wasn't already.

Terran waved one hand at the slab and the door began to close.

Inexplicably, Victor pushed me aside and tried to rush inside the chamber.

Terran grabbed the small male by the arm and flung him back. "You're not going to touch this one."

Disappointment was etched on Victor's face. "You never let me have any fun."

Fun? That creep would touch Sydney over my dead body. *She's mine to punish.* I held my hands out, ready to reseal the wards on the ancient stone door. It had taken months of studying spell books to learn how to undo them. They were among the strongest I'd ever encountered, no doubt put there by the Assembly themselves. Good thing ancient spells were my specialty.

"Goodbye, Ms. Castaway," I shouted.

Sydney's cries hit a feverish pitch. "No!" She let out a scream that was quickly muffled by the door closing with a heavy thud.

The sudden silence was deafening.

With a huff, Victor pulled away from Terran and stalked over to the lift. "Fuck you guys."

Terran stared at the closed chamber door long enough that I could see the conflicting emotions on his face. Even as a boy he'd hated to see others suffer. Rather ironic he'd become a prison warden.

"Don't pity her. She wouldn't think twice about draining your power."

Terran took a step back from the door and looked at me. "You're right. It just surprises me the Assembly threw her in there with no trial at all."

I wasn't surprised. During my convalescence I'd been visited by my father, a member of the Assembly, who'd coerced me to go along with their cover story. According to their spin on events, after collapsing during the testing ceremony, Sydney had fallen into a coma from which she still hadn't awoken.

They told everyone the loss of my affinity was due to an ancient spell gone wrong. Poor Professor Razell had dug too deeply into the mysteries of the past.

"No one can know what really happened," my father had warned.

I let out a heavy sigh. "The Assembly doesn't want anyone to know there's a spirit elemental in our realm."

Terran rubbed his chin thoughtfully. "Yeah. I don't suppose that would go over so well. Didn't a family of spirit elementals nearly conquer the hidden realms?"

I blinked in surprise. "And here I thought you slept through history class, old friend."

Terran grunted. "I paid attention to the good stuff. Hearing how that Soul Eater Silon enslaved the royals and forced them to battle each other to death was interesting."

"His name was Z'syron Quago," I said in a low voice. "And he did more than enslave the royals." Ancient scholars hinted the evil warlord had fed off their power, manipulated their minds, and turned them into his personal army. I cast my gaze back to the stone door. *Could Z'syron, the Nightmare of the Realms, be inside there too?* I shuddered at the possibility.

Terran frowned. "No offense, I know she stole your power and all, but your little witch didn't pose anywhere near the threat that guy did. The Assembly could have at least offered her due process."

I took a deep breath and tried not to feel betrayed by Terran's words. The warlock had always been a social justice warrior and I usually admired how he stood up for the underdogs. *Usually.*

"Sydney is a threat—"

A loud boom sounded behind the door.

Terran spun around. "What in the Goddess fuck is that?"

Victor raced over to where we stood, a panicked look on his face. "Is someone detonating explosives in there?"

As the scent of ice and smoke wafted from under the door, I realized what was happening. "The witch is using my power to free herself."

5

SYDNEY

I stared down at my fiery hands in shock. *How did I just make everything explode?* A minute ago, I'd been certain I would die in this cold, cursed place. But when Raze taunted me with his last goodbye, a burst of anger had shot through me. Or more specifically, a burst of fire had shot through my hands, shattering my ice coffin.

I'd immediately fallen to the cavern floor and, given the way my legs were trembling, I didn't know if I'd ever stand again.

"Nice job," Al cheered. *"Now, before you march up to that door and blow it to smithereens, can you do a girl a solid an—"*

She was interrupted by the door opening.

Raze and two unfamiliar wardens rushed into the cavern.

"There she is," my nemesis shouted. As if I could hide with my hands glowing bluish orange.

"Quick, throw a fireball at them," Al urged.

"I can't do that." I had to show the wardens I wasn't a threat. Raising my voice, I said, "I won't hurt anyone."

"Extinguish your fire," demanded the tallest, most muscular warlock I'd ever seen. As he approached, I made out the rough-hewn features of his face including his broad forehead, prominent jaw, and slightly crooked nose. His close-cropped hair was the color of buffed leather and the ropes of his muscles bunched tight as if he were a loaded weapon, coiled and ready to unleash on someone.

"Mmm-hmm. Mama likes that one," Al crooned.

I had to agree. His brawler build and green-rimmed eyes were captivating. *An earth elemental. Wow!* There hadn't been many with that affinity at the academy. Also fascinating were the deep blue swirls on his neck peeking out from under his black uniform collar. *Tattoos?* I'd never seen anyone with tattoos before.

"I don't know how to put the fire out," I confessed to him.

"Don't believe a word she says, Terran," warned Raze. "Let me deal with her."

I glared at my former Professor. He was fast becoming my least favorite elemental in the realms. "I'm innocent."

Raze's eyes narrowed. "I can personally attest that you're not."

"You should have run when you had the chance," Al moaned into my head.

I took a deep breath. *"It's okay. I'll just explain to whoever is in charge that this is all a big mistake."*

"Whatever you need to tell yourself, muffin. Look, before they cart you away, grab that soul marker."

When I didn't move, she made a sound of impatience. *"The glowing crystal in front of your face."*

"This?" I motioned at the sarcophagus I was sitting on. The intricate designs all over the stone coffin were almost as pretty as the softly glowing crystal embedded into the top of it.

"Yes!"

Realizing the wardens were almost to me, I found the

strength to rise on my knees and yank the two-inch crystal out of the coffin with my fiery hands. *"Now what?"*

Al didn't respond. *"Al? Are you still there?"*

There was no response. *Great. Just great.* My imaginary friend had disappeared at the worst time. Deciding I needed to hide the crystal, I started to stuff in into my shirt pocket. Only then did I realize I was only wearing my wet, almost entirely see-through camisole. No wonder the ugly, pock-marked warden had stopped to leer at me. *Ugh.*

The wardens were almost on me. Thinking fast, I stuffed the crystal into my skirt pocket. As I did, flames shot out toward the wardens. *Curse it!*

While the other two wardens ducked, Raze showed no fear, marching up to me. "You think to threaten me with the power you stole?"

"N-no," I stammered, lifting my flaming hands in front of me. "I don't want your power."

"Then give it back."

"Gladly. Tell me how."

His gaze narrowed. "Stop playing your games. If you knew how to take it, you should know how to transfer it back."

"But I don't. I really don't." I searched his face, looking for any trace of understanding. There was nothing in his eyes, but a rage so dark and deep it made my heart pound.

"You lie!" He dragged me to my feet, grabbed my hand, and pressed it against his face. Immediately, the flames burned brighter, engulfing his head.

"No!" I fought his ironclad grip, not wanting to hurt him.

But it was quickly apparent that the flames were not burning him. It was almost as if the fire recognized him and was happy to see him. Transfixed, I watched the bluish-orange fire ripple along his bronze skin.

Raze groaned. "I've missed this. The fire... My fire." As he nuzzled my hand, the flames disappeared. He let out a sigh of disappointment.

All at once, I noticed the feel of his goatee prickling the pads of my fingers. The sensation was intriguing. *How can it be both soft and scratchy at the same time?* Unable to help myself, I skimmed my fingers through it.

Raze wore the same dazed look he'd given me in the classroom.

He's gorgeous. If anything, Raze had only gotten better looking since I'd seen him last.

As I dared to brush my hand over his lips, he opened his mouth and nibbled my finger.

Something dark and predatory inside me stirred awake. "I need you," I said in a husky voice.

Raze shook his head. "No!" As if tearing himself from a dream, he flung me away.

I sprawled back onto the coffin.

Raze's gaze fixed on my near translucent camisole. His breathing went ragged.

I should have been horrified that I was all but bared to his gaze, but all I could think about was how good his hands would feel on my skin.

"I need you," I whispered again.

Raze staggered forward. "I need you too." He reached his hand out to me, but he was shoved away.

The huge earth elemental pushed Raze behind him and glared down at me. "Leave my friend alone, enchantress."

This close up, I could better see the ink swirls under his uniform. *So pretty.* I wondered if the tattoos covered his entire body. "Touch me," I implored.

The warlock's green-rimmed eyes widened and then locked on my stiffening nipples.

I pulled up my camisole and offered my breasts to the muscular male.

The earth elemental let out a choked sound, then his big warm hands were on me.

"Oh, yes." His touch felt amazing. Needing more, I arched off the stone coffin.

The muscular warlock pinched my nipples, dragging a wild cry from my lips.

So good. That felt so good. "More," I begged.

A shudder went through him and a second later his enormous body was settling on top of mine.

His weight forced my spine into the hard stone coffin, but I didn't care. I wanted this.

The earth elemental kissed down my face, neck, and chest while boldly pushing apart my legs.

"Yes," I cried when his fingers slid under my skirt toward that pulsing ache at my center.

"She's mine!" Raze shouted. He grabbed the earth elemental's arm and tried to drag him off me.

The earth elemental pushed him away. "No. She's mine."

Raze made a sound of frustration.

I didn't want him upset. "Raze," I said, in that strange husky tone. "Come here."

Never tearing his gaze from mine, Raze stepped around the earth elemental and knelt beside him.

"I want you both to touch me."

Both males nodded without hesitation.

Some primitive part of me knew they were mine for the taking. They'd do anything and everything I wanted them to do. Trembling with excitement, I reached for them.

Moving in a blur, the third warlock suddenly appeared next to me. Before I could even lock eyes with him, he snapped heavy metal cuffs around both my wrists.

All at once the strange compulsion driving me vanished. Blinking in surprise, I stared at the shorter male who wasn't more than an inch or two taller than me. *"W-who are you?"*

The short warlock grinned, flashing me a row of rotted teeth. "I'm Warden Merrick. But you can call me Victor."

Victor had to be one of the ugliest males I'd ever seen with skin so pockmarked it looked as if it'd gone through a cheese grater. His pale brown eyes, clear of any elemental affinity, swept over my body and gleamed.

Embarrassed, I sat up and yanked my skirt and camisole down. As I did, I realized the thick wrist cuffs I now wore had turned purple and were glowing. "What are these?"

Victor sat down beside me, so close his thigh pressed against mine. "Negators. They absorb elemental powers. All prisoners wear them."

"Oh," I said in a small voice. "Thank you."

Victor let out a laugh that sounded much deeper and richer than I expected. "Are you thanking me for rendering you powerless?"

I nodded. Surprisingly, I didn't mind his close proximity. Despite his less than appealing looks, something about Victor drew me. Maybe it was his scent, something rich and masculine mixed with a fresh ocean breeze. I found it calming although I didn't know him, and he'd just interrupted me seducing his friends.

Goddess. I'd nearly had a threesome with the wardens. My face heated as I dared to look over at Raze and the earth elemental.

Both warlocks stared at me with mirroring looks of alarm.

"Victor, get away from her! She'll enchant you too," the earth elemental warned.

Victor grabbed my wrists and held them up for him to see. "I'm not an idiot like you, Terran. I put negators on her." He let my arms drop into my lap.

"Your name is Terran?" I asked the big warden. It seemed important to get the name of the first male to touch my nipples.

He gave a curt nod. "Yes, and you're the enchantress who stole Ian's power."

It took me a second to realize he was talking about Raze. I looked over at the dark-haired warlock. "And I'm sorry about that. I don't know why I did it or why I was just trying to make you two…" A mixture of shame and confusion made my throat too tight to form words.

Victor patted my back. "There, there."

Tears filled my eyes. "I don't understand what's happening to me."

"Don't cry." Terran took a step forward as if to comfort me, and then he went motionless. "Why the fuck do I care that you're crying? What did you do to me?"

"I don't know what you're talking about." I pressed my hands to my leaking eyes, wishing that I could wake up from this horrible nightmare.

"Why does it bother me so much that she's upset?" Terran shouted in a frantic voice.

"She's enchanted us," Raze answered. "It's why I've dreamed of her every night since the attack. *Hellfire.* Even now I can barely keep myself from touching her."

I stiffened at Raze's confession. *Does that mean he is attracted to me?*

The dark-haired warlock seemed even more enraged and agitated than he'd been before. He paced around the coffins. "She's a succubus drawing us in to drain our power."

Victor scoffed. "From where I stood, it looked as if she was trying to drain something else from you two." He leaned down and whispered in my ear, "I'm happy to volunteer. I'd be a way better lover than those two losers."

Victor's warm breath washed across the side of my neck, making me shiver. "Thanks, but I don't think that will be necessary." At least as long as I wore the negators. I glanced down at the metal cuffs on my wrist. Although the devices seemed to keep my libido in check, they also seemed to be draining my energy. A wave of dizziness had me laying my head against Victor's shoulder.

Victor smiled. It might have been the poor light, but his teeth didn't look as black as they had before. And his breath smelled nice, like the corn chips Jasen used to eat all the time.

I leaned closer to him, drawn to his body heat and needing something to support my weakening muscles.

Victor slid his arm around my shoulders.

Raze cursed. "Look at her, weaving a spell on you too, Victor."

Victor arched a dark brown eyebrow. "She can weave all she wants. I'll take it where I can get it."

Raze frowned. "You can get it somewhere else. Until she gives me my power back, Sydney is mine to punish." He grabbed my shackled wrist and yanked me to my feet.

A horrendous wave of vertigo had me stumbling forward.

Before I could fall, Terran rushed over and hauled me into his arms.

Although his rugged face was etched with frustration rather than concern, I sagged against him. "Thank you."

"I don't want your thanks, enchantress. I want you to remove your spell."

Fighting to keep my eyes open, I gazed up at him. "What are you talking about? I didn't put a spell on you."

"She's lying," Raze interjected. "She'll pretend she didn't enchant you, just like she'll pretend she didn't take my powers."

"I didn't," I tried to say, but it was suddenly too hard to form words. *Why don't they believe me?*

"What are you going to do with her?" Victor asked, an inscrutable look on his face.

Raze frowned. "We have no choice but to bring her to the main prison."

The prison? That sounded terrible, but I was too tired to care.

Terran made a rumbling sound of approval. "Let's put her in tier four?"

"Excellent idea," Raze said with a dark laugh.

Black crept along the edges of my vision, and I struggled to focus on the wardens.

Victor shook his head. "You can't do that."

Ignoring him, Raze started for the door. "Come on, Terran, let's get Sydney set up in her new home."

As the big warlock crushed me to his chest and started forward, the darkness I'd been trying to keep at bay dragged me under.

6

TERRAN

The small purple-haired witch trembled in my arms as the lift brought the four of us up to the main floor of the prison.

She must be freezing.

Ice shards clung to her damp clothes and goose pimples spread across her pale smooth skin.

The subterranean prison was normally ten degrees cooler than was comfortable for a big guy like me, and Sydney was such a tiny thing. I'd wager she didn't have more than a few ounces of body fat to spare.

I should warm her.

No. It took all my self-control not to rip off my uniform shirt and wrap her inside it. The urge to comfort her, bring her to safety, and protect her from anything and everything that could harm her was nearly overwhelming. *Fuck.* I'd never felt this protective of a female I'd just met. Check that, I'd never felt this protective of any female period and that included the ones I was screwing.

I made a point of not caring. Consensual sex to release

stress was fun, but if the female ever demanded more, I ended things.

Romantic attachments weren't for me. Not now. Not ever.

Sydney shifted against me, and I caught a heady blast of her scent. My eyes rolled back as her sweet fragrance filled my nostrils—honeysuckle mixed with the musky hot scent of sex. It was spellbinding, just like her. I shook my head to clear it.

She's enchanted me with her power.

I wanted to shout with frustration. *How could I, Terran Lander of all fucking elementals, be ensnared by a female?* Unlike many warlocks of my power level, I'd lucked out by not being sworn at birth. That meant I could hook up with whoever I chose. No long-term relationships. No intimacy. No entanglements outside of my cock inside a hot, wet —

"I'm sorry I got you involved, Terran," Raze said, interrupting my thoughts. "I didn't think it would unfold like this." He waved his hand over Sydney.

"I know that," I said, unable to regret my decision to help my closest friend. 'No good deed goes unpunished,' my father would always say, before my mother's selfishness killed him.

"Is she sleeping?" Raze asked in a low voice. With his increased muscle mass from working out like a fiend and his dark facial hair, he looked different from the bookworm he used to be. None of the punk warlocks who'd wanted to bully him at the academy would fuck with him now. Not that they did back then. I'd made sure of that.

Realizing Raze was waiting for a response, I looked down at Sydney burrowed against my chest.

Her incredible indigo eyes had closed, and her breathing had taken a slow, deep, rhythmic pattern.

"I don't know." She could be sleeping or pretending to sleep. *Probably pretending.* Raze had warned me just how dangerous and manipulative spirit elementals could be. And then, like a fool, I'd waltzed right into one's arms.

Stupid.

Sydney must've used her power on me. It was the only explanation for why I couldn't shake the need to touch her. I shuddered, remembering how beautiful her breasts were and how responsive her rosy nipples had been under my hand. My cock stiffened at the memory. I couldn't wait to bite down on those stiff buds while I slid my fingers inside—

Fuck. I shook my head again, trying to clear it once more.

I checked the negators on her wrists to make sure they were still glowing. They were. *Does that mean whatever enchantment she placed on me is permanent?*

The idea that I might be under her spell forever put chills down my spine. I glanced over at Raze and found him staring at Sydney with a mixture of loathing and fascination. *Warg shit.* My friend was as lost as I was.

At least Victor was in his right mind.

The irritating warden was admiring his reflection in the stainless-steel doors of the lift. He did that all the time now. The recent streak of vanity was strange given the warlock had always been the ugliest male in the prison.

As if feeling my eyes drilling into the back of his head, Victor whirled around. His gaze dropped from my face to the enchantress. "How are you planning on explaining her to the Head Warden?"

I glared at the smaller male. "*We* aren't going to explain anything. The Head Warden rarely concerns himself with individual inmates. We'll put the witch in a cell and figure out a story for her."

"What kind of story?" Victor asked, never tearing his gaze from my enchantress.

Raze cleared his throat. "We'll tell the other wardens she's been transferred from the Asylum."

I nodded, warming to the idea. "Perfect." The Head Warden had just briefed us on the fact that the prison for mentally ill elementals was over capacity. We'd been given a heads up that some of the more dangerous patients would transfer here. Not that we weren't over capacity and under-staffed too. But neither the Assembly nor the Adjudicators gave a shit about that. If anything, over the last year they'd been sentencing more and more elementals for minor infractions. It was a colossal waste of time, energy, and resources if you asked me. But no one did.

"We'll dismiss any story Sydney tells as the ravings of a lunatic. No one will notice her," Raze added, gazing intently at her face.

Victor snorted. "You're wrong, bro. Everyone will notice her."

Raze raised an eyebrow. "Bro? Did you just call me bro?"

Victor ignored the question and pointed down at Sydney's negators. "How are we going to explain the purple color?"

I frowned. The negators always turned red for fire elementals, green for earth elementals like me, blue for those with water affinity, and silver for air users. The colors ranged from light to dark depending on the prisoner's power level. However, I'd never seen one turn even slightly close to Sydney's color.

"We'll say the Asylum is trialing a new kind of negator on some of their more violent inmates," Raze announced.

I smiled at his quick thinking. Raze had always been good on his feet like that. Me, not so much, but maybe that was part of why we'd been such fast friends. He'd been a wealthy, intellectual aristocrat while I'd been a poor, athletic, commoner. Fire and earth always balancing each other out without putting each other out.

"Fine," Victor said as the lift jolted to a stop. He turned to face the doors just as they opened and came face to face with my ex.

Damn. What is Kayla doing here?

Victor leered at the big-breasted redhead. "Hi, Warden Skye."

"Ugh, Victor," Kayla said, taking an immediate step back. As soon as Victor stepped out of the elevator, her silver-rimmed eyes swung over to me. "Hi, Terran."

I grunted. Although I'd normally avoided screwing my subordinates, the voluptuous recruit had been all over me since her first day. Bored and hard up, I'd banged her for a few weeks before calling it off.

She didn't seem to understand we were over. Just last night she'd snuck into my quarters uninvited. And given that this portion of the prison was nowhere near her post, it was clear she'd either followed me here or been searching for me.

"I was hoping to run into you, Terran," Kayla said, batting her eyelashes. "I'm on lunch break if you wanted to hang."

Her innuendo wasn't lost on Victor, who looked from her to me and grinned. "Terran, you sly dog. Okay, tell me do her curtains match the drapes?" He wagged his eyebrows suggestively.

Kayla huffed. "Fuck off, Victor."

"Is that an invitation?" Victor sidled up to her.

Kayla's face wrinkled in disgust. "It'd be a cold day in the realms before I'd allow you to touch me. Terran, on the other hand..." She pursed her glossy pink lips.

"Can you move out of the way?" I said, letting my irritation creep into my tone.

Seeming to realize she was blocking me from stepping out of the lift, Kayla moved to the side. "Who is that?" she asked, her eyes on the bundle in my arms.

"None of your concern, rookie," Raze snarled, following me out of the elevator. "Why aren't you at your post?"

Kayla flinched under Raze's glare. "Deputy Warden, I didn't see you there."

"Clearly," Raze drawled. "Why are you here?"

"I'm on lunch break." She lifted her chin and stared Raze down. "I want to know what you guys are up to?"

She was crazy to challenge Raze. The dark-haired male didn't get angry often, but when he did, he exploded. The memory of the time he set our dormitory on fire flashed in my mind.

Raze glared at Kayla. "I don't answer to rookies."

I had to bite back my smile. Raze himself had only been off probation a few short months. But in true Raze fashion, he already practically ran the place.

The Head Warden had already promoted him to Deputy and made him his number two. Normally, I'd be pissed as fuck about being passed over for a promotion by someone with less than a tenth of my work experience, but this was Raze. I could no more hate him for blazing ahead as I could hate the sun for rising.

Raze continued. "However, I will tell you we successfully apprehended the runaway inmate." He motioned at Sydney in my arms.

Kayla chewed her lip. "I didn't hear about a runaway inmate."

"Good," Raze said, managing to look relieved. He turned his glare on Victor. "Looks like you got off easy this time, Victor. Next time we won't clean up your mess."

Victor blinked twice, but thankfully played along. "How was I supposed to know the witch would run?" he whined convincingly. "She has such pretty tits." He reached over and tried to tug Sydney's undershirt up.

"Fuck off, Victor." Raze smacked his hand away. "You'd better find this one's paperwork. The Head Warden will be pissed you botched the first transfer from the Asylum."

Kayla gasped. "The inmate is from the Asylum?"

The three of us nodded.

"Apparently this is one of their most insane and violent inmates," Raze added. "Watch yourself around her, rookie."

Kayla's eyes narrowed. "She can't be worse than the other inmates in my sector."

Raze arched a brow, a telltale sign he'd accepted her challenge. "Then we'll be sure this inmate is placed in your sector once she's processed." He bared his teeth. "Be sure to show her the meaning of true punishment."

Kayla nodded. "I can do that."

Something inside me rebelled at their plans for my enchantress. Sydney didn't deserve their mistreatment. *Did she?*

"Come, wardens." With an imperious wave of his hand, Raze motioned Victor and I to follow him.

Kayla tried to grab my arm. "Stay with me, Terran." She pursed her lips and rose on the balls of her feet as if to kiss me. Her breath carried the sickly-sweet odor of Spark.

I hated when she was on the mind-altering drug. Many elementals claimed it strengthened their powers and increased their libido, but I'd seen firsthand its destruction.

I shook her off. Touching Kayla didn't affect me the way touching Sydney did. The moments with the enchantress in the crypt were among the most arousing in my life. I looked down at her.

Sydney's light pink nipples were visible through her damp undershirt.

Fuck. I gulped in a deep breath, battling the insane urge to draw those gorgeous peaks into my mouth. Then I lengthened my strides to catch up to Raze and Victor.

They'd stopped at the door that led into the general prison population.

"What's the holdup?" I asked.

"The door won't open." Raze put his face level with the biometric scanner.

The scanner flashed red.

"Why isn't it working?" Raze exclaimed after it failed on him two more times.

"Maybe the scanners are on the fritz." Victor pushed him out of the way and held his ugly face up to the scanner.

The scanner flashed green and the door clicked open.

Victor gave Raze a snide look. "Then again, maybe the scanner doesn't like Deputy Wardens who think they know everything."

"Fuck off, Victor." Raze slapped the scanner as we walked through the door. "Stupid human technology. I don't even know why we have these."

I stopped myself from explaining that the prior doors had been massive stone slabs much like the crypt door. Only high-level earth elementals had enough power to move them. But since the Assembly changed the laws allowing nulls and those with other affinities to work as wardens, they'd had to find a workaround for the doors.

"I hate the scanners too," Kayla said from behind me.

"No one asked you, rookie," Victor called back to her.

Kayla let out an aggravated gasp. "Terran, you won't let that disgusting null disrespect me like that, will you?"

I exchanged a frustrated look with Raze.

He rolled his eyes.

Shocked, I stopped in my tracks. "Raze, your eyes!" There was a sliver of crimson around his irises. Although it was barely perceptible, it must have been enough to throw off the biometric scanner.

Kayla slammed into my back. "Ouch!"

"Go around me," I shouted.

An expression of hurt flashed across her face, but I kept my focus on Raze.

He gave me a skeptical look. "Are you messing with me, old friend?"

I shook my head and whispered into his ear. "The enchantress must have given some of your power back."

Raze held out his hand, his brow furrowing in concentration. A second later, a tiny flicker of flame danced on the end of his middle finger. "I can feel my fire again!" His joyous grin was almost worth the enchantment that had been placed on me. "But it's not even close to what I had before."

"We'll get it all back," I promised.

"Yes," he agreed with a determined nod. "We just have to convince her to return it."

And remove her enchantments on me, I mentally added. "It will happen. Don't worry."

Raze looked skeptical. "How can you be so sure?"

"Because we'll figure out what she wants most and use that to bargain with her." I glanced down at the alluring female in my arms. "We'll negotiate your power back."

"Or die trying," added Raze with a teasing smile.

The catchphrase, one we'd used since we were children at the academy, made me grin. "Yes, or die trying."

❧ 7 ❧

SYDNEY

A blast of freezing water tore me from a dreamless sleep. Sputtering, I opened my eyes and found myself laying naked on a rusted metal grate with my wrists shackled together. I was in what looked like a communal bathing area, but only the shower above me was on.

"Wash yourself, inmate 18734," a hoarse voice ordered.

I twisted around to see a middle-aged female warden staring at me. Although there wasn't a trace of makeup lining her null-brown eyes and her salt and pepper hair was cut short, there was no mistaking her for a warlock. For one, her jawline and wrists were too delicate to be male and for another, the uniform she wore highlighted the bulky curves of her body the same way it had showcased the bulging muscles of Terran and Raze.

I looked around for the males, but the female warden and I were the only ones in the shower area.

"Wash with that," she called out, motioning to a thick bar of detergent smelling soap next to me.

"I-it's cold," I said through my chattering teeth. The

freezing shower water was like tiny knives digging into my skin.

"This isn't the Temple of Blessed Water," she said, clicking her tongue in irritation. "Move your pretty little ass."

When I didn't move, she pursed her lips together. "If you don't clean yourself, I'll do it." She took a step forward, her gaze running up and down my body appreciatively. "Maybe I wouldn't mind doing it."

Horrified, I found the strength to push myself onto my knees. Then I tried to wash myself as best I could with my wrists shackled. It was almost as if the glowing purple cuffs had melded together while I'd been passed out.

"W-who are you?"

"Warden Clover," she answered in a clipped voice. "I've got a backlog of other inmates to process, so finish up. Soap your hair well, the last thing we need is another lice infestation."

Inwardly recoiling from the mention of lice, I scrubbed my hair and rinsed it twice.

"Enough." She turned off the water from across the room. "Put on your tunic." She motioned at a beige garment hanging from a hook on the tiled wall.

A wave of dizziness swept over me as I tried to stand. On my third try, I got upright. Then using the wall as support, I shuffled over to the hook and grabbed the thin scrap of fabric.

Just as I was wondering how I would dress with my wrists shackled together, the warden pulled a small, black remote from her duty belt and pressed a button.

Immediately, my wrist cuffs separated allowing me to move my arms freely.

"Try anything and I'll do this." She pressed another button on the remote. The glowing purple cuffs buzzed, and pain exploded up my arms.

"Ah!" I cried, shaking my wrists as if that would make the negators stop.

Warden Clover clicked the button again and gave me a satisfied look. "That was the first setting, these puppies go all the way to fifty."

Fifty? I couldn't even fathom that level of pain.

"Now get dressed."

My hands shook as I pulled the fabric over my head. The thing was basically a potato sack with ragged holes for my head and arms. The tattered neckline hit my sternum and the bottom of the scratchy fabric hit the tops of my thighs, making me feel very exposed. I looked around for the rest of the clothing.

"Underwear?"

"A pretty thing like you doesn't need it."

Shrinking from her heated gaze, I asked, "Where are my clothes?" I'd feel better wearing my panties. As I tried to tug the tunic further down my legs, I remembered the crystal I'd put in my skirt pocket. "I had a crystal with me. Where is it?"

Warden Clover frowned. "Any possessions will be returned once your sentence is served."

"But I'm innocent and—"

She pressed the button on her remote.

Shocking pain radiated from my wrist cuffs. Crying out, I fell to my knees.

"All the inmates say they are innocent." She dragged me up. "You wouldn't be here if you were."

As I swayed on my feet, my muscles spasmed and I had to fight the urge to throw up.

"Go on. Why don't you tell me you don't belong here?" Warden Clover said, her finger on her remote.

I bit my lip. I didn't want to feel that kind of pain ever again.

"Good. Keep that pretty mouth closed." She pulled me closer. "Unless you'd like to kiss me."

I tensed as she nuzzled my neck.

"You smell good, inmate 18734. You know... I could take care of you in here." She licked my earlobe.

Oh, Goddess. No. I jerked away.

There was a loud knock on the door.

The female warden started as if she'd been shaken from a daze. "Come on." She jerked me forward.

I had no choice but to stumble along after her.

She dragged me to a door and shoved me through it.

I half fell into a brightly lit hallway where a stunning, auburn-haired warden with silver-rimmed eyes stood tapping her foot impatiently.

"What in the realms took so long in there, Rhonda?"

"Watch your tongue, Kayla," Warden Clover replied. "You think you're hot shit because you've hooked your claws into Terran, but you're still on probation."

Are Kayla and Terran together? I wondered as the air-elemental turned her glare my way.

"I heard this one's trouble."

"Not so far." Warden Clover caressed my cheek. "She's been no trouble at all."

Uncomfortable with the glazed look in her eyes, I stepped back, only to have Warden Clover tighten her grip on my arm.

"There's something about you." Warden Clover leaned in to study my face. "I almost don't want to let you go."

Kayla saved me by grabbing my arm and yanking me free of Warden Clover. "I'll take it from here, Rhonda. Inmate 18734 has been assigned to my sector."

Warden Clover blinked slowly, looking dazed. "I should start processing the others." She didn't move and her gaze never left my face.

"The hag is losing it," Kayla muttered as she dragged me down the hallway. Although she was only a few inches taller than I was, the air elemental was surprisingly strong, and I had to work to keep up to her quick pace.

"Thank you, for saving me back there," I said through panting breaths. Warden Clover had been creeping me out.

Kayla ignored me, focusing instead on the enormous door in our path. Keeping her grip on my arm, she faced a flat black panel on the wall. A faint red beam of light moved across her face. Then the panel flashed green and the door slid open.

Fascinating. I'd seen nothing like it before. Human technology was forbidden at the academy. I'd never understood why.

A cacophony of voices tore my attention from the intriguing panel to the room ahead. Room wasn't the correct word. It was a massive underground cavern with at least two hundred prison cells with electrified bars carved into the bedrock. The prison cells were tightly packed together on four different levels that circled an enormous burning wood pyre in the center of the room.

As my nostrils filled with the scent of smoke and flame, I looked for symbols of the other three elements, but didn't find them.

"All fire elementals are housed here," Kayla said as if reading my mind. "Come on. You're tier four."

"There are warlocks here?" I asked, realizing the prison cells were filled with male prisoners. *Oh Goddess.* I'd never seen so many adult male warlocks before. All of them watching me with the rapt attention of a predator.

"Obviously," Kayla sneered as she ushered me to the stairs. "Ninety-five percent of our inmates are male, and we can't very well separate you criminals by element *and* gender. It's against regulation to put males and females in the same cell though. Apparently, the warlocks kept killing the witches." She let out a disdainful laugh that crawled down my spine.

As we walked toward the stairs, the catcalls started.

"Hey, pretty witch."

"You'd look good on my dick."

"Come over here, purple hair."

"I'm going to fuck you raw."

The screams and jeers reverberated loudly in the dome-shaped room. I covered my ears with my hands, terror gripping me. Maybe staying in the burial chamber wasn't such a terrible idea.

"Quiet, or I'll zap ya," shouted Kayla. She dug a hand into her pocket and yanked out a remote that looked similar to the one Warden Clover had used on me.

My entire body trembled at the memory of the excruciating pain.

Apparently, I wasn't alone in my feelings because a heavy silence immediately descended on the room.

Not wanting to upset the female warden, I tried to keep pace with her.

My muscles, seeming to have atrophied during my time in stasis, burned and shook as I attempted the seemingly endless flights of stairs. The dizziness that I'd felt earlier returned and when we stopped at the third floor landing, I hung over the steel handrail panting for breath. "N-need a minute."

"Get up," Kayla huffed, tapping her remote again.

Gritting my teeth, I mustered the last of my strength and pulled myself up using the handrail.

Apparently, my snail pace wasn't good enough for Kayla. She made a sound of frustration and grabbed my arm. Then using enviable strength, she dragged me the rest of the way to the fourth floor.

As I stumbled after her, I noticed the cells on the top floor differed from the ones downstairs. Instead of bars, the cell doors were made of solid electrified metal. At the bottom of the glowing doors were rectangular flaps that brought to mind mail-slots. *What are those for?*

Even more baffling were the metal cages sitting across from each cell. The cages were roughly the size of an elevator and overlooked the burning pyre down below.

"Tier four houses the most violent and assaultive inmates," Kayla said, nearly yanking my arm out of its socket. "You'll be confined to your cell at all times except for every four days when you may commune with your element."

I tripped and would have fallen if not for her bruising grip. "Sounds like solitary confinement." My palms grew sweaty at the thought of being alone for so long.

Kayla continued, "During that time, we will conduct inspections of your cell. Keep it tidy if you don't want further punishment."

I couldn't imagine any punishment worse than being alone for days on end. "What about morning temple?"

"Tier four inmates don't go anywhere." She stopped at an open cell and shoved me inside.

I went flying and barely stopped myself from slamming into the jagged rock of the back wall.

"Welcome home, inmate 18734," she said, activating the electrified door between us.

Trying to keep my tears from falling, I rubbed the finger-shaped bruises on my bicep and scanned the ten-by-ten-foot cell that was my new home.

It didn't seem too bad. With the jagged rock serving as the ceiling, floor, and walls, it felt rather cave-like.

The electrified door gave off more than enough light to see what looked like a mattress on the dirt floor in front of me. It, along with the threadbare blanket no bigger than a towel, called to my exhausted body.

I crawled over to the mattress and collapsed on top of it. Ignoring the musty scent of moldy straw, I closed my eyes and prayed that when I woke, it would be to find this was all a horrible nightmare.

8

RAZE

Hunger drove me to stop by the employee cafeteria to pick up a quick bite to eat before returning to my quarters.

As I navigated through the other off-duty wardens, my mind was a jumbled mess.

I'd been so driven to find Sydney and wake her that I hadn't fully thought through what would transpire after that.

What a fool I'd been. Just a few minutes in her presence and the succubus had reduced me to my basest and most primal instincts.

It grated to know that if not for Victor's intervention, she could have drained me near to death a second time.

I clenched my hands into fists, took a deep breath, and slowly opened them. Sydney was awake, and she'd already transferred some of my affinity back.

Feeling calmer, I looked down at the tendrils of smoke curling from my fingers. Soon, I'd force her to return all my power. Then things could be what they once were. I could return to my books and teaching and leave this wretched place behind.

Taking a deep steadying breath, I pushed through the cafeteria doors. The eating area was busy at this time of night. There were at least a dozen other wardens sitting at the bench tables, not that they invited me to eat with them.

As second in command at the prison, my presence was met with wary glances and hushed whispers. A few couples seated together immediately pulled their clasped hands apart.

I barely kept in my snort of derision. I couldn't care less if they were breaking the no fraternization rules. *Hellfire*. This job was hard enough. All of us living for months underground with no fresh air, sunlight, or visits with friends and family. I would no sooner begrudge them the companionship they found than I would deny them the food they were eating.

As I grabbed a pre-wrapped sandwich from the cooler and turned to leave, two wardens from third shift walked in to grab their lunch. The males were laughing and shoving each other.

I recognized Edison by his neon green hair. The young, lanky rookie had already been counseled that the color was against regulation, but apparently it resulted from a spell his older brother had placed on him. Researching a counter spell was on my to-do list.

Catching sight of me, Edison froze. He went ramrod stiff and saluted me. "Deputy Warden, sir."

The other warden, a stocky dark-skinned rookie, stopped in his tracks and saluted me too.

"At ease, wardens," I said, feeling like a killjoy. At least at the academy, the students had seemed happy to see me occasionally. *Sydney especially*.

I forced thoughts of her out of my mind. "How are your shifts going, wardens?"

The two males exchanged nervous glances.

Edison piped up. "Good, although someone desecrated the temple this evening."

I frowned. The Lost Soul's Temple, like all temples, was a sacred space. "What do you mean?"

Edison, one of the wardens responsible for running the inmates through morning and evening temple, lowered his voice. "We found dozens of dead insects on the floor by the pentagram."

"We think someone is pranking the Head Warden," the dark-skin rookie added. "Some wardens aren't happy with the mandatory overtime."

"I imagine they aren't," I said with a frown. The Head Warden was a pompous windbag who cared more for his pet wargs than the witches and warlocks who worked for him.

In the year or so I'd been here, working conditions had continued to deteriorate. Bonuses and vacations had been canceled and now there was unpaid mandatory overtime. It was no wonder employee turnover was so high.

I gave both males a hard look. "If you hear anything about who might have desecrated the temple, come to me. Okay?"

They nodded.

I dismissed them and carried my meal toward my quarters. Terran's room was next to mine, but it wasn't him I wanted to see at the moment.

I punched the code into my door and stalked over to the L-shaped hutch desk cluttered with books and scrolls. The desk was the only piece of furniture in the room other than an uncomfortable chair and a queen-size bed. To think, these were the upgraded accommodations. My room at the academy had been so much nicer. Moreover, it'd been just down the hall from the library which had one of the largest collections of ancient texts in all the realms.

But I no longer had access to those tomes.

Letting out a heavy sigh, I dropped my unappetizing meal down on my desk and pulled a palm-size wireless video receiver from my pocket. A quick swipe of my finger and I was looking through the video camera in Sydney's cell.

The bastard in me hoped I might catch her in a state of undress, but the witch was curled up under a blanket.

Why is she sleeping again?

A flicker of worry had me zooming in on her face. Other than being drawn with exhaustion and two shades too pale, she looked fine.

She's probably tired from using so much power to free herself from the ice. My power.

The familiar burn of anger flared to life inside me. I should order her blanket removed. The witch deserved no niceties. Not after what she'd taken from me.

Cursing the very sight of her, I turned off the receiver and forced my attention to the protection spell I was translating from a third dynasty scroll. I'd need it to shield myself from the succubus.

Several times, my focus strayed back to the receiver. *Is she awake now? What is she doing?* I fought the urge to check on Sydney five more times, before finally giving in. I brought up the camera feed and found that she'd kicked off the blanket.

My mouth went dry at the sight of her long, bare legs.

For two years I'd fantasized about how those legs would feel wrapped around my waist. Of all the students I'd taught, only she had consistently robbed me of my focus and concentration.

Even before she'd attempted to seduce me, there was something about her that called to me. And it wasn't just her stunning face and perfect body.

Her adroit mind fascinated me—she was one of the few students who got some of my highbrow humor. Additionally, I'd been touched by the shadowed vulnerability in her eyes. A lifetime of being rejected and bullied had left its mark on her. I could relate to that.

My father had browbeaten me all my life. I'm certain my first memory was of him sneering at me in my cradle. I'd never been powerful enough, willful enough, ambitious enough for him.

I knew all too well what that kind of rejection could do to someone and I'd done my best to intercede on Sydney's behalf. Any mistreatment of her in my class resulted in an automatic detention. However, when I'd pleaded with the headmistress to intervene on a more wide-scale manner, she'd dismissed my concerns. Peer rejection could be character building, she'd insisted.

Bound by my position, I'd been unable to aid Sydney other than encouraging the new student, Jasen, to watch over her. I'd also been unable to deepen our connection. But deepen it I'd longed to do even though I knew it was inappropriate.

When she'd grabbed me that morning in the hall, I'd naively thought my forbidden fantasies were finally coming true. Instead, I'd walked into a nightmare.

Sydney made a soft noise in her sleep and flipped over. As she did, her tunic rode up her thighs.

Curse the Elders. Had there ever been a female with a more perfect form?

As I undid my fly and stroked myself, I replayed the most thrilling moment of my life. Sydney perched on my desk, her legs spread, begging for me to kiss her. Touch her. Make love to her.

With a guttural cry, I came in my hand. Then, an all too familiar shame followed. *What kind of professor lusts after his students?*

I stripped off my clothes, reminding myself that I was no longer a professor and Sydney was no longer my student.

She's an inmate now and I can visit her any time I want.

Anticipation pooled low in my body, and my shaft hardened again.

I'll visit her now.

No. I couldn't see her until I had a protection spell to ward off her enchantments. And then...

And then I would take back what was mine and claim her beautiful body.

Resolved, I climbed into bed and tried to banish Sydney from my mind. As always, I failed.

My dreams recast the scene of my damnation.

Sydney sat perched on my desk at the academy. She was the embodiment of temptation with her plaid skirt pulled up high enough for me to glimpse her tiny white panties.

"Teach me, professor," she said in a breathless voice.

I ordered myself to walk away, but it was no use. The dream version of myself was consumed with lust for her.

"Please," she begged, opening the buttons of her uniform shirt with aching slowness.

In my nightmare, I moved closer to her and my ultimate doom.

Then inexplicably, Sydney's fingers stilled. "W-where am I?" She blinked and looked around the room. "We're back at the academy?"

Strange. My nightmares were always the same. In all of them, I'd fallen into her arms and she'd drained me of life.

Sydney pushed her skirt down and climbed off my desk. "Am I dreaming?"

Puzzled, I shook my head. "No, this is my nightmare. You always seduce me and steal my power."

Sydney shook her head and backed away from me. "No, I will not do that."

"But you did," I said, slowly advancing on her. "Right there." I pointed at the desk.

The dream version of Sydney suddenly appeared back on

top of my desk. She looked down at herself and let out a gasp. "What's happening?"

I didn't know, but I liked that I had control. For so long I'd been forced to relive her attack. Helpless to stop her. Helpless to stop myself. Night after night.

Now it seemed I'd get the chance to enact my vengeance. A smile pulled at my lips. "I have a gift for you Ms. Castaway."

She looked up at me with those bewitching eyes, and I called on my affinity.

Unlike in all the dreams before, a ball of fire formed in my palm. I hurled it into the center of her chest.

She let out a series of blood-curdling shrieks as she immolated on the spot.

As I stared at the pile of her ashes on top of my burning desk, I felt a little of my anger ease. That felt good.

Again.

I waved my hand, and the desk returned to its previous state. I waved my hand again and Sydney, whole and unharmed, reappeared on top of it.

Her entire body shook, and tears leaked from her eyes. "That was horrible. It hurt so much."

"It's just a dream." I stalked over to her. "Do you know how it feels to be drained of your life force... of your power? Can you imagine that pain?"

I grabbed her arm and flashed her back to the memory of me waking up from my coma after her attack. A wispy dream version of myself feebly struggled to call for help from my cot in the infirmary. My throat had been so parched, but I was too weak to raise my voice. It was hours before the academy healer came to my aid.

Then I showed her the visit from my father two weeks later.

The bastard strode into the infirmary with his gold-handled cane just as the wispy version of myself was relearning how to walk.

The shock of seeing him had turned my knees to water, and I sprawled out on the floor. "Father?"

Instead of offering me his hand, Father looked down at me as if I were a stain on his shiny leather shoes. His face, a slightly older version of my own countenance, wrinkled in derision.

"You always were weak, Ian."

The hope and joy that had briefly flitted across my face snuffed out. What a fool I'd been to imagine he was there to offer me sympathy and support.

Father inspected the signet ring on his left pinky. The ring and the ornate silver robes he wore, identified him as a member of the Assembly. He treasured the symbols of power above all else.

I'd wanted to defend myself, but my words stuck in my throat. Just like when I'd been a child beaten with that cane.

Father sniffed. "Such a continued disappointment you are. Not only do you repeatedly fail to live up to your potential, you somehow lost your power. Power is everything."

The version of me on the floor lowered my head in shame.

Father sneered. "And to think a young female robbed you of the family legacy." He made a tsking sound. "It would have been better if she'd taken your life too."

Sydney, who I'd almost forgotten was at my side, let out a gasp. "That's an awful thing to say."

"Quiet." I squeezed her arm.

My memory continued playing out in front of us.

Father telling me the Assembly would blame the loss of my power on a spell gone wrong and warning me to keep my silence or face the consequences of going against the most powerful archwarlocks and archwitches in all the realms.

Sydney went pale as she heard Father tell me that my

sworn's family had broken off our engagement—an engagement he had so carefully brokered at my birth. Then he announced that the headmistress was ending my employment.

The entire time I'd just sat there taking each piercing blow of his words.

"You'll come home," Father added. "I won't allow you to become destitute. How would that look to the rest of the Assembly?"

I looked up from the floor. "How kind of you."

Father was too filled with his own self-importance to pick up on my sarcasm. "I'll see you upon discharge." He turned and walked away, leaving me even more broken.

Sydney shook her head. "I'm so sorry. I never meant for any of that to happen."

"But it did," I spat. "And no matter your contrition, you can't undo the damage." I waved my hand, and we were back in my classroom. "But you can atone for it." I waved my hand again, and she was back on top of the desk.

She licked her lips. "How do you want me to atone?"

I hurled another fireball into her chest.

❦ *9* ❦

SYDNEY

I woke with my throat raw from screaming and my nostrils filled with the phantom stench of my burning flesh. The nightmare had been so horrifyingly real.

Over and over, Raze had incinerated me.

It's as much as I deserve.

My eyes watered as I considered what Raze had lost. His health. His power. His sworn. His position. His family's regard. *Wait.* I didn't know that for a fact. My subconscious had conjured a monster for his father, but hopefully his actual parents were nothing like that cruel warlock.

Even if Raze's family was wonderful, he'd suffered, and I needed to make it up to him. But first I had to get out of here.

I rolled off the lumpy mattress and regarded my surroundings.

Last night I'd been so tired, I'd missed the metal toilet/sink combo in the corner of the cell. It was behind a half-wall of concrete. I suppressed a shudder at the stainless-steel faucet built into the toilet tank. Something about washing with toilet water seemed very wrong, but then again, beggars couldn't be choosers and I was sure I'd get used to it in time.

Time. Oh, Goddess. How long will I be here?

I stopped myself before I could run down that rabbit hole. Getting anxious wouldn't help the situation. I needed to focus on staying positive and getting the lay of the place. There was a shower nozzle sticking out of the wall above the toilet. *My own shower.*

I looked over the cell, but I didn't see any shower levers or switches in the cave walls. There was a drain near the base of the toilet though, so at least the water from the shower wouldn't creep over to the mattress.

As I searched the cell, I came across a small alcove that contained a small square of soap, a plastic toothbrush with toothpaste, and a plastic comb. *Nice.*

I forced my shaking legs to support me while I stumbled over to grab the comb and worked it through the tangled mess of my hair. Going to sleep with a wet head had done me no favors. Not that there was anyone to horrify with my appearance.

A red light on the ceiling snared my attention. As I stared at it, I realized it belonged to a small mounted camera that swiveled as it scanned the cell. *Oh, Goddess.* I didn't have an ounce of privacy in here. Anxiety rose again, but I forced myself to take a deep breath and let it out. I could hear my caregiver's voice in my head. *"Focus on solutions instead of problems, dear."*

I can handle this. The concrete wall would shield me when I was using the toilet and I could always crouch down behind it while showering.

This isn't bad at all. This cell was about as large as my dorm room back at the academy. Since I didn't have to share it with a roommate that hated my guts, it was a kind of upgrade.

My attempts to cheer myself up faltered as I thought of

the academy. What happened to Jasen and Novah? According to Raze, it had been almost two years since I'd seen them.

A sob wrenched from my throat as I remembered how scared they had sounded when I initially collapsed.

Taking another deep breath, I promised myself that I would figure out a way to reach them.

At my earliest opportunity, I'd request a meeting with the warden in charge. I'd explain that I'd been brought here by mistake. I had done nothing wrong.

What about the attack on Raze at the academy? my subconscious challenged.

I couldn't explain that, but it didn't mean they could lock me away without a trial. That went against elemental law. If the Head Warden wouldn't listen to my plea, then I'd appeal to the Assembly myself. We had rules to protect elementals. They couldn't just lock up anyone. Besides, I was innocent.

I wasn't acting so innocent back in the burial chamber. My face heated as I remembered pulling Terran down over me. His hands had felt amazing on me and so had Raze's.

Oh, Goddess. I'd behave like a total hussy. Maybe I was approaching my first fertile cycle. Normally, witches didn't cycle until their early twenties, but I could be an early bloomer.

Under normal circumstances, the onset of my cycle would have fast-tracked my consort ceremony, but that would not happen now. No doubt Logan had broken our engagement.

My throat grew tight as I thought of the attractive warlock with silver-rimmed eyes. He'd probably made a much worthier match for himself.

Which meant that... *I'm no longer sworn.* I could be with anyone I wanted.

Jasen.

My heart wrenched with pain. How ironic. Now that I could be with him, I was locked away.

Jasen is probably someone else's consort by now.

Despite my determination not to cry, tears trickled from my eyes. Then, as if I'd opened the floodgates, huge, wracking sobs exploded from my lips. It wasn't fair. My entire life had been filled with pain, rejection, and disappointment. And now I was stuck in prison away from the only two elementals who cared for me.

The sound of warlocks shouting outside my cell had me burrowing inside the thin blanket.

Buzz-clang.

It sounded as if someone nearby was throwing something hard at their electrified door.

Sobbing harder, I bowed my head low.

Oh, Goddess. Please help me.

A cynical voice inside my head whispered, "*Why would she help now when she never has before. Does she even exist?*"

"Yes," I said out loud. I may have lost my freedom, and the people that cared for me, but I would not lose my faith. There was a meaning to all of this. *There has to be.*

The exciting stories Jasen had told me flashed in my mind. The hobbit and his magic ring. The farm boy who became a Jedi. The Ripley who defeated the alien queen. They all had one thing in common—they all suffered before becoming heroes.

And wasn't the Goddess herself the epitome of suffering?

I would not allow this to break me. My pain would strengthen me so I could become a hero and maybe even a Guardian one day. Filled with resolve, I pushed myself up into a seated position just in time to make out heavy footsteps approaching my cell.

"Lunch," Kayla called out.

The electric current surrounding the door briefly wavered and a plastic plate with something brown and rectangular on it sailed through the bottom slot.

My growling stomach urged me to crawl over to the plate and inspect the brick. It was cold to the touch and carried no scent. *Odd.* I cautiously tore off one corner and discovered the brick had the consistency of beef jerky. Grimacing, I took a small bite. *Ugh.* It tasted of rotten fish, beets, and chalk. I spat it back onto the plate and decided I'd wait until dinner to eat.

Retreating to my mattress I fell into another dreamless sleep.

Hours later, I woke to another brick sliding through the food slot. I didn't need to taste it to know it was the same thing they'd given me for lunch. *Don't they serve actual food here?*

I crawled as close to the glowing door as I could without frying my face off and shouted, "Can I get something else to eat?"

Kayla laughed. "Eat the loaf or starve, inmate 18734."

I stared down at the nasty food-like substance trying hard not to whimper. And to think I'd complained about the academy food. My stomach groaned urging me to ignore the horrible taste and eat it. I took a big bite, swallowed, and then immediately rushed to the toilet and puked. It took fifteen minutes before my innards stopped spasming. Feeling beyond defeated I went back to lying on my mattress and praying that the next day would be better.

Much later I woke to the sound of water spraying. I bolted upright and immediately regretted it when a wave of vertigo slammed into me. The lack of food was definitely not helping my already light-headedness. Moving much more slowly, I crawled to the corner of the cell where the water ran. I reached my hand out to feel the icy water. *Goddess, was warm water too much to hope for?*

Deciding clean skin was worth freezing to death, I tore off my potato sack and let the icy droplets rain down on me. I was just reaching for the little bar of soap when the shower abruptly stopped. *I guess it only runs for five minutes.*

Shivering, I dressed in my potato sack and waited for my breakfast loaf to arrive. When it did, I kept down three small bites. *Win.*

I was trying to decide whether to crawl back to my bed, or just keep lying by the door, when suddenly the cell door opened.

A loud robotic voice spoke through a speaker, "Inmate 18734, step out of your cell."

What's this? I dragged myself up and stumbled out the door, only to step out into the elevator-sized cage. As soon as I stood completely inside it, the opening I'd stepped through became an electrified wall. Then the cage started moving as if on a mechanical track.

Through the metal bars I could see dozens of other cages moving around mine.

There was a loud clanging as all the cages stopped at the railing overlooking the burning flame and the lower levels of the prison. Even from this distance, I could see the cells down below were empty. *Those prisoners must be having their breakfast. I'll bet it is something better than a loaf.*

A flash of envy swept through me as I wiped away the sweat dotting my forehead. It was getting hot in here. My cage was right over the flaming pyre and the metal bars conducted the heat like an oven. *No. Imagine it's a sauna,* I told myself. Maybe if I pretended this was a kind of spa experience, I could get through this.

The clanking of doors opening and closing brought my head around.

Kayla and two other wardens were doing prison cell checks. It looked as if they were picking up plates and dropping off fresh blankets. *It's like room service.*

The prisoner in the cage behind me caught my eye. The

older warlock was only a few inches taller than my five-foot-three frame and stared at me with an intensity that made my hackles rise. I didn't know what creeped me out most. His wild frizzy hair, the crazed look in his crimson-rimmed eyes, or the fact that he wasn't wearing his potato sack and every bit of him was standing at attention.

I glanced away, my face heating even more.

"Hey, witch," came a gravelly voice.

I twisted around to see a tall, muscular inmate maybe an inch or two shorter than Terran. His entire body was covered with thick scars.

"You're a pretty piece of ass."

I bit back a scream as I saw most of the inmate's face had been torn away. The remaining mangled tissue looked like dripped candle wax clinging to bone.

The warlock bared teeth that had been filed down to look like fangs. "You look like my ex, witch."

"You killed your ex," Crazy Eyes said in a dry, raspy voice behind me.

"Fuck yeah, I did," Scar Face shouted back.

"Then you ate her," Crazy Eyes added.

Scar face let out a wistful sigh. "That bitch tasted good."

"I'll bet this one tastes better," Crazy Eyes said, moving closer to my cage. His gaze crawled over my body like tiny insects.

I tried to move back and accidentally touched the electrified wall. Pain jolted me and I cried out.

Crazy Eyes inhaled deeply. "I love it when they scream."

"So do I," Scar Face said, flashing me those monstrous fangs again.

"After I fuck this one to death, I'll let you have her body," Crazy Eyes said in a voice so calm and reasonable he could have been offering the other inmate his lunch. Given the way

Scar Face smacked his lips, that might have been exactly what he was doing.

I shrank into a ball on the floor of the cage while they continued to plan my death. When the thirty minutes was up, I ran into my cell.

Oh, Goddess. I didn't know how much more of this I could take.

The wardens who had inspected my cell had left me another potato sack, a clean blanket, and a laminated sheet of paper that listed the prison rules. Almost none of them applied to the tier four inmates since we weren't allowed to go to the cafeteria, rec yard, or day room.

For a moment, I wondered if the edge of the laminated paper was sharp enough to slit my wrists.

Sadly, it wasn't.

TERRAN

I t'd been a long ass double shift made worse because one of the Head Warden's pet wargs had been found dead inside the prison temple. To say the Head Warden had lost his shit was an understatement.

Whoever had flung the poor creature into the portal as a joke had just written themselves a one-way ticket into the slammer. Killing bugs was one thing. Murdering one of the Head Warden's prized pets was another.

After listening to the blowhard shouting for hours about the warg killer, all I wanted to do was clock out for the night. As I pushed the door to my room open, I discovered a complication to my plan.

Kayla was sprawled out naked on my bed. As I cursed under my breath, she held up glasses filled with blue liquid. "Hi, Lead Warden."

Not this again. I'd already broken up with her and ordered her to stay out of my quarters. Aggravated beyond reason, I stepped in and slammed the door behind me. "What the fuck are you doing in here?" As a mid-level air elemental, Kayla could use her power to move air currents and objects in space. Objects that apparently included my locked door.

Kayla sat up slowly as not to splash the nasty shit in the glasses. "I thought we could celebrate our first month anniversary."

Our anniversary? "We *were* fuck buddies." I emphasized the past status of our relationship. "Fuck buddies don't have anniversaries. Or follow each other around their place of employment. Or break into each other's rooms." I scrubbed the stubble on my jaw trying to rein in my temper.

Kayla's too bright smile didn't dim for a second. "You seem wound up. This will help." She floated one of the glasses over to me.

I wrinkled my nose at the sickly-sweet blueberry scent. "You know I hate Spark." Not only had my mom favored the semi-hallucinogenic liquid before her death, at least a quarter of the inmates had Spark addictions prior to their apprehensions. I'd long thought we should outlaw the highly addictive substance, but apparently the Assembly didn't agree.

Kayla pouted and made the floating glass circle my head. "Don't be a spoilsport. This is top of the line. I spent almost my entire paycheck on it."

"Then you're an idiot." I wondered how she got her hands on the drug down here. Deciding it was probably for the best I didn't know, I stepped around the floating glass, undid my duty belt and set it on my dresser. My aching hips and lower back immediately breathed a sigh of relief. "Look, I'm tired and I want to sleep. Take your Spark and go."

"You don't mean that." Kayla set the glass she was holding on my nightstand and dipped her finger in it. Then she traced her nipple with a drop of the blue liquid. "Come over here and lick me clean." She parted her legs and moved her fingers between the thatch of red hair at the apex of her thighs.

Instead of turning me on, her actions turned my stomach.

Why can't she take the hint? Letting some frustration out, I said, "How many times do I have to tell you it's over between us?"

She reared back on the bed. "But you said you needed me."

Is she already high? "No, I didn't." I'd never gone after any female. I just occasionally fucked the ones that went after me.

She shook her head in denial. "Yes, you did. That time you came to my academy job fair."

I had a foggy recollection of speaking to her and dozens of other students at the recruitment event. She'd been flirtatious and I liked the look of her in the short plaid skirt. "I probably said I needed someone like you here at the prison, which was true. We need more wardens and I wanted to recruit you. But I didn't tell you anything I didn't tell the other students."

She blinked rapidly. "I turned down much better assignments to be a warden... because of you. And then when we started sleeping together, I thought it meant something."

I shook my head. "Don't put that on me. I was clear from the start that you and I were only to have a bit of fun. Remember, I said no strings attached."

"I didn't really think you meant that."

Clearly. My eyes felt grainy and my head throbbed with exhaustion. I needed this over and her ass out of here. "I never say things I don't mean. Now, if you wouldn't mind..." I motioned at the door.

Her eyes flashed with emotion. "There's more to it. There's someone else, isn't there?"

What? Surprised, I didn't immediately respond.

Kayla sucked in a breath. "Fuck. I knew it. Tell me who she is?" Her hands curved like claws into my sheets.

Unexpectedly, a pair of indigo eyes flashed in my mind. Deciding Kayla might move on sooner if she thought there was someone else, I said, "It's the new purple-haired inmate, if you must know. Now find some self-respect and get the fuck out of my room."

Kayla let out a barn owl-like screech and threw her hands out.

An invisible wind slammed me against the wall.

Kayla's lips drew back in a feral sneer. "I came down here for you and you throw me over for some crazy criminal!"

Holding me in place with one hand, she waved her other hand at the glasses.

Both the floating glass and the one on the nightstand torpedoed at my head.

I ducked the first one which shattered over my right ear, but the second glass slammed into the side of my forehead before smashing on the floor.

Ouch. That'll leave a mark. I wiped away the sticky blue syrup. "Now, who is acting crazy?" I shouted.

"Fuck you!" Kayla waved her hands and my ceramic lamp followed the trajectory of the glasses.

"Stop!" I ordered, twisting away.

The lamp smashed into the wall next to me.

Kayla then waved at the framed photo of my dad hanging on the wall. It was my favorite picture of him. The same one that hung in the prison's hallway of heroes.

Not that!

Reflexively, I snatched it out of the air before it could hit me and set it safely on the floor. "Stop now!"

Her gaze roamed my room and landed on my duty belt.

She wouldn't.

With a flick of her hands, my radio slid out and flew into my stomach.

I tried to catch it, but it smashed to the floor.

Fuck. Those human devices were costly to repair. "Are you done now?"

"No!"

I sucked in a breath as my duty handgun unholstered and turned to point at my face.

Her tantrum had taken a deadly turn. "Enough!"

The gun wavered in the air.

Sensing her weakening resolve, I crunched through the glass to grab the weapon. I could have sent the jagged glass pieces flying at her face, but I didn't. Call me classy and shit.

Instead, I walked over to the door and yanked it open. "You're dismissed, Warden Skye."

Kayla's face crumpled at my cold, but professional tone. She gathered her clothes and darted naked into the hallway. "You'll regret this!"

"I already do." I slammed the door and mopped the Spark off my face. *Never again will I fuck around at work.*

Stepping over the glass on the floor, I set my gun on my dresser. Then, I kicked off my boots and dove into my bed. *Ugh.* My sheets smelled like Spark. I hated that scent. It reminded me so much of the only female to break my heart.

As my eyes closed, my subconscious cued up the worst fucking day of my life...

⚜

DADDY WAS WORKING LATE. HE WAS ALWAYS WORKING late. I missed when he'd throw me up in the air and tickle me. I wished I was bigger so I could be a warden and help him too.

Mama was in her room, like always. I wasn't to bother her, but I was hungry. She hadn't gotten me breakfast or lunch and my belly sounded like a growling monster.

Mama could make lunch. Then we could play like we used to in the sandbox. *Mama makes the best sandcastles.*

I put down the rocks I'd been playing with and slowly

walked toward Mama's room. The hallway was dark and it seemed so long. Mama's door was open a crack. The sliver of harsh bright light from inside made me blink.

"Mama." I put my small hands up to the door.

No! I knew what I'd find inside, but I couldn't stop the younger version of myself from pushing against the heavy wood.

"Hey, little guy," a female voice called out.

I twisted my head around to see Sydney standing in the hallway behind me.

She was dressed in a prison tunic.

What the fuck? It wasn't enough that I fantasized about her all day, now she was visiting my dreams too.

Sydney crouched down. "Are you looking for your mama, little guy?"

Her presence snapped the compulsion to relive the pain of this day.

"Not at all," I said, growing to my full adult height. "And no one calls me little guy."

"Terran?" She blinked up at me in surprise, while our surroundings shifted to my quarters.

I leered down at the witch still crouched on the floor. "If you stay in that position, I could put you to work."

Those incredible indigo eyes of hers expanded as she stood. "Am I in your dream now?"

"Apparently," I said, watching her study my room. There wasn't much to see beyond my dresser and bed. I came here to sleep and occasionally fuck.

Just thinking of the last romp I'd had with Kayla, soured my stomach. I pushed thoughts of the air elemental away and focused on Sydney.

She looked at the picture of my dad that, in my dream, was still on my wall. "Is this your father?"

"Yes."

She looked between me and the photo. "You look a lot like him."

"I've heard that before." Seriously, if my subconscious was going to summon my enchantress, I wanted more than bullshit small talk. My balls tightened as I imagined all the ways I wanted to take this female.

"He was a warden too?" she asked, studying the uniform Dad was wearing.

"He was the Head Warden here for years."

"Is that why you wanted to become a warden too?"

I moved closer to her. "Why don't we talk about something else like what you're wearing under that tunic?"

She blinked. "I'm not wearing anything under here."

"Are you sure?" I stepped behind her. "Maybe I should check."

"I'm sure." She shied away and inspected the duty belt lying on my dresser. "Wow. There are a lot of things on here. What does this do?" She pulled out a tube of mace.

I grabbed it from her hand. "Nothing you want to experience."

"These are heavy," she said, pulling out my spare pair of negators.

Now we're talking.

I plucked them from her hand. "Should I cuff you?" Every female I'd been with got off on the whole warden-prisoner role play.

I opened a cuff and started to snap it around her bare wrist.

She jerked her hand away. "Why would you do that?"

I leaned down and whispered in her ear, "So I can hook your arms to my headboard and lick every inch of your body."

"What? No." She backed away from me until the back of her thigh hit my dresser.

Well, fuck. "Figures," I said more to myself than her. I

tossed the negators on my dresser. "I can't even get my sexual fantasies to go right today."

Sydney wet her plump lips. "Is that what this is? A sexual fantasy."

"Why else would you be here," I grumbled.

"So we could talk and get to know each other."

I groaned and sat down on my bed. "I don't do that shit with females in the real world, why the fuck would I do that in my dreams?"

"Maybe it would be refreshing." She hopped up on the bed next to me. "I'd like to get to know you. Maybe we could be friends. My only friend is Jasen."

"Who's Jasen?"

"He's a water elemental from the academy." Her indigo eyes sparkled. I didn't like that they did that for another male.

"He's your only friend."

She blinked. "Yes."

"Did you fuck him?"

Her mouth dropped open. "N-no."

"But you wanted to, didn't you?"

She didn't respond, but her face flushed a pretty shade of pink.

She's a virgin. Interesting that my subconscious would generate this kind of fantasy. I usually avoided virgins like the plague.

Still, variety was the spice of life. And the idea of introducing my dream enchantress to every depraved thing on my mind turned my cock to granite.

"How about this, enchantress? I'll play your getting to know you game if you play one of my games."

Her eyes narrowed suspiciously. "What game is that?"

"It's called the kissing game." I tried for my most innocent smile. "For every question I answer of yours, I get to kiss you."

"Aren't you and Kayla together?" she asked, sounding breathless.

How in the realms does she know about Kayla? Deciding it was another inexplicable figment of my dream, I said, "No. Kayla and I are over."

"Oh." Sydney relaxed. "Okay then. I'll play your game."

Fuck yeah. Shit just got interesting.

SYDNEY

In my dream, Terran gave me a wicked smile that made my heart pound.

It's just kissing. No big deal. And I'd get the chance to learn more about the huge warlock. So what if I'd only kissed Raze before. I'd seen other witches kiss their sworn, and I'd read about kisses.

My face heated as I thought back to the erotic scenes in Andrea's books. We wouldn't kiss like that. Just a peck on the lips.

I stared at Terran's mouth noticing for the first time how full his bottom lip was. *Perfect for nibbling.*

Terran shifted his weight on the bed, and I had to hold my body straight to keep from crashing into his hulking frame.

He really was the biggest warlock I'd ever seen. Even seated, the top of his close-cropped brown hair was at least a foot taller than my head.

Being this close to him made me feel so small and delicate.

He can snap my neck with one of his giant hands.

Or pleasure me with those long fingers.

I flushed at my dirty thoughts. It seemed even in my dreams I was acting like a hussy.

"Well?" Terran said in his deep velvety voice.

I realized he was waiting for me to ask the first question. "Um..." My brain blanked. I'd had a million questions just a minute ago and now... nothing.

He waited with patience I wouldn't have expected from a male like him. Back in the burial chamber, he and Raze had been so fierce and intimidating.

Suddenly, a question popped into my mind. "How do you know Raze?" I sensed a long history between the two males.

He blinked as if I'd gone in a direction he hadn't expected. "We went to school together."

I leaned forward. "Really?"

"Yeah, we were roommates at the Arcane Academy for over a decade."

"That's a long time," I said thinking of Andrea. She'd been my longest running roommate, and we'd only shared a room for a year. All my roommates usually left at the end of the semester. I wasn't sure why she hadn't, maybe she requested a transfer and there had been no other rooms available. "You must have gotten close."

"We did. We got into a lot of trouble together." He gave me a lopsided smile that brought to mind that tow-headed child I'd encountered at the beginning of my dream. "Although Raze ended up taking a Scholar assignment, and I ended up here," he motioned around his room, "we stayed in touch."

"And now he's a warden too."

Terran nodded. "He needed a gig after you stole his power and he lost his job."

I flinched at the coldness creeping into his eyes. "I never meant to hurt him. I promise you."

He smiled again, but there was no warmth to it. "As if I would ever believe a promise given by a female."

Feeling as if he'd slapped me, I sat back. "Why would you say something like that?" He hadn't struck me as a misogynist, but then again, what did I really know about him?

Terran cocked his head to the side. "That's your second question. I won't answer that until you've paid for your first."

Fair is fair, I guess. "Okay." I pursed my lips and leaned over to give him a quick peck on the mouth.

He jerked back, shaking his head. "I never kiss on the lips."

I blinked in surprise. "Where then?"

He looked down at my chest. "I want to kiss your nipples."

"Oh." My breath lodged somewhere between my heart and my throat. What he was asking was scandalous, but this was just a dream, right?

"Okay." Summoning what was left of my bravado, I arched my chest out toward him. My nipples had hardened into little nubs the moment he'd mentioned them, and they jutted against the scratchy fabric of my tunic.

Terran made a low sound halfway between a growl and a purr.

It sent a bolt of liquid heat straight to the juncture of my thighs.

He reached out and pushed my tunic off one shoulder, exposing my right breast.

I tensed as he moved closer. My nipple seemed to swell under his intense gaze.

He lowered his mouth and gave the turgid peak a teasing lick.

I gasped as pleasure jolted through me.

Then he brought my nipple into his mouth. At first, the

pull of his lips was gentle. Then the suction grew harder and he bit down just enough to make me cry out.

Raw need pulsed from where he was latched straight down to my core.

As if he knew how hot and aching I was, he put one of his enormous hands onto my bare thigh.

The scorching heat of his palm startled some sense into me.

Catching my breath, I scooted away. "My turn to ask a question."

He leaned back and regarded me with a hooded gaze that made me squirm with desire. "Ask away."

"Why don't you kiss your lovers on the mouth?"

He clenched his jaw, passion leeching from his green-rimmed eyes. "I don't want to get attached."

Sensing I was closing in on something very important, I waved him on. "Because?"

He sighed and looked over at the framed photo of his father. "It's complicated."

I could feel him withdrawing. *Curse it.* Some unseen force drove me to discover more about this male. Knowing I had but one tool in my arsenal, I pulled both of my arms through the top of my tunic. Then I shimmied the scratchy fabric down to my stomach, exposing both my breasts to his hungry gaze.

That had the desired effect.

He bit back a groan, reached for me and then caught himself. "Because if I don't care about them, then they can't hurt me the way my mother hurt my father. His soul died when she left him, and he never recovered." Terran's gaze held such pain, my eyes burned in sympathy.

It was the same bleak look the little boy had in the beginning of the dream.

A dark realization choked me. "Your mother killed

herself."

Terran looked away. "She slit her wrists. I'll never forget the sight of all that blood." He swallowed thickly. "Who the fuck does something like that knowing their kid will see it?"

I shook my head mutely, feeling the anger and grief reverberating from him.

Terran took a deep breath. "I hated her for what she did. To me. To my dad. He followed her in death two years later. By then he was just a shell of his former self. They'd been consorts for over twenty years before they had me." He gave me a tight smile. "They didn't think they could have children and then, surprise." He motioned down at himself.

"You must have been a wonderful surprise," I said in a gentle voice.

Terran shook his head. "Not so much. The healers concluded that after my birth, my mom spiraled into a postpartum depression which was exacerbated by Spark use. It was my fault she killed herself and my fault that my dad died of a broken heart."

Tears stung my eyes. He couldn't really believe that could he? "No, it wasn't. You can't believe that for a second."

He pressed his lips together in a firm line.

I reached out and put my hand over his. "She was mentally ill, Terran. No one is to blame."

He took a ragged breath and wound his fingers through mine. "I don't know why I'm telling you all this. I've told no one. Not even Raze."

"Well, it's a dream, so it doesn't count," I said, trying to lighten the mood. "Besides, we're playing a game, aren't we?"

The raw pain in his gaze was quickly replaced with passion. "Yes. My turn to claim my reward."

"Claim away." Anticipation thrummed through me as I arched my chest toward his lips, but he surprised me by sliding off the bed.

He knelt on the floor in front of my legs. Then he slowly nudged my knees apart and pushed up my tunic.

When he brushed his fingers over my core, I gasped. "What are you doing?"

"I'm going to kiss you here."

I struggled to speak—to refuse his scandalous proposal. But then he was moving his fingers in concentric circles around the epicenter of my desire. A strangled moan escaped my lips as heat spiraled out from his touch.

Taking that as consent, he lowered his head. His hot breath washed across my damp flesh.

"Oh, Goddess!" I dug my fingers into his sheets, holding on for dear life.

He gripped my hips and brought me to his lips.

The first swipe of his tongue along my seam ignited every single nerve in my body.

As if my moan had flipped a raw and primal switch inside him, he shoved me down onto my back, yanked my legs over his shoulders and began to feast.

The things he did with his tongue, teeth and lips, had me sobbing incoherently. I was bombarded with pleasure unlike anything I'd ever experienced. Lust coiled tighter and tighter inside me until I could no longer breathe. It was too much.

"Please," I cried, not sure exactly if I was begging for him to stop or keep working the magic with his tongue.

"Not so fast," he chided, pulling away.

The frustrated cry I gave died when he crawled over me. My breathing went even more ragged as the hard point of his manhood pressed against my aching heat.

My tunic was balled around my stomach, leaving the rest of my skin bare for him to touch. And I wanted him to touch me... kiss me... put himself inside me.

I cursed the fact that he was still fully dressed in his

uniform. The swirl of blue ink near his collarbone drew my gaze. "I'm ready for my next question," I panted.

He arched one brow, his face only inches from mine. "What's that now?"

"Can you show me your tattoos? All your tattoos."

The sexy grin he gave me made my toes curl.

"As you wish, enchantress."

He rolled off me and landed smoothly on his feet next to the bed. Then he brought his hands to either side of his shirt and ripped the fabric in two.

His body was such a thing of beauty. I sat up marveling that every inch of his muscled flesh, aside from the area above his collarbone and the area below his forearms, was covered in intricate blue tattoos. I'd seen nothing like it before.

"You're so pretty."

Terran scoffed. "Males aren't pretty."

"Handsome then," I offered.

"I'll take that." He rested his hands on the waistband of his black pants. "Are you sure you want to see all my tattoos?"

I nodded, not trusting myself to speak.

He worked his fly open. His thick, swollen shaft fell out and bobbed in the air. It was massive, as thick as my wrist, and tattooed from root to its smooth pink crown.

I sucked in a breath. I wanted to touch it, taste it, and press it inside me.

He pushed down his pants and kicked them off along with his boots. His thickly muscular legs and thighs were as gloriously tattooed as the rest of him. "Is your curiosity quenched?"

"No," I whispered. "I have another question, Handsome. How can that fit inside me?"

His shaft jumped under my gaze. "Let me show you."

As he prowled back to the bed, I lay back and parted my

thighs. From my roommate's saucy books, I technically knew what came next, but I couldn't wait to experience it with him.

No matter how icy his demeanor, I now knew he was at his core a good male. He'd been traumatized at a young age, but it wasn't something he couldn't come back from with help from the right female. I wanted to be that female.

Terran grabbed my hips and dragged me to the edge of the bed. Then he flipped me around onto my stomach.

I let out a startled sound as my face hit his bed sheets.

"Get on your hands and knees," he ordered, his voice deeper and sexier than ever.

"Okay." Excitement and trepidation coursed through me as I pushed up into the position he requested.

The mattress dipped as he moved behind me.

I trembled at the feel of his hairy legs pressing against the backs of my smooth ones.

One of his hands gripped my hip. Then something huge and hard bumped against the inside of my thigh.

"I can't wait to be inside you, enchantress," Terran growled. Then he was pushing forward. I felt him breeching me, filling me, ending my innocence forever...

Suddenly, Terran was gone. His bed was gone. And I was seated on Professor Razell's desk dressed in my school uniform.

What in the realms?

I glanced around the classroom, cringing at the sight of the sinfully gorgeous, dark-haired warlock approaching me with balls of fire in his hands.

No. I don't want this.

My entire body ached with a need so intense, I ground my molars together. *I want Terran.* I closed my eyes, willing myself back to his bed.

Raze made a tsking noise. "There you are, Miss Castaway. Are you ready to atone for your sins tonight?"

❧ 12 ❧

RAZE

Excitement thrummed through me as the witch appeared on my desk as if I'd conjured her.

Incinerating her over and over had brought me immeasurable satisfaction last night, and I was looking forward to enacting more revenge.

I lifted my hands enjoying the sight of the flames sparking off the ends of my fingers. If only I had my power back in real life too. But she had taken it. Rage made my flames spike higher. I'd burn her to ash quickly and then take my time with her on the next go round.

Sydney's eyes were shut tight as if she anticipated the oncoming pain.

"Are you ready, Miss Castaway?" I asked her again.

"No." Her purple eyes flew open. "I was having the most incredible dream before this..." She let out a pained moan and rubbed her thighs together. No amount of my anger could stop my gaze from zeroing in on her nipples, stiff as berries against her crisp white shirt.

I had to ask, "What were you dreaming about?"

She licked her swollen looking lips, the passion in her eyes unmistakable. "Terran."

And just like that the fire in my palm fizzled. "What? Why?"

"He's an incredible lover," she said in a breathless voice.

Curse the Elders. What kind of dream is this?

"He's cruel to females," I said, feeling the ridiculous need to warn her.

Her eyes flashed. "Only because he doesn't trust them. Someone he loved very much hurt him."

I blinked at her insight. I'd never really sought to understand my friend's hostility to the fairer sex. "But he's not cruel to you I take it?"

"No, you are the cruel one," she said, lifting her chin in challenge. "And I want to be with him now instead of you."

I tried to hide my stung ego with an icy laugh. "As if you have a choice in the matter, *My'ilana*." The nickname, which meant purple one in the ancient tongue, fell smoothly off my lips, the way it had when I'd called on her in class.

She gave me an injured look and took a deep breath. "Prof... Raze, why do you hate me so much? In your lectures, you said the Ancient Ones shouldn't be blamed for destroying the Goddess because they didn't understand the ramifications of their actions. But now, you blame me for something I couldn't control."

I went motionless, finally seeing the frustration and grief in her beautiful face. She was such a puzzle. Innocent and seductive. Sweet and malevolent. Of all the mysteries I longed to solve, I ached to understand her most of all.

She took a deep breath and continued. "Something happened to me during the testing ceremony. I-I think I came into my power for the very first time. But neither you nor any of my other professors prepared me to handle it."

I wanted to blurt out we didn't even know spirit elementals still existed, but I held my tongue. What she was saying did make sense. Prior to her attack, Sydney demonstrated no signs of any affinity. If she'd been hiding her power, she'd deserved the highest acting awards. The most likely explanation was that she'd suddenly come into her power and it had overwhelmed her. But that didn't excuse her attack on me. *Did it?*

She stepped off my desk and paced around it. "It consumed me... the hunger." Her cheeks flushed. "It makes me want sex."

"I'm well aware," I replied.

Her head snapped around so quickly, her hair flew in her face. "Well, I wasn't aware. I didn't understand what was happening to me or why I craved your touch. All I knew of sex came from romance novels and the fantasies I had of you and Jasen."

Her confession blindsided me. Although I'd suspected she was inexperienced up until her attack, never had I guessed she might reciprocate my romantic notions.

"You had sexual fantasies of me?" That shouldn't have been relevant, but somehow it was all I could focus on.

She nodded, that tantalizing blush spreading down her neckline.

Are the tops of her breasts flushed too? My breathing quickened. "What did I do in these fantasies of yours?"

"You pleasured me with your..." She glanced at the tent my arousal had made in my pants.

Lust gripped me as it had in all my dreams before. But this time it felt different. I sensed I could walk away.

To test my theory, I stepped behind a row of students' desks, increasing the distance between us. She did not hold me in thrall. *I can walk out of this classroom if I want.* But I didn't want to do that. Instead, I longed to bring every one of our wicked fantasies to life.

Sydney turned her back to me as if embarrassed to look me in the eye. She stared at the spells written on the blackboard. "I wish I could go back to the day of the testing ceremony. Maybe if I'd walked out before the headmistress called on me…"

"Your affinity would have eventually manifested. Remember the quote from Z'solemn the wise."

She tipped her face in my direction and said, "You might as well try to stop a storm with a kiss as stop inherent magic."

It wasn't the exact quote, but the essence was there. "So, you see, there would be no avoiding what happened to you." *Or to me.* I let out a shaky breath and along with it much of my anger.

She shook her head. "I just wish it hadn't been you that I… attacked."

I moved toward her, stopping just behind her. I wasn't overly tall for a warlock, but the top of her head only came to the middle of my chest. "If not me, then who? One of the other students? They would not have survived." Of that I was confident. I'd barely recovered, and I was more powerful than most all of the students and faculty. With a burst of clarity, I realized that me bumping into her in the hall had saved someone's life.

"I'm so sorry," she said with a sniff.

I bent my mouth to her ear and whispered, "I have an idea for how you can atone for what you did."

She stiffened. "You're going to burn me again."

"No." Slowly, I wrapped my arm around her and pulled her against me. "What would you say if I told you I had fantasies about you too?"

She rested the back of her head against my chest. "I'd say you were lying."

I pressed my erection against her. "Does this feel like dishonesty?"

She let out a gasp.

"Do you want me to show you one of my fantasies?"

She nodded.

"We can stop anytime, just say the word." I guided her over to my desk. "Put your hands there next to the papers."

She obediently leaned over and placed her hands on my desk.

I gathered her hair in my hand and tugged her head back. "You've been such a naughty student, Miss Castaway. You must be punished."

She looked back at me with a mixture of excitement and trepidation. "How will you punish me?"

"You'll be spanked." I reached down and lifted her skirt. The sight of her little white panties made my throat dry. Swallowing hard, I lifted my shaking hand and brought it down on her ass, hard enough to cause a momentary sting.

She gasped.

I spanked her again, a little harder.

A pleasured moan escaped her lips.

"Do you like that?" I said into the shell of her ear.

"I-I think I do," she confessed, her eyes on my desk.

"Let's see how much." I slid my hand between her legs, finding her panties soaked through.

She made a keening sound as I moved my hand under the elastic and rubbed her damp flesh.

"Oh, Goddess!" She writhed against me when I pinched the swollen jewel at the top of her sex.

When her thighs trembled and her cries grew loud enough to shake the blackboard, I spun her around and sat her on the desk.

The motion threw papers into the air where they momentarily fluttered like wingless doves.

"Off," I ordered, waving my hand.

Sydney's clothes disappeared, and after months of questioning her existence, I found the Goddess again. For only she could have created a female as beautiful as this.

"Exquisite," I murmured, following the perfect curves of Sydney's body to the tantalizing center of her sex.

"That's handy," she panted, her beautifully shaped breasts heaving. "Does it work both ways?"

"Why don't you find out?" I challenged, loving how her brow furrowed in concentration.

"Off!" she ordered.

At once my clothes evaporated and I was as nude as she. For a brief moment, I felt self-conscious. Although muscular because of my exercise regime, I was nowhere near Terran's mammoth build.

However, Sydney's eyes held no recrimination as she stared at my hairy chest. She crooked her finger at me. "Come here."

I fought the urge to take back control. This was my dream... my fantasy. But then she opened her legs and the visual of those pale thighs spread across my desk was too powerful to resist.

I fell over her as I had during the attack. I kissed down her neck and breasts, licking her nipples while I delved my fingers inside her.

She arched off the desk, letting out wild cries that furthered my own lust.

I started to drop down to my knees so I could taste her honey, but she shook her head. "I need... I need..."

I tensed. *This is the part where she drains me to death.*

But instead of trying to fuse our mouths together, she wrapped her hand around my aching shaft.

The sensation nearly blew off the top of my head. Letting out a hiss of breath, I forced myself to stillness as she worked her hand up and down my flesh. Lust speared through me with every pass of her fingers. My knees buckled, and I leaned against the desk for support.

Her strokes quickened. "Please," she pleaded, trying to pull my shaft to her sex.

I couldn't deny her, or myself. Gripping her legs, I slid her to the very edge of the desk and aligned our bodies. Then with one punch of my hips, I claimed her. She was so tight. Magnificently tight.

Sydney let out a wild sob as I moved. "Yes!"

Delighted by her cries of pleasure, I increased the pace, rocking my pelvis to the frenetic beat of my heart.

She took everything I gave her, chasing every thrust with her hips.

It was incredible—everything I'd ever imagined and more.

As we moved together in a rhythm as old as magic, the papers on the floor took to the air around us, swirling as if captured in some imaginary wind tunnel. Faster and faster they whirled as if they were responding to the rising tension in our bodies.

Sydney made a keening sound and arched off the desk. She was close. So close.

Wanting us to fly across the abyss together, I moved my hand between us and rubbed her swollen little bud.

Her eyes flew open. She screamed my name and—

A shrieking alarm tore me from my dream.

I thrashed against my bed covers, my shaft seeking her wet heat.

Slowly, I came to my senses, although I swore her cries still rang in my ears and her sweet scent still clung to my skin.

The alarm I'd set for morning shift continued to ring.

With a curse, I raised my hand and sent a fireball into the annoying device. As the acrid smoke stung my nostrils, I looked down at my hands.

Without thinking I'd conjured more power than I had

since the attack. *Are my dreams of Sydney bringing my power back?* They certainly were reigniting my libido. The insistent throbbing at the center of my body was distracting.

Closing my eyes, I stroked myself to the image of my witch crying out for me.

✻ 13 ✻

SYDNEY

I woke akimbo on my mattress, a furious ache between my legs. My breath was ragged, my heart was pounding, and my nipples were so hard they could cut glass.

The back-to-back dreams of Terran and Raze had left me desperately wanting. I let out a groan of frustration. Perhaps this was just more punishment the Lost Soul's Penitentiary doled out. First, they isolated you. Then, they starved you. Finally, they bombarded you with sexy dreams that went nowhere.

I let out a sigh and stared up at the ceiling of my cell. The words "fear is the only prison," had been painstakingly chiseled into the rock.

I scoffed. This place certainly qualified as a prison. And, if I was being honest, so had the academy. I might not have been stuck in solitary confinement there, but I'd been forbidden from leaving the school and I'd been treated as the lowest kind of life form by everyone other than Jasen, Novah, and Professor Razell.

The moment my former professor's face came to mind, I moaned in longing. I could almost feel the ghostly echo of his lips moving across my skin. In the dream, it seemed as if he believed me and forgave my attack. Of course, it was just a dream. The real life Raze still hated my guts.

I sighed. I completely got why I would dream of Raze, but what was up with my dream of Terran?

Surely, my subconscious didn't need to generate childhood trauma for the ruggedly handsome earth elemental. That poor male. If anyone was in a prison of fear, it was him. The suicide of his mother had given him major trust issues and no wonder. I shuddered thinking of that tow-headed little boy finding his mother's lifeless body.

My subconscious was probably trying to come up with an explanation for the male's surliness.

But he hadn't been so surly in the dream. I flushed remembering Terran's mouth on me. It had felt incredible. And his magnificent inked body had been mouthwatering. I clamped my thighs together remembering his huge colorful manhood. *What would it feel like inside me?*

Raze, who had a slightly shorter length and a thinner girth had filled me perfectly in my dream. *Could my body accommodate anything bigger than that?*

Turning my back to the camera, I pulled my blanket over me and slid an exploratory finger between my thighs. It didn't feel as nice as the wardens' fingers, but it still made my breathing quicken.

Experimenting, I slid two more fingers inside. *Oh!* That felt nice. I bit my bottom lip to keep from moaning. The increased fullness felt so good. I moved my fingers in and out, just how Raze had moved in my dream. *Yes. Oh, yes.*

As pleasure mounted inside me, water spewed out of the shower.

Curse it. Orgasm or shower?

Knowing I had a limited time to bathe, I rolled out of bed, pulled off my potato sack, and crawled into the freezing shower. A few days of experience had me maximizing every second. I quickly soaped my body, hair, and even brushed my teeth before the spray cut off.

I stayed sitting behind the half wall, where the camera couldn't see me while I air dried. The previous days, I'd thrown on my potato sack right away, and then had to sit in the uncomfortable damp fabric for hours. I was learning.

When I finally felt dry enough. I crawled back over to my mattress, again avoiding the camera, and redressed.

The sound of something clattering against the door of Scar Face's cell told me it was almost breakfast. My neighbor got more animated the closer it came to mealtimes.

I glanced over at the door knowing the arrival of my next loaf was imminent. It'd been days since I'd tried to force a bite of that nasty food down, but surprisingly, the hunger pains were gone. It could be all the water I was drinking. I'd been trying to trick my stomach into constant fullness, but it probably wouldn't keep working for long.

I'd always been naturally thin and the few curves I had were fast being whittled away. Sighing, I waited for my food slot to open.

My ritual had become, grab the food from the plate, break it into bits, and flush it down the toilet. Initially, I'd made the mistake of leaving the loaves out and quickly found myself with several dozen creepy crawly roommates. Now, I didn't mess around.

The electric field on the door buzzed off.

Is it already time for the cages? I didn't think four days had gone by, but the hours were running together. I should start marking the days in the wall like one of the former occupants of the cell. His or her check marks had ended on day forty-two. I liked to think that was when they were released. If only I too would be so lucky.

With a loud click, my door swung open.

I pushed myself to my feet and started toward it, only to freeze when I saw a huge male standing in my doorway.

For one heartbeat I thought it was Terran, then the male turned his face toward me, and I saw the mangled web of scars.

Scar Face.

What's he doing here?

A wide grin split his twisted face. "Hello, little witch." As he stepped inside, his scent—sulfur and rotten onions— wafted over.

Recoiling in horror, I screamed for help.

Scar Face chuckled. "No one will come." He motioned at my camera. "No one will see."

The camera was turned to face the back wall. The light was off.

I felt the blood drain from my face. *Someone orchestrated this. Who? Raze? Did he hate me so much he wanted me dead?*

Scar Face moved closer. "I'll take my time with you. I need to make this last." The gleam in his crimson-rimmed eyes filled me with terror.

No. Goddess no. I shook my head in denial of what was happening.

His grin widened, and he cupped himself.

I backed up until the jagged rocks of the cell wall dug into my spine. *What do I do?*

Scar Face suddenly stiffened. He let out a surprised yell, then his eyes rolled back, and he collapsed. Only then did I see the blood pouring from his neck and the smaller male standing behind him.

Crazy Eyes held a long, jagged piece of stone, wet with blood in his hand.

A shriek tangled in my throat. *Did he murder Scar Face to save me, or to claim me for himself?*

As I huddled against the wall, Crazy Eyes wiped the blood

from his makeshift knife on Scar Face's potato sack. Then he gave me a chilling smile. "I could not allow him to harm a child of night."

Child of night? Deciding my best bet was to play along, I forced a smile. "Thank you for protecting me."

His eyes were as black as coal and glinted with insanity. "Become my apprentice and I'll teach you to protect yourself."

Become his apprentice? The warlock was as mad as a mateless wyvern. "Thank you, no," I said again, trying not to tremble.

His smile took a hard edge. "You do not yet understand your power. Let me help you. Together we will escape and destroy them all." He extended a bloody hand.

My stomach churned. "I'm fine right here." No way was I going anywhere with him.

"You are not safe..." Crazy Eyes stiffened as if he heard something I couldn't. "Very well. I will leave you for now." He grabbed one of Scar Face's arms and dragged him out of my cell.

Struck dumb by the impossible amount of strength the tiny warlock displayed, I didn't dare move.

Crazy Eyes returned only to scrape up the bloody dirt, which he placed on top of a blanket he'd brought with him. Then he left, closing my door behind him.

Not five minutes later, the electric field over the door buzzed back on.

I'm not sure how long I stood there in shock and horror, before my legs finally gave out.

Someone had tried to kill me. No, more than that. Someone had tried to have me killed by Scar Face and an even more insane inmate had saved me.

The temperature in my cell seemed to drop twenty

degrees. I crawled over to my blanket and wrapped myself in it.

It was Raze. It had to be. He had the motive. He blamed me for losing his power and position. And as a warden, he could turn off my camera and open a few prison cell doors.

Tears burned my eyes as I realized just how close I'd come to dying. Never had I felt so vulnerable and alone.

I rocked back and forth trying to comfort myself the way I had when I was a child and the jeers of the other students had become too overwhelming.

Their taunts rang inside my mind.

"Freak!"

"Purple monster!"

"No one wants you, not even your parents!"

I rocked harder. It'd all been true. Even my last name denoted I'd been castaway by whatever female had given birth to me. I was unclaimed and unloved—destined to be hated by all.

A sob caught between my throat and sternum. *Why is this happening to me?* What had I done to deserve this?

Tears poured from my eyes as I gave myself over to the grief and fear. The sound of the door slot opening and a loaf sliding through didn't calm me. I continued to rock and rock for hours.

Eventually my eyes grew heavy, but I didn't dare sleep. Not when there could be another attempt on my life.

I needed a weapon. Trying to cobble together some strength, I looked over the walls of my cell. There didn't seem to be any loose rocks. I'd have to use something else. I stumbled over to the loaf, set it aside, and inspected the plastic plate. If I could break it, I'd have two pieces with jagged edges.

I brought the plate over to the wall and tried repeatedly slamming it against the rock. It wouldn't break.

My shoulders sagged in defeat.

The electricity on my door thrummed off.

Oh, no! Raze must have realized I was alive and sent someone else to kill me.

My door slowly creaked opened.

Clasping the plate to my chest, I flattened myself against the wall. My only chance was to surprise my attacker.

The silhouette of a small male appeared in the doorway.

Maybe it's Crazy Eyes again. Would that be a good thing or a bad thing?

The male strode inside and closed the door behind him.

Hiding in the shadows, I raised my plate preparing to strike.

"Syd?" a familiar voice whispered.

My heart stopped. "Jasen?"

Shocked by the impossibility of hearing my best friend's voice, I lowered the plate.

The male turn on a light revealing himself to be the short, ugly warden I'd met in the burial chamber. "There you are!"

I blinked as he held the light up to my face.

Why does Victor sound like Jasen?

Victor smiled as if he knew a secret. Then his lips pulled up and the ugly warden's face stretched. His pointed chin became a square jaw, his teeth whitened, his pockmarked complexion transformed into smooth skin, and shaggy blond hair replaced his greasy-looking locks.

Victor, who had morphed into Jasen, raised his arms. "Give me some love, Violet Eyes."

After what I'd just been through, it was too much. I let out a cry and blacked out.

14

JASEN

Of all the ways I hoped Syd would respond to my big reveal, having her pass the fuck out wasn't one of them.

"Syd!" I bent down and shook her much too slim shoulders. Her head lolled back, and her magnificent violet hair fanned out over the dirt floor.

Shit. The shock of seeing me shapeshift must've been too much for her. I should have waited. I'd been so excited for our reunion that I'd rushed it.

Professor Razell always said my reckless impatience would be my downfall. That guy always seemed to see straight through me with an uncanniness that set my hair on end. He'd been the only one to guess at my feelings for Sydney, which hadn't been too hard given the first time I saw her I went into some friggin' trance.

In my defense, I'd been confused as hell at being kidnapped walking home from San Diego High and drop kicked into the Elemental Academy by these strange fuckers who claimed to be members of some Assembly. They told me that my long-lost bio dad had been a warlock and although he and my human mom hadn't been together long, he'd apparently gifted her with me and gifted me with an affinity for water.

If that wasn't screwed up enough, the Assembly people wouldn't tell me who my bio dad was, and they wouldn't even let me say goodbye to my family. No doubt my mom and stepdad had lost their minds when I disappeared.

To make matters worse, I'd been tossed into class with a bunch of stuck up witches and warlocks. I was getting ready to bust my way out of there when I'd caught sight of the most beautiful girl I'd ever seen.

One glimpse of Sydney's wide violet eyes and I'd been thunderstruck. I was shaking at the knees just like that AC/DC song. I swear to fucking God that my heart stopped beating for a few seconds and my soul sang, as cheesy as that sounds. All the while I couldn't do anything but stare at her like some brain-dead moron while the other students laughed at me.

Probably out of pity, Professor Razell assigned me to the desk right next to Sydney. And I'd be forever grateful he'd asked me to watch out for her. His request allowed me to go all crazy-ass stalker on Syd and when my following her everywhere didn't freak her out, befriend her.

She was more than just my friend though. Syd was my confidant. My family. My everything.

My chest grew tight as I tenderly stroked a finger down Sydney's beautiful face.

For two years I'd waited for her to recognize the special connection we had. The way we finished each other's sentences. How just being together could calm each of us down. But she hadn't. She'd held on to the notion that her sworn, that asshole Logan, was her future. *Fuck him.* He didn't deserve one brightly colored hair on her head.

Just thinking of how sad she'd been when Logan stood her

up during their arranged visits made me gnash my teeth. But we had bigger problems than Logan these days.

I glanced over my shoulder to make sure the camera in the cell was off. Early this morning, I'd remotely disabled it from the command center.

Since we were safe from any inquiring eyes, I shucked off the warden uniform and took my true form.

It felt fucking amazing to stretch to my full height and relax the iron-clad focus required to hold onto Victor's shape. I did a quick all over body shake and sank down next to Sydney. Planting a kiss on her forehead, I said, "Come on, Violet Eyes. Wake up."

She didn't stir.

Not liking the paleness of her skin and how shallow her breath was, I turned my attention to the negators I'd placed on her wrists. The cuffs glowed a little too brightly. *Shit.* They could be sapping too much of her strength.

I'd slapped the restraints on her wrists for two reasons. First, to stop whatever freaky shit was happening between her and those other wardens back in the crypt. Second, so I could put a hacked version of the cuffs on her.

Unlike regular negators, these cuffs had a low setting. Additionally, I could turn off any attempts at increasing their intensity.

I dug my remote out of my pocket and changed the negators' settings.

Almost immediately, color crept back into Syd's face. Her eyes fluttered open. "Jasen?" She said my name softly as if she didn't quite believe her eyes.

"In the flesh," I replied, motioning down at my souped-up naked body. I'd gone ahead and given myself some chiseled abs and some hulk-like biceps along with a few extra inches on my winky. All chicks liked big dicks. Or so I'd heard.

Syd followed my gaze, her cheeks reddening. "Why aren't

you wearing any clothes?"

"Warden Merrick's uniform doesn't fit the real me." I flexed my muscles hoping she'd find them hot.

She averted her gaze. "Can you cover yourself?"

Rolling my eyes, I tossed her ratty blanket over my junk. "Better?"

She turned and wrapped her arms around me. "Thank the Goddess you're here."

I returned the embrace, savoring the feel of her in my arms. My heartbeat slowed and the tightness in my chest eased up.

I hated how she trembled. I wanted to get to her sooner, but it had been nearly impossible to find a time when there weren't a dozen wardens working this sector.

Today, for whatever reason, half the shift hadn't come in and I'd been able to make my move. "Are you okay, honey?"

"No. Scar Face tried to kill me today."

I pulled away. "What are you talking about?"

"My door opened this morning and he came in. Thankfully, before he could kill me, Crazy Eyes stabbed him. Right there." She pointed to the middle of the floor.

There wasn't a trace of blood. "Okay," I said slowly. Solitary was getting the best of my girl.

"It was Raze who opened the doors. He wants me dead. Look he turned the camera off." She pointed up at the camera.

My poor Syd. I hated to see her brought so low. "I disabled the camera so I could sneak in here." I cupped her face. "It's going to be okay, honey."

Sydney frowned. "You don't believe me."

I lied. "Of course I do. But you have nothing to worry about now. I'll protect you and get you out of here." I wrapped my arms around her.

She slowly melted into my embrace. "Thank the Goddess.

I didn't know how much more I could take. Wait." She pushed away to look at my face. "How are you able to shapeshift? It's something only the arcane water elementals can do. You're not an arcane, are you?"

If only. On my best day, I could conjure rain and heal minor injuries. No way could I transform on my own. But there were other ways of accessing that power. I pulled a shiny stone out of the leather strap tied around my bicep.

"I have this."

She looked down at the stone, her mouth dropping open. "Is that a soul stone?"

"You bet your sweet ass it is," I said with a grin. "It gives me the power to take whatever form I want." I left out the part where I'd stolen the stone from the headmistress's office and used it to assume the identity of a warden here. The real Victor Merrick had been all too happy to take my offered payment and lay low while I kept watch over my girl.

Keeping watch was a relative term as I couldn't figure out how to open the door to the crypt where she'd been stashed. But I visited regularly to make sure it was undisturbed. Thank fuck, I'd been there to intercept Raze and Terran on their way to see her.

Sydney took the stone from my hand and peered at her own reflection in the mirror-like surface. "Can I use it to transform?"

"Unfortunately, no," I said, taking the stone from her. "You'd have to have a strong affinity for water, and you have…"

"An affinity for spirit." She wrapped her arms around herself. "Jasen. I'm a monster."

"Don't say that. Don't even think it." I didn't understand why the other elementals treated her like the boogeyman just because she had a rare affinity. This was Syd. One of the gentlest, sweetest girls I'd ever met.

It was freaking insane that the Assembly had hidden her away in that crypt over whatever had gone down with Raze. What a tool that guy was. And to think he used to be my favorite professor.

I'd overheard Raze bitching to Terran long enough to know his version of what happened with Sydney. But now that she was awake, I'd get her version of the story and get her out of here.

I didn't have a plan yet, but I'd come up with something. Until then, I needed to get Syd into better shape emotionally and physically.

I cupped my hands around her oval face, trying not to be distracted by her beauty. "You're one kick ass witch and I'm going to get you out of this place."

Syd gave me a weak smile. "You will?"

"Bet on it. But in the meantime, I brought you a few things to make your temporary stay a little better." I ran over to grab the bag I'd dropped by the door. Inside were some of her favorite foods along with a few items I'd been able to save from her dorm room. Andrea had tossed everything in the garbage. *What a bitch.*

When I turned to show Syd what I'd brought, I found her staring at the back wall, her face flushed. "Jasen, not everyone is as comfortable with nudity as you are."

I rolled my eyes. "Seriously, Syd. It's just a body. I can take any shape." To prove my point, I morphed into my favorite form.

Syd peeked over and let out an outraged cry. "You turned into me."

I looked at my gorgeous breasts. "Sexy, aren't I?" I couldn't resist tweaking my nipples.

"Stop that!" Syd shouted, her face turning an even deeper red.

"Why? You have the most beautiful breasts in all the

realms, they should be played with." This wasn't the first time I'd complemented her breasts in the history of our relationship, or even the hundredth time. I knew my constant sexual innuendos flustered her, but it was a way of getting out some of my pent-up lust.

Instead of chastising me for being inappropriate like she always had in the past, Syd's breathing hitched.

Suddenly, the air between us seemed to thicken.

Syd licked her lips and the sight of her pink tongue made my stomach twist with need. In my true form, I would have been harder than stone, but in her form, I grew wet and achy between my legs.

"You didn't get my body right," she said in a breathy voice. Her pupils dilated so large that her eyes almost looked entirely black.

"What?" It took me a second to follow her words. The sweet sultry scent that was filling the cell, muddled my brain. *Is that amazing scent coming from her?*

In an uncharacteristically bold move, Syd rose on her knees and dragged off her prison tunic.

Seeing her body in all its glory scrambled my brain.

"See my breasts are smaller than yours," she said, cupping her gorgeous tits. "And I don't have any hair between my legs." She pointed down at the most perfectly bare pussy I'd ever seen.

I let out an inarticulate sound and lost my focus. Immediately, I reverted to my true form. I expected her to freak at the sight of my throbbing cock, but she only smiled and crooked her finger at me.

"Come here, Jasen. I'm hungry."

Like a dumbass, I lifted the bag. "I brought you that sweetbread you love."

"I don't mean food." She reclined back on her mattress. "I want you."

This isn't right. I rubbed the sides of my head. *How did my girl go from blushing and refusing to even look at me, to propositioning me like a porn star?*

Holding my gaze, Syd parted her slim thighs and showed me a glimpse of paradise. "I need you, Jasen."

Holy shit. I'd been praying for this moment every night for years. Part of me never thought it would happen. But it was. Right here and now, this was happening.

I stuffed the soul stone into the tether on my arm and told her how I really felt. "I want you, Syd. I want you so goddamn much. I've always been in lo—wanted you, right from the start. I'm sorry I didn't say anything sooner. I didn't want you to freak." *And I'm a cowardly fuck who can't bear the thought of losing you if you didn't return my feelings.*

Syd didn't react to my confession other than to open her thighs wider. "I ache for you, Jasen. Touch me."

With fucking pleasure. I fell over her like a starving man. For that's exactly what I'd been, starving for her touch, her kiss, her body.

I licked and sucked her neck, throat, and then her gorgeous stiff nipples, while my hands slid between her legs. I groaned at finding her hot and slippery wet.

"Kiss me," she begged, trying to pull my face up to hers.

But I was too busy latching onto her nipples. I tried different levels of suction until I found one that made her moan.

Other than having Sonja Mendez give me a hand job during a sophomore year field trip—best bus ride ever—I'd never been with anyone. But I'd been watching porn for years and that along with my vivid imagination gave me enough confidence to kiss my way down her flat stomach and settle my head between her legs.

"I'm going to send you to the moon, Violet Eyes."

Then I made good on the promise.

15

SYDNEY

My dream encounters with Raze and Terran hadn't prepared me for Jasen's erotic assault on my body. This was the real thing. My head spun as I desperately tried to process that my best friend and forbidden crush was making love to me. *How is this happening?*

One second Jasen was transforming into a prettier version of me, then a strange hunger urged me to act provocatively, and now he was touching me, kissing me, putting his mouth there...

My heartbeat thundered like the hooves of a thousand racing horses as he thrust his tongue inside my body.

Oh, Goddess!

As he licked every inch of my core I was thrown into a churning vortex of sensation and hunger so intense it seared away everything but the need for more. More touching. More kissing. More Jasen.

"You taste amazing." The vibration of his lips against my sensitive flesh made me moan.

I dug my fingers into his tanned shoulders not sure if I wanted to push him away or hold him tightly to me.

"If you like that. You'll love this." He drew my bud into his mouth and sucked hard.

Pleasure like nothing I'd ever experienced slammed into me. I came so hard and fast, my entire body convulsed. I pleaded his name as soon as I could form words. I needed to catch my breath, to process this... whatever was happening between us.

Jasen had other ideas. He forced my thighs even further apart and lifted my knees over his shoulders. This position allowed him to thrust his tongue deep into my channel. He thrust so deep he had to be doing a shapeshifting thing, but I didn't care because it made me come again and again.

After my fifth orgasm, he finally showed pity on me and set my quivering body down. But there wasn't any time to come to my senses, because the moment my butt hit the mattress, I felt the scalding brush of his manhood against my inner thigh.

I froze transfixed by the intimacy of the moment. *Is this really happening?* I'd never even touched a naked male in real life and now I was about to go all the way with one.

But not just anyone. *My Jasen.*

He let out a ragged breath, which drew my eyes to the wetness around his mouth. I should have felt embarrassed by the evidence of my desire, but all I felt was the burning need to fuse our mouths together.

"Kiss me."

Ignoring my plea, Jasen slid his erection back and forth through my wetness. Passion burned in his heavy-lidded eyes. "I want to be inside you."

The erotic brush strokes turned my focus from his mouth to where he pressed against me. "I want that too," I confessed. Each pass of his rigid length sent a jolt of desire straight through me.

"Are you sure?" he asked, rising over me.

I'd never been surer of anything. I wanted to know what it felt to have this connection in real life. I moaned my consent and tried again to pull him on top of me.

Jasen pulled out of my grip. "No, honey. I want to watch you take every inch of me."

His words made my toes curl. "Yes." I went still and breathless as Jasen nudged my thighs apart and guided himself into me.

There was no warlock in the realms I trusted more than Jasen. It felt so right that he was my first. The urge to confess my feelings bubbled to my lips, but I bit the words back. *Later. I'll tell him later.*

The insistent press of his throbbing shaft made me gasp. It hadn't been like this in my dreams. My flesh seemed to fight his sweet invasion, but Jasen was patient.

He pushed in slow, so achingly slow. As he breeched me his lanky muscles were tense, his jaw clenched, and his beautiful blue-rimmed eyes were locked on where we were joined. Gone was his cocky smile and the teasing glint in his eye.

In place of my jokester best friend was an almost feral looking warlock intent on claiming my virgin body. And claim he did with a single thrust of his hips.

I inhaled sharply as his shaft ripped through my inner barrier.

Jasen froze, completely sheathed inside me. "Are you okay?"

I nodded. The tiny bite of pain meant nothing. Not when he was deep inside my body. I rotated my hips, acquainting myself with the unfamiliar sensation.

Jasen let out a hiss of breath. "Don't do that, honey. You'll make me lose control."

I don't know what darkness in me made me swivel my hips again, but when I did Jasen let out a guttural moan and started thrusting wildly.

Although my inner muscles burned with the unfamiliar workout, a delicious fire built inside me, growing hotter and hotter.

Jasen kissed and licked my neck and breasts all the while he thrust in and out of me dizzyingly fast.

When I reached up to caress his sweat-dampened chest and back, he interwove our hands together and held mine down. Somehow that made his claiming even more primal.

Our moans and the slapping sound of us coming together over and over echoed throughout the small space like a sinful melody. Incredibly, it felt as if we'd left our separate selves behind and become one magnificent being. If only we could stay like this forever. Jasen and me. Our bodies undulating in passion.

"I'm close," he panted, his breath tickling my ear. "Need you to come with me." He arched his hips and something that felt like a finger brushed against my clit.

I glanced at our clasped hands. *How can he be touching me there when his fingers are in mine?* "W-what's that—"

"Don't think. Just feel," he whispered into my ear. Whatever was rubbing against my bud moved faster and faster, matching his wild thrusts.

Giving myself over to the bone-melting sensation, I threw back my head and rocked my hips frantically, grinding against his cock and his amazing cock-finger or whatever it was that worked my nub with the hottest most incredible friction. Suddenly the cock-finger turned into a suckling mouth.

The unbelievable sensation shoved me right off the edge. I screamed my release so loud, the cell shook and dirt rained down on our heads. I clamped my thighs around his hips and rode every wave of the soul-shattering orgasm.

Jasen went rigid and bellowed my name. His cock jerked and filled me with liquid heat along with a rush of energy that invigorated every cell in my body.

Along with a return of my strength came an incredible feeling of bliss that eased the strange hunger and tightness in my chest.

With his fingers still entangled with mine, Jasen rose over me and stared into my eyes. His gaze was filled with emotions so intense they electrified me.

Years of memories suddenly played back in my mind. All his teasing sexual innuendos. Every long hug we'd shared. The menacing looks he gave any warlock who wandered in my direction. The hurt expression he wore anytime my sworn was mentioned. It all suddenly made sense.

He loves me.

I saw everything so clearly in that moment. All those forbidden feelings I'd bottled up all these years bubbled to the surface. "Jasen, I lo—"

Loud cursing from outside the prison cell interrupted me.

JASEN JERKED HIS HEAD IN THE DIRECTION OF THE DOOR. "Oh shit!" His face lost color. Then he was shapeshifting on top of me. One second he was my gorgeous, lanky best friend, the next he was that short, ugly as sin warden with greasy hair and a pockmarked face.

And he was inside of me.

Even though I knew it was still Jasen, I couldn't help crying out and trying to push him off.

My shriek of surprise must've confused the two warlocks who rushed into the cell.

"Son of a bitch," Raze yelled. He flung Jasen off me.

Terran hauled Jasen up by his neck. "I'll kill you for this, Victor." Holding the smaller warlock by the neck, Terran slammed him into the wall repeatedly.

"Stop!" I screamed.

Jasen's face turned purple and his bare feet kicked against the rock.

Terran will strangle him. "Let him go!" I tried to push my way between Terran and Jasen but Raze dragged me to the other side of the cell.

Raze stared down at me, a horrified expression on his face. "She was a virgin, Terran. That cocksucker raped her."

I followed his gaze to the blood smeared on my inner thighs.

"You piece of warg shit!" Terran shouted. He threw Jasen down and stomped on his stomach.

Jasen cried out in pain and curled into a ball.

Realizing Jasen would not expose himself by summoning his element, I tried unsuccessfully to push past Raze. "Don't hurt him!"

The fire elemental seemed to have forgotten how much he hated me. "We won't let him hurt you again." His eyes flashed with a bright crimson light as he shot a huge fireball directly at Jasen.

"Move!" I shouted in warning.

Jasen twisted away from the ball of flame before it could hit him in the face.

"Stop! You were the one who tried to have me killed," I screamed at Raze.

The fire elemental stared at me in confusion. "What are you talking about?"

"You allowed the inmate next-door to attack me."

Raze's jaw dropped. "I would never do such a thing."

I read the truth in his expression of outrage. *If he didn't try to kill me, who did?*

Raze took another step toward me. "Terran and I came as soon as we realized your camera wasn't working. Victor, did you mess with her camera?"

"Yes," Jasen groaned from the ground.

"When we get through with you, you'll never hurt an inno-cent witch again," Terran growled. He grabbed Jasen by the back of his hair and lifted his other fist over the smaller warlock's face.

"Stop! He didn't hurt me. I asked him to have sex with me."

Terran and Raze froze, then looked from me to Jasen, who'd raised his arms to protect his face.

"Is this true, Victor?" Terran asked in a deadly soft voice.

Jasen glanced over at me, a flicker of indecision in his eyes.

Curse it. It looked as if he was trying to protect my virtue.

Swallowing hard, I summoned my most sultry voice. "I seduced him." I threw back my hair and pursed my lips in what I hoped was a sexy pout. "I wanted an orgasm since neither of you two delivered last night."

Terran dropped Jasen in a heap and he and Raze spun around to look at me.

"What did you say?"

Trying not to cringe at being the focus of their intense gazes, I straightened my spine. "I-I wanted to fuck." The vulgar word seemed to stick in my throat. Licking my lips, I said louder, "I need to fuck."

"She needs to fuck," Raze echoed.

Terran exchanged a long look with Raze. "Now we know what she wants."

Seeming to forget about Jasen, the two males prowled over.

Terran, with his huge rippling muscles loomed over me on my left, while Raze with his dark, swirling energy pressed in on my right.

My traitorous body thrummed with excitement at their proximity. *How can I be turned on by them when I've just made love to Jasen?* I dared to glance at my friend.

He was trying to push himself up on shaking arms. One of his eyes had swollen closed and his throat was darkening with bruises.

Can he heal himself by shapeshifting? I hoped with all my might he could but knew he couldn't expose himself by using the soul stone.

A warm hand cupped my breast, dragging my attention back to the two warlocks surrounding me. "What are you doing?"

"She's got beautiful breasts, doesn't she, Terran?" Raze said, running his finger lightly over my nipple.

My nipples, sensitized by Jasen's loving, stiffened instantly and I couldn't help the moan that escaped my lips.

Terran ran his hand over my butt. "And a beautiful ass. I'll bet you're a virgin here too."

I sucked in a breath as his finger slid between my cheeks and brushed against my back hole. His actions sent a thrill through me. *What would it feel like to have sex there?*

My Goddess. What kind of witch am I? I'd just been loved hard by Jasen and now I was getting turned on by two other males.

"How about this?" Terran said, moving his hand back around my hip to touch my still sensitive core.

I let out a hiss of breath as one of his large fingers pressed against my mound.

"Raze and I will fuck you senseless, if you give him back his full power, and you remove your enchantments on us."

I blinked. "My enchantments?"

Terran turned me to face Raze and dipped a finger inside me. "Don't play dumb, enchantress."

My core burned, but the pain faded as Terran began rubbing my bud. "Oh, Goddess." My legs shook, and I fell forward into Raze's arms.

The dark-haired male held me upright and lowered his head to take one of my nipples in his mouth.

I threw my head back at the onslaught of sensation.

"We'll give you everything you want if you just release us from your spell." Terran rubbed me faster as he ground his pelvis against my back. I could feel his impossibly huge erection through his pants. Just imagining that massive length sliding inside me made me gasp.

Terran looked over my shoulder at Raze. "Are you down for this?"

Raze answered by biting my nipple.

The burst of pain amid the pleasure fried my brain. "Please!" I gasped brokenly. I was so close to coming again.

Terran's smile was cruel. "Not until you give us what we want. Stop your enchantments now. I don't want you haunting my dreams at night." As he continued to tease me, he undid his pants. The flash of color made my mouth fall open.

"You're as pretty as you were in my dream." How in the realms could my subconscious have guessed that his shaft would be completely tattooed?

Terran went perfectly still. "What happened in your dream?"

"We played a kissing game and you got naked."

"The fuck." Lust ebbed from Terran's gaze and an expression close to fear crossed his face.

The hair on the back of my neck rose. "Y-you had the same dream, didn't you?"

Terran said nothing, but I could see the answer in his eyes.

"How can that happen?" I turned to Raze who'd taken a step back. "You made love to me on your desk. Did you dream that too?"

The dark-haired warlock looked stricken.

"You might as well try to stop a storm with a kiss as stop inherent magic," I quoted from our dream.

"Impossible." Raze reeled back as if I'd slapped him.

"Obviously not." Terran's gaze narrowed. "She must've used her power to enter our dreams."

"I did not." At least not intentionally.

On the other side of the cell, Jasen yelled, "Leave her the fuck alone!" Then he let out a guttural roar and attacked Terran.

Terran flung his arm out, sending Jasen into the back wall.

Jasen's pained grunt was drowned out by a thunderous rumbling.

Chunks of dirt and rock rained down on our heads. Jagged cracks appeared in the walls and the ground vibrated with such force that I lost my balance and fell down in a sprawling heap.

Jasen crawled over and cradled me in his arms. "I've got you."

"What's happening?" I cried.

As suddenly as it started, the shaking stopped. The four of us looked at each other in shocked silence for a moment. Other than being covered in a thick layer of dirt we all seemed to be unharmed.

"What in the realms was that?" Raze shouted, releasing his death grip on the wall.

"An earthquake," Jasen answered, loosening his tight embrace enough that I could sit up.

"No," Terran said, a grim expression on his face. "The prison wards were activated. Someone tried to escape."

16

RAZE

The shrilled wail of the prison alarm underscored Terran's words.

Hellfire. Only a fool with a death wish would try to escape Lost Soul's Penitentiary.

I rushed to the front of the cell and opened the door. *What about Sydney?* Unable to resist the urge, I spun around to ensure she hadn't been harmed by the earth tremor.

Seeing her naked in Victor's arms hit me like a punch to the gut. The bastard had taken her virginity. I hated that.

Sydney's first time should have been with me, like last night in our shared dream. *Bless the Elders. She wants me as much as I want her.*

"Are you, okay?" I shouted over the blaring alarm.

She pushed out of Victor's arms. "I'm fine."

Victor reluctantly let her go.

Sydney looked dazed, and her lips were swollen and bruised. *Had Victor hurt her during sex? That bastard.*

I glared at the null, wanting to hurt him for taking what was mine. *Mine? Get a hold of yourself, Ian.* "Are you sure?"

As Sydney nodded, her teardrop-shaped breasts shook.

The hypnotic sight made my mind go blank. Never had I seen a more perfect pair. They were perky and on the smaller side, but that had always been my preference. I couldn't wait to caress them and—

The radio on my duty belt crackled with static before the Head Warden's voice wheezed out, "Raze, are you there? We have an emergency."

I grabbed the radio. "I'm here, sir. What's happening? Did a prisoner escape?"

"No. But we've had another incident at the temple. You and Terran need to come ASAP. I can't get a hold of the Lead Warden."

"I'll find him." I glanced at Terran who was inspecting his radio. He'd mentioned it had been malfunctioning. Turning my attention back to my handheld device, I said, "We'll meet you there."

Ending the communication, I motioned Terran and Victor to follow me out.

Victor pressed his lips against the witch's forehead in an act that seemed too familiar. Then he grabbed his clothes and hurriedly dressed. The sight of the blood smeared across his flaccid cock made my fingers erupt in flames. I clenched my hands into fists and smothered the fire before I could turn him into kindling.

Never would Victor see Sydney again. That was for damn sure.

Terran stared at Sydney, his expression flashing with indecision. Likely, he was struggling with the same overpowering urge to stay and protect her.

Damn enchantment.

"We have to go," I said, all but dragging the other two wardens out of the cell. Once I'd closed the door and sealed Sydney inside, I took a deep breath. The scent of unwashed male prisoners mixed with dust and dirt cleared my mind.

Victor, who'd thankfully buttoned his pants, rubbed his bruised neck. "Deputy Warden, I—"

I threw him against the railing. "You will never visit her again."

The smaller male glanced at the four story drop behind him and paled.

His fear did nothing to calm my aggravation. All I wanted to do was shove him over and watch his brains splatter on the concrete floor below. "She's mine. Sydney is mine."

He stared at me as if incredulous. "In your dreams, bro."

For a split second, the challenge in his eyes and his cocky smile seemed so familiar. I leaned forward. "Do I know you from somewhere?" The ugly warden was considerably older than I was. *Where might I have met him before?*

Victor laughed. "Nah, but she does. Syd knows me extremely well." He wagged his eyebrows suggestively.

He dares taunt me. My hands erupted in flames.

Terran's heavy hand fell on my shoulder. "Calm down, Raze."

The irony of the moment wasn't lost on me. I'd always been Terran's voice of reason. *Guess the tables have turned.*

The prison alarms suddenly stopped their ear-splitting wail.

Getting ahold of my emotions, I smothered the fire in my hands. "Go," I ordered Victor. "Before I throw you into the fire."

"What fire?" he said, pushing himself off the railing.

"Fuck off, Victor," Terran shouted.

The smaller male fled toward the stairs.

"He's right," Terran said, peering over the railing. "The fire is gone." He pointed at the empty pyre on the ground floor.

"Impossible." I shook my head in confusion. The

Assembly had warded each affinity symbol in the prison themselves. The flame should never go out.

"About Sydney..." Terran said, looking back at her cell.

"We'll discuss her later." I wasn't in a good place to talk about her and we needed to meet with the Head Warden. "What's the fastest way to the temple?"

"Through sector three," Terran replied.

"Lead the way."

We rushed down the stairwell, passing Kayla and several other sector four wardens.

Kayla, who was covered with dust and dirt, looked startled to see us.

Although Terran continued on, I grabbed Kayla's arm. "Did you know the camera in inmate 18734's cell was malfunctioning?"

The air elemental shook her head. "Is she dead?"

"Sydney is fine." I didn't feel the need to apprise the rookie of what happened between Sydney and Victor.

"Oh." Kayla's disappointed look jarred me.

Remembering what Sydney had said about an attack on her, I tightened my grip around Kayla's elbow. "And she'll stay that way, won't she?"

Ignoring my question, Kayla's gaze tracked Terran's movements down the stairs. "Terran, can we talk?"

He ignored her and jumped down the last rung of stairs.

Kayla cried out. "Terran!"

He strode to the sector door and stalked through it not once looking back at her.

I shook the female warden to force her attention back to me. "You won't do anything to hurt inmate 18734. That's an order."

She trembled. "You said to show her the meaning of true punishment."

I had said that. *Curse the Elders.* "Forget what I said. From now on she is not to be mistreated. We'll speak more on this later." I pushed Kayla away and rushed after my old friend.

I found Terran talking to the wardens congregating around the prisoner intake area.

"Is everyone okay here?" I asked.

"Yes," retorted the bull-faced Warden Clover. "Who tried to escape?"

"No one, but we're headed to the temple to find out what's going on. Radio the other sectors and see if they need assistance."

"Yes, Deputy Warden." Warden Clover straightened her spine. Although many wardens found the older witch abrasive, I appreciated her no-nonsense attitude and her ability to follow orders. *Unlike some.* Victor's face flashed in my mind. *Who does he remind me of?*

"Come on, Raze." Terran motioned me through an unfamiliar door that led us through a narrow passageway. "Watch your step." He waved at a slab of rock that had fallen onto the floor.

Curse the Elders. The prison was a damn labyrinth. Even with a map I often became hopelessly turned around. Not Terran though. He knew the prison inside and out.

For a moment, I felt a twinge of guilt over my recent promotion. It should have been Terran who got the Deputy spot. He deserved it far more than I did. Not only did he have more experience, he seemed to love this cursed place. It was unfair that I'd usurped him after being here only a short time.

It wasn't hard to figure out why. The Head Warden, like everyone else, wanted to curry favor with the Assembly. He'd erroneously assumed that if he promoted me, he would get in good with my father. *Right. As if my father cares about my fate.*

Terran and I stepped out of a door and immediately found

ourselves at what should have been the base of an immense air vortex.

"What happened to the air affinity symbol?" Terran asked spinning around.

It was hard to hear him over the cries of the prisoners and the wardens trying to calm them down.

"Do you think the affinity symbols in the temple are damaged too?" Terran shouted.

His question chilled my blood.

With the prison being over a mile underground, the portal in the temple was the only way in or out. If the affinity symbols and wards around the portal were damaged, we'd all be trapped here. Even worse, without a continuous infusion of energy from the hidden realms, every elemental here, prisoners and wardens alike, would die.

"Let's find out." I ran toward the sector door, noting an enormous crack above it.

This sector had definitely sustained more structural damage than the other areas we'd seen. *Hellfire.* Just what we needed.

Terran stopped and stared at the crack. "That has to be fixed." He held up his hands to summon his element.

"Let them handle it." I pointed at the wardens doing prisoner checks. There were at least two earth elementals among them.

"Come on." I strode through the door knowing Terran would follow.

We walked past central control and then pushed through the doors to the prison temple.

At first glance, everything looked fine. Although there were several cracks in the arched walls of the rounded room, the portal in the center of the floor was still open and active. *Thank the Elders.*

The luminescent energy swirling inside the portal lit the

room in an otherworldly light and gave an eerie harshness to the Head Warden's corpulent face. He stood at the altar next to the portal speaking to two warlocks who were nearly as large as Terran.

"What are Adjudicators doing here?" Terran murmured as he studied their grey uniforms.

The Head Warden caught sight of us and waved us down. At the motion, the foot-long, scaly beast on his thick shoulder flicked its forked tongue in our direction.

Ugh! He's carrying a warg again. The cursed creatures resembled reptilian cats and often bit anyone in reach with their razor-sharp fangs. I hated the nasty creatures as much as the Head Warden loved them.

Terran went still. "Who the fuck is that?"

I followed his gaze to the twisted body behind the altar. "It looks like Hugo."

The cantankerous alcoholic had never been one of my favorite employees, but it was jarring to see him with his eyes wide open and his face contorted in an expression of pain.

"What happened to him?"

"It looks as if he tried to go through the portal without a key," Terran said, his voice filled with confusion.

"No." I refused to believe anyone, even Hugo, would be that stupid. For obvious reasons, the portal had been warded by the Assembly. Only the Assembly, the Adjudicators, and members of prison command staff had portal keys. Any attempts to use the portal without a key would cause an immediate and painful death.

The Head Warden stepped away from the visitors and joined Terran and me in the aisle. His green-rimmed eyes were bloodshot, and his bushy white mustache quivered in agitation. "I always knew Hugo's drinking was a liability, but I never thought he'd do something like this. Poor fucker. He was set to retire next month too."

"What a shame," I said without feeling. Hugo's drinking and insulting attitude had made him few friends. *Could one of the other wardens have pushed him?*

"Are you sure he tried to go through the portal on his own?" Terran asked, his mind clearly traveling down the same dark road as mine.

The Head Warden sighed and rubbed the bridge of his bulbous nose. "Edison saw the whole damn thing. The rookie said he'd been checking the pews for contraband when Hugo ran into the room and jumped straight into the portal. The resulting explosion took him out and triggered the tremor. Thank the Goddess we didn't have a cave in."

Terran and I murmured our agreement.

The Head Warden continued shaking his head. "I don't understand it. First the bugs, then my sweet warg..." He reached up to stroke his remaining warg's fluffy purple mane. "... And now Hugo."

"Where is Edison now?" Terran asked, looking around the temple for the rookie.

The Head Warden absently waved in the direction we'd come. "I sent him to his quarters. A falling rock hit him in the head. He didn't seem himself."

No doubt the rookie was in shock. The green-haired youth was barely older than my students at the academy. Way too young to witness death up close like that.

"Why in all the realms would Hugo do something so stupid?" I wondered out loud.

The Head Warden shrugged. "Your guess is as good as mine." He let out a weary breath. "Anyway, to make matters worse the Adjudicators just showed up. They've launched an investigation and want to interview my staff. That's why I called you two down here."

Terran's heavy brows came together. "Why do they need

to investigate Hugo's death? You said Edison witnessed the whole thing."

"Oh, they're not here about Hugo." The Head Warden plucked the warg off his shoulder and cradled the creature as if it were a baby. "They're here because the Assembly sensed one of their wards had been broken—the ward on the burial chamber. Do either of you know anything about that?"

The floor seemed to sink under my feet. In our rush to deal with Sydney, we hadn't thought to shut the burial chamber door much less reseal the wards.

A glance at Terran showed he recognized our mistake too.

Hellfire. If the Assembly discovered what we'd done, we'd exchange our warden uniforms for prison tunics. Then it wouldn't matter if I got my power back.

Terran, who'd always been a shit liar, stammered. "N-no, sir."

The Head Warden's green-rimmed eyes sharpened. The male was a pompous ass, but no fool. "Are you certain?"

Thinking fast, I stepped between them. "The earth tremor took out all the affinity symbols in the sectors. It stands to reason it damaged the burial chamber wards too. I'd be more than happy to bring the Adjudicators down to see for themselves."

The furrows on the Head Warden's forehead smoothed. "Thank you, Raze. That would be excellent."

I paused and rubbed the side of my face as if I was pondering something. "You know, it would probably be best to send an earth elemental like Terran down there ahead of us to make sure the passageways are safe. We don't want to risk the Adjudicators' lives."

The Head Warden's head bobbed up and down. "Good thinking." He slapped my shoulder with a familiarity he hadn't earned. "This is why I promoted you over your competition. Brains will always supersede brawn." He turned to

Terran as if he hadn't just insulted him. "Go check out B3 and make sure it's safe for visitors."

Terran snapped to attention. "Yes, sir."

"I'll inform the Adjudicators." The Head Warden waddled toward the two warlocks who studied Terran and me intently.

There was barely veiled suspicion in their crimson-rimmed eyes.

"What the fuck?" Terran said through clenched teeth. "They'll find us out."

I turned my head so the other males couldn't read my lips. "Not if B3 is impassible." I held his gaze until he got my meaning. Raising my voice, I said, "Radio in with your update, Lead Warden Lander."

"Will do, Deputy," Terran replied before turning and leaving.

I thought about accompanying Terran, but the Head Warden beckoned me over.

"Gentlemen, I'd like to introduce Deputy Warden Ian Razell."

Both Adjudicators' eyes widened a fraction.

The taller one scanned my face. "Any relation to Archwarlock Forge Razell?"

"Ian is the archwarlock's only child," the Head Warden answered for me. "And we expect great things from him." As he delivered another bone-shaking back slap, his warg snapped at my arm.

Curse the Elders. Terran better be quick.

17

SYDNEY

I sat on my cell floor long after the wardens left. Dazed and more than a little shaken, I looked down at the blood on my thighs.

Jasen and I had made love. And it had been everything I'd dreamed it would be.

I inhaled deeply, picking up the fresh ocean scent of him still clinging to my skin. I should have felt ecstatic, but instead I felt confused.

My body had come alive at Jasen's touch and at the touch of the two other wardens. Goddess, if the earthquake hadn't interrupted us, I might have had sex with both Raze and Terran too.

My aching cleft throbbed with excitement at the idea.

I shook my head. That was so very wrong. *What kind of witch craves multiple males?*

A very wicked one...

My grumbling stomach intruded on my self-castigating. It had to be getting close to dinner.

Just the thought of trying to choke down another nasty

piece of loaf made my stomach churn. At this point, I might just eat my blanket instead. It certainly would taste better.

I looked over at my mattress and noticed something on the floor. It was the bag Jasen had brought me.

Didn't he say he brought food?

No sooner had the thought floated through my head than I was scampering across the cell, snatching up the bag and emptying the contents over my mattress.

Food!

My mouth watered at the sight of sweetbreads, candied fruits, chocolate covered nuts, and preserved meats. *All my favorites.* With a moan, I dove into the food. I meant to save some for later, but my hands and mouth had other ideas.

I ate every morsel and then hunted down the few crumbs that had fallen onto the mattress. Only then did I sit back patting my belly in satisfaction. For the first time in forever, I was satiated. Even that strange gnawing hunger in my chest had gone away.

Sighing contently, I looked over the other items Jasen had brought me. Most of them had come from my dorm room at the academy.

I ran my fingers over the oval-shaped silver frame that contained a rendering of Novah and me when I'd been only two. Her arms were locked tightly around the toddler version of me as if she feared someone would snatch me away.

She loves me.

My eyes misted as I set the frame upright near my mattress. I knew I couldn't keep it out, but right now it felt good to have a visual reminder of the only family I had.

I riffled through the other items on the mattress and discovered the large wood jewelry box Novah had given me for my fifth birthday. It was filled with medallions awarded for perfect attendance and progressing through my levels. I'd never got any academic distinctions, but then none had ever been expected from a null like me.

No. I'm not a null. I had to remind myself as I eyed the remaining contents of the jewelry box. There were a few pieces of obsidian jewelry. I'd always liked the smooth, glassy black stone and Novah used to gift me pieces from her collection. I dug through the bracelets and earrings looking for my star pendant. I felt naked without it. I'd been found wearing the pendant as a baby and I'd continued wearing it up until the testing ceremony.

Although my pendant wasn't inside the box, I found a small glass snow globe. *Jasen must have put it inside as a gift.*

As I shook the globe, iridescent flakes whizzed around a miniature replica of the academy. The tiny buildings were so detailed, I could almost see imaginary birds flocking to the mossy walls and stone turrets.

Will I ever see the academy again?

I never thought I'd miss the place, but my throat tightened as the faux storm subsided inside the globe. I carefully set the piece back inside the jewelry box and turned my attention to the small pile of clothes Jasen had brought me.

With a flash of excitement, I realize they were the clothes I'd been wearing in the burial chamber.

Even though I was sure I'd hallucinated my conversation with Al, I jammed my hand in my skirt pocket and pulled out the two-inch crystal I'd stashed there. It still pulsed with that black light I remembered from the crypt.

"Thank, the Goddess. We can talk again!" Al shrieked into my mind.

So surprised to hear her voice, I accidentally dropped the crystal. Thankfully, I caught it before it hit the ground.

"Don't go dropping my soul marker, miss butterfingers."

"Sorry." I cradled the crystal in my palm noticing that the

small crack in the side looked a little bigger. "What's a soul marker?" I'd never heard the term before.

"It's a crystal that has the ability to trap spirits. The Assembly affixed soul markers to our coffins to make sure we couldn't escape and possess anyone."

My hand shook slightly. *"You can possess people?"*

"Arcane spirit elementals can possess animals, elementals who are weak of mind, or elementals who invite them in."

She hadn't exactly answered my question. "But what about you, can you—"

"Damn girl, I almost forgot to congratulate you for losing your V-card. That was some prime-time fucking."

I gasped. "You saw that?"

"Hell, yeah I did. Nabbing a shapeshifter for your first time, lucky girl."

My insides twisted as I went over all the intimate moments Al had witnessed.

Al continued. *"And I was thrilled to see you getting your shine on with the other two wardens. Figures my brother had to ruin the first ménage I've seen in a millennium. He always messes up my fun."*

"Your brother? What are you talking about?"

"One of your idiot wardens must have damaged his soul marker. That's a colossal mistake if you ask me. He's the biggest pain in the ass you've ever met."

I glanced down at the crystal. "So, you can move around outside of your soul marker if it is damaged?"

"Mmm-hmm. Mine was fractured when they dropped your ice tomb on top of my sarcophagus. I've been able to float my ass around ever since. Do you know Saguaro Valley is only twenty miles away? Fun little town. There is this club there called Eros where the shit goes down for real."

Suddenly, Al's weird speech and pop culture references made sense. *She's been observing humans.* "Why don't you just stay there? Why come back here?" I couldn't help asking.

"*I can't stray from my soul marker for more than a couple hours.*"

Interesting. I put my finger over the pulsing black light wondering if it was her soul. "What happens if the marker is destroyed? Would you be free?"

"*Without a body, I'd evaporate into the aether.*"

Yikes. I tightened my grip around the crystal. Despite her voyeuristic ways, I didn't want her disappearing just yet. "We'll ensure that doesn't happen."

"*Good deal. I don't want to miss all the action you'll have around here. You wouldn't believe how dull it is to watch inmates jerk themselves off for days and months on end. And most of the wardens are a boring lot. Although the kinky shit that big earth elemental is into makes mama hot.*"

Part of me wanted to demand she tell me what Terran was into, the other part of me wanted her to bite her tongue. "Al, you can't watch us having sex."

She made a sound of frustration. "*But that's the most excitement I've had in over a thousand years.*"

She's that old? "Friends don't watch friends have sex."

"*My friends do... did.*" She caught herself, her voice growing tight.

"Well, we'll be different kinds of friends. The kind of friends with boundaries."

She sighed. "*Fine. But you have to promise to share all of the dirty deets with me. I mean, I want to know positions, what he smelled like, how he licked your pussy—*"

"I promise," I said quickly to shut her up.

"*Damn, you will have so much fun with that shapeshifter.*" She whistled. "*The closest I came to tapping that was when I was banging a Vulcari. He took his beast form while inside my ass—*"

Ew! I shuddered. "Stop, just stop." I'd never get that visual out of my head.

Al sniffed. "*To each their own. Just be sure you get yours while the getting is good. Tomorrow is never guaranteed, cupcake. I learned that the hard way."*

Filled with curiosity, I sprawled out on my mattress with her crystal in my hand. "What happened to you?"

"The War of the Realms happened. There I was, minding my own business in Acacia. I was the most famous dancer in the land, I'll have you know. The Prince of Acacia once offered me a castle for just one dance."

"That must've been some dance."

"Girl, you have no idea. I had moves that could seduce a hundred-year-old spinster."

When she didn't say anything for a minute, I prompted her. "So, you were in Acacia?"

"Yeah. I was in my damn fine castle living my best life and one morning the royal army rides up along with members of the Assembly. Naively, I invited them in. I shouldn't have invited them in." Her voice tightened. *"An arcane water elemental knocked me out and when I woke, I was inside my sarcophagus in the burial chamber. Took me three weeks to die."*

"Oh, my Goddess. That's terrible." I couldn't imagine the horror of slowly starving to death.

"I was in good company. They did the same to every spirit elemental in the realms. They even captured my brother which I'm sure was no minor feat."

I wondered if he was around. "Can I talk to him too?"

"Girl, you don't want anything to do with him. He makes the monsters in human movies look warm and cuddly."

Lovely. "And he can watch me the way you've been watching me?" My stomach rolled at the thought.

"Yes, but enchanting females were never his obsession."

That reminded me. "Raze and Terran accused me of putting an enchantment on them. But I swear I didn't."

She giggled. *"Well, of course you didn't. You don't need to. Our kind exudes pheromones that attract others. I've always called it the shine. Kind of our element's way of keeping us fed.*

I'm sure you've experienced elementals flocking to you your entire life."

I shook my head. "It's been the total opposite. Everyone always rejected me. Well, except for Jasen and my caregiver."

"Hmm. Could your parents have put a repulsion spell on you? It's not unheard of for overbearing fathers to want to protect their daughters from that kind of attention. I mean, I had my first stalker by the time I was five."

A spell? I'd never considered that before. "I don't know who my parents are. I was abandoned at birth."

"Aren't you just a walking lifetime movie. An orphan searching for her family. A virgin searching for her mates. A criminal longing to free herself from her prison sentence."

"I'm none of those things," I countered. "I've never cared who my parents were." I had no interest in meeting anyone who discarded me like trash. "I'm no longer a virgin." Jasen had seen to that. "And I'm not a criminal."

"Aren't you though? Even back in my day, stealing another's power was an offense punishable by death."

My face grew hot. "I didn't mean to steal Raze's power. I-I didn't even know what I was doing."

"Of course you didn't, cupcake." Al's voice was soothing. *"We've already covered that you drank too deep and his power will replenish in time so no harm no foul."*

"Really?" Sparks of hope exploded inside my chest. "I didn't steal it forever?"

"Did you see that fireball he tossed at your shapeshifter a few hours ago? I'd say Raze is already close to full power."

That's true. I'd been too overwhelmed to really notice Raze's use of power, but he had summoned a large flame. *Ha! If I hadn't stolen his power, they couldn't keep me in prison, right?*

Al continued talking, *"And you kept yourself in check when you fed from the shapeshifter, so I'd say you are a fast learner."*

"Wait. I-I fed from Jasen?"

"It sure looked that way to me. Even my best orgasms never made my skin, hair, and eyes glow."

I looked down at my arm, noticing my skin looked radiant. And I felt amazing. "He didn't seem adversely affected."

"Adversely affected?" She scoffed. *"The warlock is on cloud fucking nine, sweetheart. You've got what no witch has had in a thousand years. Spirit. Communing with spirit is a gift like no other. Think of it as having magic pussy. Witches and warlocks will line up for a taste of you. You'll have your pick of whoever you want whenever you want."*

"All I want is Jasen," I said defensively.

She laughed. *"You can't lie to your pal Al. I saw you getting your shine on with those other wardens."*

I opened my mouth, then closed it.

Seeming to pick up on my embarrassment, she said, *"Don't beat yourself up, kid. No spirit elemental in the history of spirit elementals has ever been monogamous. It's just not in our nature."*

I lifted my chin. "Well it's in my nature." Jasen was more than enough warlock for me.

"Aw, you're cute." Her laughter was starting to grate. *"Our kind needs sex as much as we need food. Can you imagine eating the same thing for every meal?"*

As if she'd conjured it, the food slot swung open and one of those nasty loaves coasted into the middle of my cell. *Ugh. Thank Goddess for Jasen's treats.*

Al continued as if she hadn't noticed my meal being served. *"Aren't you super lucky to have a new best friend to show you the ropes?"*

My breathing hitched. "Are we really friends?" I'd always wanted a female friend, not that Jasen wasn't wonderful.

"Of course," she said with a conviction that won me over. *"And as your best friend, I'm advising you to do a little post-coital clean up, unless you want to wear blood on your thighs as a badge of honor."*

"Ugh, definitely not." I stood and walked over to the toilet.

"Let's do something about that hair too. Bed head is sexy, rat's nests aren't."

"Oh." I touched my hair self-consciously.

"You'd look good with curls. Let's get it damp and braid it. After that, we need to work on your lingo. No one in the human realm talks so formally."

The strangest feeling of happiness came over me as Al continued prattling in my head.

I'm no longer alone...

18

TERRAN

With Raze's orders ringing in my ears, I strode through the prison using the side passageways only me and a few veteran wardens knew about. My father, who'd been the Head Warden at Lost Soul's for decades, had taught me the ins and outs of this place when I was young. Most of my fondest memories involved imaginary adventures zipping in and out of these secret rooms.

But when he died, my childhood antics had ended. With both parents gone and no family willing to take me in, I'd become a ward of the Assembly who'd promptly thrown my ass into one of their academies. I guess the joke was on them though because even though I tested higher than most earth elementals, I refused their Cultivator assignment. I'd made it crystal clear that the Warden assignment was the only one I'd accept.

A formal letter of disapproval had been issued, but they'd sent me back here. To my home.

I frowned at all the fractures in the walls. *They need to be repaired.* I lifted my hand to fix them when I remembered I had more pressing issues to deal with.

Adjudicators.

If they discovered what Raze and I had done...

Sydney's stunning face and body appeared in my mind's eye. *Ah, fucking hell.* The gorgeous enchantress had messed my life up good.

More than that, she'd deliberately invaded my dreams.

But why?

To see me at my most vulnerable? To find my hidden secrets? To disarm me and lay her hooks deeper in my heart? My heart? Fuck.

Sydney had snared me in a way no other female had before. I obsessed about her night and day and when Raze told me her camera wasn't operational this morning, I'd half lost my mind trying to get to her. In the prison, when cell cameras malfunctioned, inmates died.

Prison gangs were always arranging hits on their rivals. And I could think of half a dozen wardens who would turn a blind eye for the right price. If I were in charge, I'd root out all those bad apples and lock them up myself. But I wasn't in charge, and no one seemed to care if inmates didn't make it out alive.

Just the thought of something like that happening to my enchantress was enough to make me see red. I'd nearly lost my mind when I saw her struggling underneath Victor's naked body. In that moment, I could have smashed him to pieces for hurting her.

My breath went ragged. I'd never thought I'd encounter a female I'd kill for.

Trying to outrun my thoughts, I jogged the rest of the way to the lift and slammed my thumb on the call button.

Hurry up.

I needed to get down to the crypt and make sure the corridor to the passageway was impassible, and I needed to do it now.

Where's the lift? It should have opened immediately.

I hit the call button again.

When the doors didn't open, I realized the lift was on one of the lower levels.

My pulse jumped. Trying to calm myself, I reasoned someone had gone down to get supplies.

The level directly below the main prison was used for storage. Some of it food, but most of it was laundry supplies, extra prison uniforms, and commissary goods the prisoners could purchase. Often rookies were dispatched to pick up a pallet of fresh blankets or some shit.

The longer the lift took to rise, the greater my anxiety. The lift wasn't sitting on B1. The inmate property room was the next level below that, but I didn't imagine any wardens were impounding or checking out property right now. In the tremor's aftermath, all wardens had been ordered to their posts.

That left B3. *Fuck.* Sweat dotted my brow. Someone had taken the lift to the crypt and since they hadn't come back up, they were still down there.

We wardens were a superstitious lot, and I couldn't think of anyone brave or dumb enough to go down there.

I could still hear my father's warning in my head. *"Monsters are best left undisturbed, son."*

Even as an adult, it'd taken Raze begging me for weeks before I'd finally ventured down. And look where it had gotten me. Enchanted by a witch and in jeopardy of losing my job, and probably my freedom too.

What if there's an Adjudicator down there right now?

Raze and I had assumed there were only two of those fuckers, but what if there had been more? Maybe the others had immediately gone to inspect the wards on the door.

They'd know immediately that someone opened the crypt. It wouldn't take them long to point a finger at Raze, as the only warden knowledgeable enough about spells to break the wards, and me, the only warden with enough earth elemental power to move the colossal stone door.

Warg shit.

I ran a sweaty hand across the stubble starting to sprout over my jaw as I waited for the lift. *What will I do if I find them down there?*

Two scenarios played out in my mind. One resulted in my immediate arrest. The other resulted in me committing a crime so horrific, it left a foul taste in my mouth.

The lift doors opened.

Frustration and panic beat at my chest as I stepped inside the metal contraption and pressed the button for B3. *What do I do?*

Raze was my best friend, but I never thought helping him would cost me everything. I should have known better. By opening the crypt we'd broken not just the prison rules, but elemental law. The Assembly placed the wards on the door for a reason—they didn't want anyone going into that room. *And they certainly wanted nothing coming out.*

When the Adjudicators figured out what we'd done, we'd end up becoming inmates here instead of wardens.

My throat tightened as I imagined the fresh hell that would be. We wouldn't survive long in this place.

And worse. What would happen to Sydney? Would they lock her away again? Would they kill her?

Ice water filled my veins. I can't let anything happen to my enchantress. *But am I prepared to do what it takes to save her?*

I shuddered. I was many things, but I wasn't a killer.

The lift lurched to a stop and the doors opened with a whoosh.

Unfortunately, the corridor was entirely passable and clear of debris. Even worse, the torches anchored to the wall had been lit. *Someone is definitely down here.* The shadows of the flames dancing across the empty passageway taunted me with visions of my imminent arrest.

The Adjudicators must be in the crypt. If I acted fast, I could close the door and trap them inside. Then I could bring enough earth down to block entry to the passageway.

The problem would be taken care of. No arrest. No imprisonment. Raze, Sydney, and I could go on with our lives.

But could I live with that?

One of my father's favorite sayings rang in my ear. *If you can't do right, then at least don't do wrong.*

I curled my hands into fists, my insides churning with indecision.

Seeming to have enough of my deliberating, the lift doors closed.

I held my hand out, stopping the slates of metal from meeting. As the doors opened again, I made my decision.

I stepped out into the corridor and grabbed my radio. "This is Lead Warden Lander, over."

Raze's voice crackled over the device. "What's the status of B3?"

"It's safe to traverse, over."

There was silence, as if Raze didn't understand my words. "Can you confirm that the area was undamaged by the tremor, Lead Warden Lander?"

"It's undamaged, sir."

I could sense Raze's desire to curse.

I took a deep breath and continued. "It seems the other Adjudicators are already down here investigating the crypt."

Raze inhaled sharply. "What other Adjudicators?"

Radio static belched from my handheld device. I shook it and pressed the talk button again. "Raze?"

Nothing but more static. It shouldn't have surprised me. My radio had been acting up since Kayla threw it at me. Sighing, I shoved it back onto my duty belt. Then, feeling like a male walking to his hanging, I marched the length of the corridor and stopped at the entryway to the crypt. No way was I setting foot in that cursed place again, but I could at least lock eyes with the Adjudicator that would take my freedom.

The inky darkness of the tomb was pierced by a single torch carried by the last person I expected to see down here.

Edison?

The twenty-year-old stalked from coffin to coffin. Although there was no mistaking his shock of bright green hair, the quickness and fluidity of his movements was completely at odds with his normal clumsy gait. Further, instead of his normal goofy smile, his wide mouth was pressed in a harsh line.

What the fuck is he doing?

I squinted and watched him yank something from the front of a coffin. *He's pulling the soul marker. Why in all the realms would he do that?*

"Edison, get over here." My hoarse order came out louder than I'd intended, and it echoed throughout the chamber.

The rookie glanced over at me, his sallow face paler than usual. "I will attend to you shortly."

The fuck? The little null would be lucky I didn't break his gangly neck. "Rookie, get your ass over here now."

Edison held the torch up as if to better see my face. "I think not."

My eyes nearly crossed. This day was already fucked. The last thing I needed was a lippy subordinate. "Edison, if you don't get your scrawny ass over here, I swear to the Goddess I'll shut the door and let you rot in here for eternity."

That got the little fucker's attention.

The warden leveled his gaze on my face and let out a battle cry.

What in all the realms? I was struck almost stupid at the sight of the kid rushing at me.

His eyes were wild and as black as the deepest recesses of the crypt as he lifted the torch in front of him.

Fuck.

Just before he reached me, I knocked the makeshift weapon out of his hand hard enough to fracture his wrist.

He hissed like a serpent but kept coming. He slammed his other fist into my stomach.

I barely felt the contact. "Stop. What the fuck, Eddie?"

This was insane. *Did seeing Hugo die snap his sanity or something?*

Edison made a sound of frustration and jumped onto my back like a deranged warg.

My shock turned to anger as he tried to gouge out my eyes.

I pounded him repeatedly in the face with my fist.

He countered by wrapping his arm around my throat and trying to strangle me.

"Enough." I reached up, grabbed him by the neck and flung him at the arched entryway.

Edison hit the stone with a crunch and landed on the floor in a boneless heap. His legs twitched and a long hiss escaped his lips, not unlike the sound a carbonated bottle of liquid made when twisted open.

I tensed, readying myself for another attack, but the rookie stayed down with his eyes closed and head lolled to the side. There was no pulse at his throat.

He's dead. Guilt and sorrow arrowed me in the chest.

The sound of boots thundering in the corridor had me turning my head toward the lift.

"Stop right there." The Adjudicators ran toward me, their fiery hands raised pointed at the center of my chest.

I quickly raised my hands. "He attacked me." I nodded at Edison's corpse.

The two agents looked from me to him as if they didn't know what to believe. At least the fireballs in their palms disappeared.

"I swear on the realms, I was only defending myself." I hoped the blood running down my face would convince them of my innocence.

"What's going on?" Raze demanded. He'd run behind the Adjudicators and now leaned against the corridor wall panting hard.

Keeping my hands in the air, I looked over at my friend. "I have no idea. I came down here to check the passageway and found the rookie inside pulling a soul marker from one of the coffins."

Raze's eyes widened. "Why would he do that?"

I shrugged. "No idea. But when I ordered him to come out, he attacked me."

"That's even more suicidal than Hugo's jump into the portal," Raze said, watching the Adjudicators speak in low voices to one another.

Their grim expressions weren't giving me the warm fuzzies. But at least Raze and I were off the hook. The Adjudicators would think Edison broke the wards on the tomb.

The taller Adjudicator plucked the soul marker from Edison's pocket, and then carefully placed it back inside the crypt as if it was an armed explosive.

The shorter Adjudicator peered inside. "Where's the witch encased in ice?"

Warg shit. They'd noticed Sydney was gone. I slowly lowered my hands and played dumb. "I don't know what you're talking about."

"A while back we brought in a young female trapped in a

block of ice." The short Adjudicator pointed near Sydney's former location.

"That's above our pay grade," Raze interjected. "You'll have to take that up with the Head Warden. Hey, what are you doing with him?"

The taller Adjudicator grabbed Edison by the arms and dragged him into the crypt. He paused and looked at Raze. "We need to seal him in there."

Even though Edison had attacked me, I shook my head furiously. "No. You can't do that. His family will want to bury him." Another wave of sorrow hit me. *I've taken a life.*

"His body can never leave this cursed place," the taller Adjudicator said, a haunted look in his crimson-rimmed eyes.

A preternatural wind came out of nowhere and threw us against the corridor wall.

Both Adjudicators made the sign of the Goddess before backing away.

"This is much worse than we anticipated," the taller Adjudicator muttered.

"Much worse," echoed the shorter Adjudicator. "We need to report this."

In unison, they turned and ran toward the lift.

The sight of two grown ass warlocks running away as if their lives depended on it, made the hairs on the back of my neck stand up. "Wait. Tell us what the fuck is going on."

"What are you going to report?" Raze shouted at the same time.

Ignoring us, they rushed into the lift.

As the doors were closing, the shorter Adjudicator called out, "There's a Soul Eater among you. The Goddess help you all."

19

SYDNEY

Days passed without another visit from Jasen or the other wardens. If not for Al's running commentary, I might have sunk into a deep depression.

Where's Jasen?

Just before he left, he'd kissed my forehead and promised he'd come back.

Initially, I'd freaked out thinking Raze and Terran had seriously hurt him, but Al assured me Jasen was fine. She said all the wardens were working overtime on repairs to the prison after the earthquake. Surely, he could still find a moment to see me or at least bring me something edible to eat.

I eyed the three-foot-high stack of plates I'd accumulated. Even starvation wouldn't drive me to eat an entire loaf, but Al had coaxed me into eating a few gag worthy bites from each one.

I needed to keep up my energy for the dance moves she was teaching me.

"Do it again. Squat. Good. Now thrust your hips," she ordered. *"Faster."*

My thighs burned in agony as I gyrated my pelvis for the umpteenth time.

"Yes! You've got the twerk down, you sexy wench! You should be proud of yourself. In only three days you've mastered the booty bounce, the lap dance, and the striptease. You know how to undulate like a serpent and can shake your ass better than any dancer I've ever seen. Except me."

"Of course," I said, rolling my eyes. "And why exactly are you teaching me all these moves again?"

"Well, for one, every witch should be well versed in the art of seduction and for two, it's a damn fine workout."

"No argument there," I said, hobbling over to my mattress. Every muscle in my body was sore from the headstands, splits, and other body contortions she'd talked me into.

"You can't rest now, cupcake. You haven't learned the art of the hair flip yet."

"I need a break," I whined at her soul marker. I'd woven it into my hair with a piece of torn blanket. Because of Al's nonstop mile a minute talking, I hadn't had more than a few hours of sleep the past few days and it was taking a toll. "Just let me rest for a little while." My heavy eyelids were just starting to close when Al let out a huff.

"You can sleep when you're dead. Shake that money maker."

"Too tired," I mumbled. Then to keep her from bugging me again, I untied her soul marker and slid it inside the mattress where I'd hidden my jewelry box and picture frame.

Blessed silence.

I sighed and let my eyes flutter closed again.

Two breaths later, I was back in my homeroom, clad in my uniform, and perched on Raze's desk.

But it wasn't just Raze standing across from me in the dream this time. Terran stood next to the dark-haired warlock, his thick muscles bunched as he folded his arms across his chest.

Both males wore black warden uniforms and matching scowls.

Neither of them looked happy to see me.

Terran gave Raze a grim smile. "Your dream spell works. You win."

"I always win," Raze replied, swinging his dark gaze my way. "Ms. Castaway, I'm glad you could join us."

"You don't look very glad," I said, nervously pulling my skirt down to cover my legs.

Terran took a step forward. "What do you expect? That we would be happy to see you after finding out you were invading our dreams?" His icy tone gave me goosebumps.

"I'm not doing it on purpose."

A tic jumped in his jaw. "Sure. Just like you're not enchanting us... or making us desire you."

I started to defend myself but Raze grabbed Terran's arm and tugged him back by his side. "Let's stick to the plan."

What plan? I was feeling as if I'd fallen into a trap.

Terran gritted his teeth but didn't object when Raze stepped in front of him to approach me.

"Ms. Castaway, we have an offer we'd like to make you."

"Okay," I said slowly.

Raze stopped a few feet away from the desk. "We are prepared to give you what you desire most, if you meet a few of our demands."

Intrigued, I leaned back on the desk. "What do you want?"

Raze gave me a smile that didn't reach his eyes. "We want you to return my power."

I opened my mouth, but he raised his hand to stop me from speaking.

"We also want you to remove your enchantments on us and help us track down a dangerous rogue spirit elemental."

That got my attention. "What do you mean rogue spirit elemental?"

Terran stepped forward. "A Soul Eater escaped the crypt and has been destroying the wards and killing... things."

I gasped. *It must be Al's brother.* She said he was a monster.

Raze nodded. "We think you can help us locate this elemental and return it to the burial chamber."

I didn't know if I could, but I needed to know what was at stake. "And what are you offering me to do this?"

"Us," Terran said, stepping around Raze and walking up to the desk.

I blinked. "Come again?"

"Exactly." Terran leaned over me and nuzzled my neck. "We'll make you come again and again."

My breathing hitched as he rested one of his huge hands on my thigh, just below the hem of my skirt. "And you think that is what I desire most?"

Raze walked around the desk and stood behind me. "Isn't it? You said back in your prison cell that you need to... how did you put it?"

"She needs to fuck," Terran finished for him. His eyes darkened, and he slid his hand under my skirt.

I couldn't help the shocked moan that escaped my lips when his fingers brushed over my suddenly aching flesh.

"I like you dressed as a schoolgirl," Terran said as his fingers moved under my panties.

"Oh, Goddess." My insides melted as he delved inside me.

Raze brushed his mouth against my ear. "We're prepared to give you everything you desire for as long as you desire it." To underscore his point, he cupped my breasts through the fabric of my shirt.

My breasts seemed to swell in his palms as he massaged them.

Terran flicked his thumb over my bud, making me cry out. "We'll make it so good for you, enchantress."

"So good," Raze echoed, his hands pushing under my shirt and camisole.

Pleasure bombarded me as I writhed against the desk and their hands. "Both of you? Together?"

"Together," Raze answered.

"We'll share you." Terran leaned down and nipped my ear. "But I get your virgin ass first."

The scandalous image of the two gorgeous warlocks making love to me at the same time heated my blood. I trembled, my heart pounding in my ears. *But what about Jasen?*

"I think she needs more convincing." Raze pulled me so I was lying over the desk with him standing near my head and Terran standing near my legs. He waved his hand over me. "Off."

My clothes disappeared and I lay bare before them.

Terran let out a low whistle. "Fuck worshiping the Goddess. I'm worshiping this from now on." He sank to his knees and buried his face between my thighs.

I let out a wild cry that Raze captured with his lips. The pleasure was so intense, I saw stars.

Terran went to work on my core, sucking my bud as he thrust his fingers inside me.

All my senses fired at once. Shrieking in pleasure, I tried to grab his head and force a slower rhythm.

Raze stopped me, grabbing my arms and pinning them down on top of the desk. Then the dark-haired warlock licked his way down my chest and clamped his lips around my nipple.

It was overwhelming. Terran's mouth on my core. Raze's mouth on my nipples. My body drew as tight as a bow. I could taste the rapture of the oncoming orgasm. Then, right before I came, both males jerked away.

"Wait." I reached for them, but they moved to stand side by side in front of the rows of student desks. Although I could plainly see the erections tenting their pants, their jaws were locked and their expressions granite.

"If you want us to continue, you must agree to the terms," Raze announced.

"What terms?" I pushed myself up on the desk, my core throbbing painfully.

"Agree to the bargain, enchantress," Terran urged in a low voice.

So overwhelmed with their loving, I'd completely forgotten about the bargain they were trying to strike.

The big elemental strode back over to me. "I think she needs even more convincing. Raze, eat her pussy this time. I'll play with her nipples." He pushed me back down on the desk, his eyes glittering with wicked promise.

As Raze prowled over, I realized they planned on sexually tormenting me until I agreed. They were using pleasure as a weapon against me.

Terran pinched one of my nipples. "We can do this all night, enchantress."

As Raze pushed my thighs apart, my desire fizzled. They didn't care for me. I was merely a means to an end for them.

"No." I kicked Raze and twisted out of Terran's grip. Then I rolled off the desk, taking a pile of graded papers with me.

As I stood, chest heaving, the papers containing the names of all the students who'd hurt and teased me my entire life rained down on me.

I caught one paper with Andrea's name on it and tore it in half. I was done being bullied. Al had taught me that I wasn't a freak. I was a kick ass spirit elemental, and no one would push me around anymore. Including Raze and Terran.

I marched toward the two males, who exchanged a what-in-the-Goddess is happening look. "It's time to set the record straight, wardens. Number one, I didn't enchant either of you." I motioned between them.

Al had given me a crash course in everything spirit elemental, and I wouldn't let them accuse me of things I wasn't capable of.

When Raze started to say something, I cut him off. "All spirit elementals exude pheromones that attract others. It's not personal. Even Warden Clover propositioned me in the shower."

Terran blinked.

Thanks to Al, I also knew the cure for the shine. "If it bothers you all you have to do is avoid my presence." I turned my gaze to Raze. "And I didn't rob you of your power, I merely drained a lot of it when I fed for the first time. Your power needed time to regenerate and you already have most of it back based on the fireball you threw at…" I caught myself before I gave up Jasen's name.

Raze glanced down at his hands, a thoughtful expression on his face.

"And I could help you find the escaped spirit elemental, but only in return for what I actually desire most."

"And what's that?" Terran asked quietly.

"My freedom. I want out of this prison."

As the males chewed that over, I shut my eyes and imagined myself clothed. All at once my entire body was covered in a soft fuzzy blanket.

Raze's black brows shot up. "What in the realms are you wearing?"

I stroked the grey fleece and smiled. "Al calls it a Snuggie." I'd laughed when she described the wearable blankets, but they were really freaking comfortable. *Freaking. Ha! Listen to me.* Al's human lingo lessons were really starting to rub off.

"Who is Al?" Raze demanded.

Curse it. I needed to watch my tongue. "It's not important. What is important is that I won't put up with these shenanigans anymore."

Raze exchanged a confused look with Terran. "Shenanigans?"

Apparently, I would have to spell it out for them. "No using sex as a weapon. Not now. Not ever." I might have been sexually inexperienced, but it didn't mean I'd let them use it against me. "I really can't believe you thought sex with you two is what I'd desire most." I snorted. Al was right, males were dense.

Terran looked stricken. "So, you don't want me."

There was a vulnerability in his gaze I hadn't seen before. It struck a chord in my heart and I softened my words. "I didn't say that." I lifted my hand to touch his lips. "But I want you to kiss me on the mouth and treat me like more than a booty call." Al had given me the four-one-one on those.

Terran flinched.

"And me? Do you desire me?" Raze asked, going motionless.

I moved closer to him, letting my gaze move from his inky black hair, to his gorgeous crimson-rimmed eyes and muscular body. "Of course, I desire my sexy professor."

His shoulders sagged as if in relief.

"But I want you free of anger. I won't be your punching bag any longer. You must forgive me once and for all."

Raze's gaze softened. He opened his mouth to say something, but suddenly the terrifying sensation I was drowning ripped me from their dream.

❧ 20 ☙

RAZE

"Where did she go?" Terran spun around my old classroom in a circle.

"The most probable explanation is that she woke up," I replied, still lost in thought. I lifted my hands and summoned fire. Orange and blue flames ignited on the tips of my fingers the same way they had during my confrontation with Victor.

Sydney had spoken the truth. *Hellfire.* Everything she said was true.

Twelve months ago, smoke appeared on the tips of my fingers as I lamented the loss of my power. Six months ago, I'd been able to summon a few small sparks, but I didn't think much of it. All this time the fire had been reigniting inside me while I'd been plotting how I'd get it back.

I sat down hard on top of one of the student desks. "I've had my power all this time."

Terran gave me a strange look. "Does that mean you don't hate her anymore?"

I snorted. "I never hated her. In fact, I've been half in love with Sydney since the first day I saw her in my class."

All around us, hazy versions of students appeared. They clutched their textbooks and chatted with each other. None of them seemed aware of Raze and me as they walked through us.

Terran came to attention when a wispy version of Sydney walked through the doorway. He never took his eyes from her as she navigated around the other students to sit in her usual seat in the back.

Several students I recognized as my troublemakers immediately surrounded her desk and jeered at the beautiful purple-haired female.

Sydney, who'd unpacked her water bottle and books, froze.

Clayton, a self-entitled air elemental, used his power to send Sydney's book flying over her head.

Sydney climbed on her desk, trying to grab it.

Andrea knocked over Sydney's water bottle, coating her chair with water.

Unaware, Sydney yanked her book out of the air and sat back down in her seat. She let out a cry and jumped up, her skirt dripping wet.

The students around her let out gales of laughter.

Even though it was only a memory, I was tempted to march over there and throw those students into detention all over again.

Terran cursed. "Who are those fuckers?"

I shrugged. "Students who got off on bullying Sydney."

"Why? She's sweet, and beautiful, and smart, and—"

"If I didn't know better, I'd think you were in love with her." I'd meant to tease him, but Terran didn't smile.

"She's incredible, Raze. I've never felt this way about a female before." The longing in his voice shocked me.

"I have to force myself not to visit her. It actually hurts

me when she's upset." He rubbed a hand over his chest. "I thought she'd enchanted me, but…"

"But this is something else," I finished for him. Just a few moments ago when she'd demanded I forgive her I'd been ready to do so. I could no longer hold on to my rage, not when my heart was demanding I hold on to her.

As all my anger finally evaporated, I could finally see what was happening and pheromones were not to blame. "She's our fated mate."

There was no other explanation for my obsession with her. And, if I was being honest with myself, the attraction had been there long before her attack on me at the academy.

Terran shook his head, denying what he had to know to be true. "I don't have a fated mate."

"No. You don't have a sworn," I corrected for him. The Seer, one of the most powerful archwitches in the realms, supposedly matched each elemental to their fated mate at birth.

But I'd suspected for years it was all a farce. My father had long boasted he'd brokered my match with Jessalyn's family. He'd thought Jessalyn and my combined fire affinities would give him even more powerful grandchildren.

"Not possible," Terran whispered, still swimming in the sea of denial. "And even if she was my fated mate, how can she be yours too?"

"I don't pretend to know," I confessed. "But I can tell you feel as deeply connected to her as I do, and I don't feel any jealousy towards you. When you suggested we share her back in her prison cell, I was all for it. Even us sharing her in this dream felt right. Did it not?"

Terran slowly nodded. "Yes, it felt… natural."

That confirmed it. "She belongs to us, Terran. She's our mate." And it was our imperative to care for her, protect her, and ensure her happiness. We'd done such a piss-poor job of it so far.

Terran paced through the phantom students still milling about the desks. "Goddess fuck. Raze, we've treated her like total shit. We're no better than those bullies." He pointed at the ghostly version of Clayton and Andrea.

"I know." A heavy weight settled on my chest as I thought of what we'd put her through. My accusations. The terrible things I'd said to her. *Hellfire.* Besides threatening to leave her in the burial chamber, I'd incinerated her in my dream over and over. As I tallied my crimes against her, my mouth filled with a bitter taste. "We'll make it right."

"How?" Terran gave me an anguished look. "We locked her up in tier four, Raze. Even the most hardened criminals don't survive long in there."

My shoulders sagged for a moment. *He's right. We should have never put her there.* "We'll move her," I said, shoving past the guilt and self-recrimination. "She can share our quarters while we track down the Soul Eater and—"

"You're assuming we can find it." Terran paced around the desks. "We haven't been able to detect any further sign of it and neither could the Adjudicators."

I scoffed. "They didn't really bother to look, did they?"

After the Adjudicators had briefly spoken with the Head Warden, they'd rushed back through the portal.

Not an hour later, the Assembly had summoned the Head Warden. Before leaving, my superior had put the entire prison on lockdown.

No one was allowed in or out until we found the Soul Eater. The portal was closed except for thirty minutes a day —the minimum to keep us all alive.

In the three days since, we'd had no word from the Head Warden and although we had all the wardens watching for unusual behavior among the prisoners and their coworkers, no one had reported anything so far.

The Head Warden still hadn't returned and the longer he was gone, the more concerned I'd become.

Terran's pacing grew more erratic. "How are we going to track down the Soul Eater without Sydney's help?"

Good question. However, I hadn't been keen on involving Sydney in the first place. By Terran's account, this rogue Soul Eater was dangerous, and I couldn't stand the thought of her in danger.

The floating students were irritating me. As I waved them away, an idea came together in my mind. "We need to figure out who we are searching for."

Terran spun around. "You mean go back into the burial chamber?"

I nodded. "We'll identify the sarcophagus with the missing soul marker. I should be able to translate the runes on the coffin and then we'll know who we are up against. My father always said to destroy your enemy, you must understand your enemy."

Terran huffed. "My father always said there are no enemies, only teachers." He got a far off look in his eyes. "Sydney wants to leave the prison."

I cocked my head to the side as if he were daft. "Of course, she does. No one actually wants to stay in this place."

He looked down at his boots. "It's not so bad really."

"Terran, look at me."

The enormous male lifted his head and gave me an accusatory look. "Now that you have your power back, you'll leave too."

I sucked in a breath, not really having thought it through. "Eventually." The promise of gaining employment at another academy filled me with excitement. There were so many more libraries to explore, scrolls to translate, and ancient mysteries to solve.

Terran's voice filled with bitterness. "Everyone I care for leaves..."

I put a hand on his shoulder. "You and I will always be close, you know that. And now with this dream spell we can speak whenever we want." I waved my free hand about the room. The dreamwalking spell I'd translated from ancient scrolls years ago was surprisingly easy to cast.

The tension in his face eased. "We'll be able to bring Sydney to our dreams at night too, won't we?"

"Of course." The spell could summon any elemental into a dream or nightmare. "But we're getting ahead of ourselves, old friend. We must find that Soul Eater or we risk the unthinkable happening."

"The Assembly won't shut the portal down and murder us all."

I sighed and pinched the bridge of my nose. "They can and they will. When I attended warden training last fall, my instructor spoke of the incident at the Fallen Penitentiary."

Terran rolled his eyes. "Drill instructors love to warn recruits about the Vulcari prisoner that escaped and was found by the human military."

He was missing the point. "Do you know what happened to the prison after that?"

Terran shrugged. "It was a hundred years ago."

"No one ever heard from anyone at that prison again."

An uneasy looked crossed Terran's face. "The Assembly could have fired the wardens and shut down the prison."

"Oh, they shut it down all right. The Assembly closed their portal... Permanently. They killed every warden and prisoner because of one escaped inmate." My father had given me the unvarnished truth when I'd asked him about it. "Let's not kid ourselves. If we don't find the Soul Eater, the same thing will happen to us."

Terran's eyes widened.

He's finally understanding.

"Let's wake up and go back to the crypt," Terran said, his back ramrod straight.

"Or, we could just visit your most recent memory of the burial chamber now," I countered.

The relief on his face was almost comical. "Yeah, we could do that." Terran closed his eyes and when he opened them, we'd flashed from my old classroom to the doorway of the burial chamber.

A ghostly version of Terran shouted at a hazy version of Edison, who was standing near a sarcophagus deep inside the chamber. Neither of them reacted to our presence.

Terran watched the dream version of himself scowl at the young, green-haired rookie. "Fuck. If only I'd known the kid was possessed."

I knew from experience, there was no point in fantasizing about changing the past. But we could learn from it. "Let's get a closer look at where he is standing."

Terran followed me as I stepped into the darkness of the chamber.

The light of Edison's flickering torch was too weak to illuminate our way, so I summoned my fire.

All at once I glimpsed the magnificent riches around us. I gasped in awe.

When I'd visited the chamber before, it was with the single-minded focus of freeing Sydney. So filled with pain and anger, I had paid little notice to my surroundings.

But this... this was incredible. I spun around with my hands raised, dazzled by the sheer weight of the history in this room. The closest sarcophagus was etched in hieroglyphs dating back to the dawn of the Elders. The one next to that was covered in runes from the second dynasty. Every inch of the stone coffin was etched in symbols depicting the life story of the occupant. "Remarkable."

"If you say so," Terran said, turning to watch the fighting match between the dream version of himself and Edison.

"Look over here." I waved my hand toward the cave walls etched in devotional carvings.

"What does it say?" Terran asked, not looking remotely interested.

"My ancient Numerian is rusty, but I think it says spirit is within us and all around us. It holds all creation together. It is without end."

"It sounds as if it's praising spirit, not condemning it."

I nodded excitedly. "This must have been a tomb for spirit elementals long before the War of the Realms."

Terran's brows drew together. "Why would they build a prison on top of a graveyard—Oh, I get it. They wanted us to guard the crypt."

"Indeed. This is an incredible find, Terran. If we could study the artifacts in this room, we could understand more of our history and more about the spirit element."

"Those will probably help too." Terran pointed at piles of tattered scrolls stacked around an ornately decorated sarcophagus.

"Amazing!" *What knowledge do those hold?* A thrill shot through me and I tried to bolt in that direction. Terran's heavy hand gripped my elbow, holding me in place. "Not so fast, bookworm. Remember why we're here."

"You're right." With considerable effort, I turned my focus back to our mission. "Where was Edison standing when he pulled the soul marker?"

Terran frowned, his brow furrowing. "I think there." He pointed toward the center of the chamber. "Yeah, he was standing near that coffin."

As we maneuvered around the sarcophaguses, I could see the stone coffin he pointed at was relatively simple compared to the others. There were no ornamentations on it or inlaid gems adorning it. Also, and most importantly, it had no soul marker.

"This has to be the one," Terran said, looking down at the empty hole in the coffin lid where the soul marker had once been. "There looks like writing here. What does it say?"

I stepped around him and wiped at the dust and dirt on the sarcophagus. Age and the underground elements had eaten away the stone, but Terran was right, there were runes here. The symbols predated the oldest language I knew, but I could extrapolate the meaning.

I took a step back, horror washing over me.

Terran gave me a nervous look. "What is it? What does it say, Raze?"

I swallowed hard. "Here lies the Nightmare of the Realms."

Hellfire. The thing roaming the prison wasn't just any Soul Eater, it was Z'syron Quago, one of the deadliest and most powerful of all.

21

SYDNEY

I awoke feeling as if I was choking on dry ice. The invisible vapor tasted and smelled like licorice. I coughed trying to expel it from my mouth and nose, only to have it travel deeper inside my body which was moving without my control.

Helpless, I could only observe as I stood and stretched sinuously. Then I twirled around in a circle over and over, kicking my leg out in repeated movements that spun me dizzyingly fast.

Am I dreaming? No. This felt too real to be a dream. Despite my lack of control, I was aware of the sensation of cold dirt floor on my feet.

Through my mounting fear, I sensed the alien presence within me. Al was here, and worse, she was in total control.

"Al, get out!" I shouted telepathically.

I sensed her guilt and immediate awareness of me.

Anger and that gnawing hunger swelled up inside me, giving me the added strength to shove Al out of my consciousness.

For a brief second I felt as if I were coughing up licorice syrup and then finally, I was alone. *Thank the Goddess.*

I dug through my mattress and yanked out her soul marker. "What in the realms was that?"

"I thought you were sleeping," she said, sounding defensive.

"So, it's okay to possess someone when they are sleeping?" The pitch of my voice was high enough to break glass. "I thought we were friends."

"We are," she said in a small voice.

"Friends don't possess each other," I snarled at the crystal. I had half a mind to break the damn thing in half and vanquish her to whatever hell awaited creatures like us.

I waited for her to tell me that her friends possessed each other all the time, but she just sighed. *"You're right. I'm sorry. I shouldn't have done that. It's just that it's been so long since I danced. That's all. I just wanted one last dance."*

I massaged the twitching muscle of my right thigh. "Then you should have asked me."

"You'd let me take your body for a spin? For real?"

"Maybe," I replied, uncertain I should trust her with my body or anything at this point. "But you can't do that again."

"I won't. I swear to the Goddess, I'll never possess you without your permission." Her voice rang with truth, but I was leery of trusting her.

I rolled her soul marker back and forth. "You said only arcane spirit elementals could possess someone."

"Yes," she answered. *"And only an arcane sprit elemental stronger than myself could toss me out like I was last week's loaf."*

It took me a moment to grasp the meaning of her words. "You mean, I'm an arcane elemental?"

"Sure as shit you are. In fact, you're the most powerful spirit elemental I've ever encountered and, given who my family is, that's saying something."

Shock glued me to my mattress. "What kind of things can an arcane spirit elemental do?"

"*Well...*" Al drawled out the word until I was ready to snap her crystal. "*All of us can dreamwalk, absorb life force energy, and possess other creatures, but we have our own specialty, so to speak. Take me, for example. I can seduce any living being in the realms. And I don't mean just beguiling them with my shine. Nearly every elemental I danced for was willing to abandon their positions, their consorts, and their families for the merest chance of being with me.*"

"Wow." I didn't know whether to be impressed or horrified.

She continued. "*My brother could mind control other elementals and make them do his bidding. My grandfather could raise the dead.*"

Ugh. I shuddered. "I hope that's not my ability."

"*It's not,*" she said soothingly. "*You have an even rarer ability. You can absorb and retain another elemental's powers.*"

"You mean like Raze's fire affinity?" I looked down at my fingertips, half expecting to see flames dancing at the ends of them.

"*Yes. And some of the shapeshifter's water abilities.*" Seeming to register my shock, she added. "*I can sense the water elemental power inside you now. The negators are keeping you from using it.*"

The idea that I'd inadvertently taken some of Jasen's powers while we made love sickened me. "Oh, Goddess." I was worse than a Soul Eater. Feeling chilled to the bone, I wrapped my arms around myself. "I won't do it again. I won't steal elemental powers." If that meant I could never touch another, then so be it.

Al's husky laughter grated on my nerves. "*Oh, stop being a drama llama. Like I've already told you, an elemental's power comes from deep within. It will naturally replenish.*"

"Right." Just like I'd told Raze in the dream, not that he believed me. I let out a deep breath and rubbed my temples.

"No harm, no foul, remember?"

Al's words took a few notches off my anxiety. At least I hadn't permanently injured either warden, and I hadn't fed from Raze or Jasen intentionally. My seduction of them had been innocent, unlike Raze and Terran's seduction attempt of me.

They'd been horrible to me in the dream. If they had just asked me nicely, I would have gladly helped them find Al's brother. Now, I wouldn't lift a finger unless they met my demands.

I wanted my freedom. And when I had it, I'd make a fresh start. "With my power, I could get a Guardianship," I said, voicing my hope out loud.

"You're missing the big picture here, sweetie," Al said, sounding like she'd gotten the punchline of a joke I'd missed. *"You can gain all the elemental powers. Earth. Air. Fire. Water. Every time you feed, you'll grow those powers more and more until you're an arcane in each element. That combined with your arcane spirit elemental affinity will make you the most powerful motherfucker in existence."*

My heart missed a beat. "I'd be an arcane in all the elements?" There were rumors of exceedingly rare elementals that had dual arcane powers, but I'd never heard of someone having three or more. And the prophecy of the Omni—an all-powerful elemental that would save the realms from the apocalypse was just a legend.

"Shit, girl. You could start infernos with a snap, fly in the air, heal with a touch, and make crops grow. Oh, and let's not forget how you'll be able to punch a motherfucking hole between realms whenever you wanted."

My mouth fell open. It took an entire cadre of Assembly members to create a portal, but I'd be able to create one myself. That was crazy. Insane. And something the Assembly wouldn't like one bit.

The truth knocked over my hopes and dreams like a

house of cards. "The Assembly will never allow me to leave the prison, will they?"

Al said nothing for a moment. *"No. You're too powerful."*

Well, screw me sideways, to borrow words from Al. "What if I agreed to wear negators for the rest of my life?" I inspected the softly glowing cuffs on my wrists.

"Do you want me to lie?"

"No." I knew the answer deep in my bones. *Curse it.* What irony that I'd mourned having no power all my life, when the truth was, I'd had too much. Tears stung my eyes.

Al made a tsking sound. *"Don't you cry, baby girl. We don't need those paranoid, power-hungry, pitiless fucks to grant your freedom, do we?"*

I sniffed. "W-we don't?"

"Nah, my beauty. We'll free ourselves."

"Ourselves?" I asked, looking down at her soul marker.

"Well, since we're best friends and all, I thought you'd take me with you."

Before I could respond, a loud robotic voice belted, "Inmate 18734, step out of your cell."

Curse it. I'd lost track of the days. It must already be time for the cage which meant Kayla and the other wardens would inspect my cell.

I looked at my mattress in panic. That would surely be the first place the wardens would look. They'd find my things. I yanked the jewelry box and picture frame out of the straw and spun around the room. *Where can I hide these?*

"There's a loose rock in the base of the wall by the shower," Al interjected. *"The inmate in this cell before you hid his shank there?"*

His shank?

The robotic voice said again, "Inmate 18734, step out of your cell."

I ran over to the shower, dropped to my knees and felt around the rocks in the wall until I felt a wobbly one. With a little coaxing, it slipped out revealing a space wide enough for my jewelry box and the frame. *"Sorry, Al, but I'll have to put you in here for a little while too."* I couldn't risk being found with her soul marker.

She started to argue, but I opened the box and slipped her crystal inside. Already grieving the loss of my friend, I quickly pushed the rock back into place and stood just in time to see Kayla and another male warden I didn't recognize march into my cell.

Kayla scowled at me. "Inmate 18734, you failed to follow the rules."

I looked down at my feet. "I was just—"

"Doesn't matter," she snarled, interrupting me. She pulled out her remote and pressed the button.

My wrist cuffs buzzed with a slight electric current.

Her spiteful expression morphed into one of confusion. "You should be writhing in pain." She glanced at the stocky, pasty-faced warden standing by the cell door. "Gerry, you zap her."

The warden dutifully pointed his remote at me and pressed a button.

Once again, all I felt was a tickle on my wrists.

"Her negators must be malfunctioning," Gerry said, staring at my wrist cuffs. "I thought they were a strange color."

Kayla's eyes glinted with malice. "Then I guess we'll have to teach her to follow the rules the old fashion way." She pulled a black wand-shaped item from her tool belt and flicked her wrist. The device expanded into a sixteen-inch solid metal baton.

Fear skated down my spine. I raised my hands in front of me. "You don't have to use that. I'll get into the cage."

"She's cooperating, Kayla," Gerry said, his null brown gaze

crawling up and down my bare legs. "Let's let her off this time."

"Seriously?" Kayla glowered at him. "She's got you wrapped around her cunt too?"

Gerry licked his lips as his gaze undressed me. "Let's call this a first-time offense."

"Let's not," Kayla sneered. She advanced on me with her baton. "I hate bitches who think rules don't apply to them."

As she swung, I brought my arms up to protect my head.

Kayla's metal baton clanged harmlessly against one of my negators.

The redhead cursed. "You fucking bitch." She slashed at me again.

This time I didn't react quickly enough and the baton swiped across my upper arm and shoulder. I let out a cry and fell on the shower floor.

She followed me, straddling me with her baton raised and said in a low voice, "Those other inmates were supposed to kill you, bitch. Why didn't you die?"

Kayla is the one who tried to kill me? Shocked, I tried to push her off. "Why are you doing this? What did I ever do to you?"

"You stole Terran from me," she snarled.

"Terran?"

"Don't even say his name." She raised the baton again.

I was sure she would beat me unconscious, but something seemed to catch her eye.

"What's this?" Giving me a hard push, she went over to where I'd hidden my treasures. She worked the stone free and yanked out the jewelry box and picture frame. "Look at this, Gerry. Contraband."

Panicked, I reached for the jewelry box. "It's not contraband. Just a few things from my childhood. Please give them back."

"Sure," she said as she hurled the jewelry box straight at my head.

"Stop it, Kayla." Gerry stepped in front of me and my wooden box bounced off his chest.

I tried to grab it before it hit the floor, but suddenly the box and picture frame were airborne.

Kayla laughed as all the items in the box flew out and circled around the cell. One by one, the items smashed against the far wall—the picture frame, my school awards, and the snow globe followed by...

"Not that!" I screamed, shoving myself to my feet and rushing for the one thing I cared about most—the soul marker. I leaped for it, my fingers skimming the base, but a powerful current of air yanked the crystal from my grasp and hurled it against the stone.

Grief stricken, I watched it smash into a thousand pieces. "No!" Sobbing, I rushed over to the tiny shards trying to put them back together. "Al! Talk to me, Al."

There was no response.

The glowing black light was gone.

Al was gone.

Tears poured down my face as I realized I'd truly lost her. My new friend. The only one who truly understood who I was and what I could do.

Feeling as shattered as the soul marker, I collapsed on the floor. As I sobbed, I scented the faint odor of licorice. Maybe it was Al's way of saying goodbye.

"You can have this back too," snarled Kayla. She sent the jewelry box smashing down on the ground next to me.

The wooden box splintered, but I didn't mourn its loss the way I mourned Al.

"You're a monster," I cried.

"Let me show you a monster," she raised her baton over me.

I didn't bother protecting myself this time. *What's the point?*

"Stop right there." A loud male voice boomed from my cell doorway. A heavy-set, white-haired warlock, carrying a lavender and cream warg perched on his shoulder, glared at us.

Kayla's face lost color. "Head Warden. I-I can explain."

Gerry, who'd retreated to the corner of the cell, quickly tried to cover for Kayla. "The inmate refused to get into her cage, and she had contraband."

The Head Warden rubbed his bushy mustache and gave me an assessing look. "Did the inmate attack you two?"

Gerry shook his head.

The warg jumped off the Head Warden's shoulder and nosed the shattered pieces of Al's soul marker.

Kayla moistened her lips, "N-no, Head Warden but—"

"But you beat an unarmed, non-aggressive inmate?"

Kayla lifted her chin. "Her negators weren't working?"

The Head Warden made a sound of frustration. "I can't have this kind of bullshit going on in my prison. Especially with the Assembly breathing down my throat."

Gerry rubbed his hands together nervously. "I-I tried to stop Kayla, but she wouldn't listen to me."

"Is this true?" the Head Warden shouted.

The warg, seeming to pick up on its owner's anger, hissed at Kayla.

The female warden lowered her head. "I'm sorry, sir. It won't happen again."

"You're right it won't. You're terminated. Clean up this mess, turn in your badge, and pack your things. When the lockdown is lifted, you'll leave."

"But—"

"Not another word," the Head Warden boomed. "I never want to see you in my prison again."

Kayla's face went bone white. "Y-yes, sir."

The Head Warden swung his green-rimmed gaze to the male warden. "Gerry, you can expect a letter of reprimand. Now assist with clean up and get back to your duties." He scooped the warg off the ground and gently placed the small creature back on his shoulder.

Gerry moved his head up and down so fast his jowls slapped together. "Y-yes, sir."

"I'm taking this inmate to the infirmary to be checked out." The Head Warden stepped around Gerry and grabbed my arm. "Come with me, Violet Eyes?"

Jasen? The Head Warden is Jasen?

Feeling my grief turn to hope, I let him lead me out of my cell.

My heart thrashed a percussive drum circle beat against my ribs as I led my girl through the prison. I was taking the biggest risk of my life right now. Impersonating the head dick dragger while he was meeting with the Assembly off-realm was a big gamble.

But it was do or die time. Go big or go home, as my stepbrother used to say. After I sprung this fucked up chicken coop with Syd, I'd track him down along with the rest of my human family. But first I had to get my girl to safety.

As if feeling my anxiety, the Head Warden's unearthly cat-dragon creature dug its razor like claws deeper into my shoulder. I smothered my grunt of pain, happy that I'd been able to cajole it onto my back. The Head Warden rarely went anywhere without one of his pets and wearing one now made my charade more believable.

I dared a quick look back at my girl. Syd's piercing beauty dazzled me as always, but my chest tightened at the sight of her tear-stained face. *I can't believe that bitch Kayla destroyed all Syd's things.* It was my fault. I'd brought them to her not considering what would happen if they were discovered.

I'd make it up to her when we got out of here. I'd been looking for any opportunity to rescue her, but Raze and Terran, who'd taken over operations in the Head Warden's absence, had been tracking my every move like Sharp-Shinned Hawks. I swear the pains in the asses hadn't slept in days.

Finally, the fire elemental and the earth elemental had retired to their quarters, and I'd played my ace in the hole.

"Head Warden, I didn't know you were back," Rhonda said, intercepting us in the hallway.

God dammit. I glanced over the woman's linebacker shoulder. We were so close to the meeting room where I'd stashed a change of clothes for Syd. Unable to hide my irritation at the notorious busybody, I said, "I wasn't aware my itinerary was your business, Warden Clover."

She flushed. "You're right. Sorry, sir. But the comings and goings of inmates are my business." Rhonda shifted her gaze to Sydney. "Where are you taking her?"

I stiffened my spine and snorted the way the Head Warden did when he was about to blow a gasket. "Warden Clover, am I or am I not in charge of this prison?"

The warg snapped at her face.

Rhonda took a step back and blinked furiously. "Y-yes, sir."

"And are you not my subordinate?"

The oh-shit look on her face was fucking priceless. "Y-yes, sir," she stammered again.

"Then you will mind your fucking business and go back to work."

Rhonda bobbed her head. "Of course, sir."

I watched the female warden with narrowed eyes until she walked down the hall. "Cow," I muttered under my breath.

Syd let out a muffled giggle, but I didn't dare look back at her, not when I knew several cameras were on us and freedom was still a hike across the prison.

I tightened my hand around Syd's cuffed wrist and led her down the hallway past rows of visitor meeting rooms, stopping at the last one. "In here," I said, opening the door for her.

Syd stepped into the dimly lit, windowless room. I watched her inventory the only items in the space—the wide metal table, the two bolted down chairs, and a set of floor shackles. "What is this?"

"It's the only visitor room that's unmonitored, honey," I said in an apologetic voice. The Head Warden's warg jumped down as I secured the door.

"Jasen!"

At the sound of Syd's cry, I spun around just in time to catch her.

Syd threw her arms around my neck. "I'm so glad to see you."

"Just how glad?" I leaned down to kiss her, but she shied away.

"You're as old and fat as Professor Wyndham. Could you transform back?"

I laughed and morphed into my true self. This time when I leaned down again, she met my lips with her own. The feel of those soft lips parting under my teasing tongue, made me harder than Stoney Point.

She let out a small moan and pressed her perky tits flush against my chest. "I've missed you so much."

That incredible smell wafted from her. I could almost get high off it. Honeysuckle and something else. Something that brought to mind the taste of her when she was orgasming around my tongue. It fogged my mind with desire.

I grabbed her ass to lift her higher and my fingers met

bare skin. She wasn't wearing a goddamn thing under that misshapen prison tunic.

The devil made me slide my hand an inch over.

Hot, wet pussy grazed my fingers.

Fucking hell.

High octane lust slammed into me, searing away all conscious thought. I needed to touch her. Taste her. Fuck her. And if I didn't do those three things in the next five minutes, I'd combust and take her and this goddamn prison out with me.

Sydney whimpered and shifted against my fingers.

I was so far gone I hadn't even realized I'd shoved half my hand inside her.

Way to go, Carlow. Let's introduce my girl to fisting during her rescue.

I needed to back this train up big time. Summoning all my willpower, I pulled my hand away and set her down. "Sorry, honey. It's hard to control myself around you."

She looked up at me with those gorgeous violet eyes. "I don't mind. In fact, I want more of that."

My dick throbbed as she licked her swollen lips and reached for me again.

I held my hands up as if warding her away. "I want that too, but first we have to get you out of here."

"But I'm so hungry," she pleaded. It might've just been my imagination, but her irises seemed darker. And her scent was getting stronger. It filled the room and my nostrils, threatening to rob me of my last bit of self-control.

Have to fight it.

I took a deep breath through my mouth and pointed at one of the bolted down chairs. On it was a folded warden's uniform and one of the portal keys attached to a lanyard I'd swiped from the Head Warden's office.

"Change into that and then we'll head to the temple."

Since the prison was on lockdown, the temple should be empty. We could hide behind the pews until the portal opened—whenever the fuck that would be—and get the hell out of dodge during the thirty minutes it was active.

Thankfully, instead of arguing with me, Sydney moved over to the chair. "So, you want me to take this off?" She played with the hem of her tunic.

"Syd," I pleaded. We didn't have time for sexual games. As soon as I got her out of this place, I was going balls to the wall with her beautiful body, but not now.

"Okay," she said, lifting her tunic. She turned her back to me and slowly revealed every inch of her heart-shaped ass and the smooth pale skin of her back. Then she bent down to pick up the clothes on the chair with exaggerated slowness. She parted her thighs far enough that I glimpsed her plump pink folds.

The warg looked up from licking its front paw to purr at Syd's display.

I groaned, no doubt looking like one of those looney tunes characters with my jaw dropped and my tongue lolling out of my mouth. "Damn, woman." I had no idea where my chick had gotten a crash course on seducing a dude, but it was working.

Fuck was it working.

My dick felt as if it was about to hulk smash through my pants.

Keep your eye on the prize, Carlow.

I couldn't jeopardize our one chance of getting out of here for another taste of her no matter how much I ached to do that. I forced myself to turn around and face the door.

"Jasen, I need help," Syd said moments later.

I cranked my head around to find her kicking bod encased in the standard warden uniform. Well, her lower half any way.

She was struggling to put her arm through the cuff of the

tight, long-sleeve shirt. The thick metal of her negator blocked her attempts. "I can't get it through."

"Let's get your negators off." I walked over and grabbed her arm, trying hard not to admire the perfect pink color of her nipples peeking out of the shirt.

Syd yanked her arm away. "I-I don't think you should do that. I'm barely in control with them on. The hunger—it's so strong. I don't trust myself."

She couldn't put on the uniform shirt with the cuffs in the way and if she wasn't in uniform, we'd be stopped by Guardians the moment we stepped out of the portal. "You can control it." Syd could do anything. I pulled my remote from my pocket and started to press the button to unlock her cuffs.

She tried to stop me. "Jasen, no. Let's come up with another plan."

The warg, who paced around the table, let out a yowl as if agreeing with Syd.

"There is no other plan." I pressed the button. The negators fell off and hit the floor with a metallic thunk.

"I'll bet you feel better without them on." Those cuffs did a number on an elemental's strength and energy. I stuffed the remote back in my pocket and looked at her expecting to see a relieved smile.

Her eyes were closed and her breathing ragged.

The warg hissed and backed into the corner of the room.

Worry harpooned me in the gut. "Syd, what's—" The words died on my lips when she opened her eyes.

Her irises and the whites of her eyes had gone completely black. "I'm hungry," she said in a preternatural voice.

What the fuck? Her strange voice, her shark eyes, and the way she stalked toward me had me stepping behind one of the chairs.

What's going on with my girl?

"I need you." She grabbed the chair between us and ripped it out of the floor, bolts and all. Then she hurled the metal seat across the room as if it weighed nothing.

The warg howled and ducked under the table.

Holy fuck balls.

Not good. This was not good. "Syd, you're freaking me out right now."

"Hungry." She grabbed hold of the sides of my shirt and ripped it open.

Buttons went flying and pinged off the wall.

"Syd?" I didn't know what to make of her animalistic behavior. I'd never seen this side of her before.

Making a soft growling sound, she wrenched my head to the side.

I half expected her to bury her teeth into my neck, like a goddamn vampire but she only licked my pulse.

"Syd, please," I pleaded.

She started kissing down my chest. Her hot breath washed across my abs, making my stomach muscles jump.

I tried one more time to reason with her. "We can do this later, honey."

"Now." She ripped open my pants and sank to her knees. Then she wrapped her hands around my cock, and I forgot why we needed to go. *Hell.* I forgot my name.

She gave my cock one long pump and then brought me to her lips.

Fucking A.

I inhaled sharply, forgetting to breathe through my mouth. Her intoxicating scent clouded my mind as she explored me from crown to base. It was incredible.

Every lave of her tongue sent an electric shock straight to my balls. And just when I thought it couldn't get any better, she drew my full length into her mouth and sucked.

My head fell back against the wall in surrender. Unintelligible words slipped out of my mouth. *So. Fucking. Good.* I rocked against her lips, gently at first and then rougher as she took me deeper.

Fuck. My girl was deep throating me like a pro.

Shuddering and panting, I grabbed the back of her head and fed her my cock, hard and fast.

Her lush lips took every thrust. Even the light scrape of her teeth against the underside of my dick was incredible.

Pinpoints of light flashed before my eyes as I tried to hold my orgasm off.

Then she cupped my sack.

A guttural shout burst from my chest as I blew apart in her mouth.

She moaned and drank me down. Then, as if she couldn't get enough, she continued sucking.

The suction extended my buzz, making my head spin like the few times I'd smoked pot.

My knees gave out, and I collapsed to the floor.

She followed me, still sucking my dick.

It felt as if she was taking part of me into her.

"Syd, stop." My voice came as a croak. I tried to push her away, but I felt so weak.

She looked up at me with those hooded obsidian eyes and kept going.

I was dying. I knew it, but what a motherfucking way to go.

Dimly, I was aware of the door being kicked open.

Raze and Terran stalked into the room.

Terran cursed. "Look at that Raze. We thought Sydney was in danger, instead she's giving that fucker a blow job." He raised his voice. "You can stop sucking his cock now, enchantress."

Raze stepped in front of the huge earth elemental and

glared down at me. "You're a bigger fool than I first surmised, Victor, or should I say, Jasen Carlow. I figured you out, *bro*."

Syd hummed her pleasure against my flesh, each draw of her lips bringing with it a wave of dizziness.

"Sydney, stop that," Terran shouted.

I fell unconscious before I could warn them.

SYDNEY

Overwhelmed by my dark hunger, I fed. Each pull of my lips brought in more and more revitalizing energy.

As that seemingly empty tank inside the center of my chest filled, Jasen's eyes closed and his head lolled to the side.

Pleased he no longer resisted, I settled into my feast.

The warg let out a shrill sound from under the table, but I ignored it. It wasn't big enough to be tempting.

An enormous hand grabbed my shoulder and wrenched me away from Jasen.

What's this?

I twisted around to see both Raze and Terran standing in the room.

Mmm. Such gorgeous males. I slowly stood, appraising them. Their muscular chests rose and fell as if they'd been running and a sheen of sweat covered their skin. Even more mouthwatering was the invisible power that crackled in the air around them.

Terran took a step back and gave a worried look to Raze.

"What's wrong with her eyes? And what's with that amazing smell?"

"Hellfire. Her affinity has overtaken her. That fool Jasen must have taken off her negators."

The dark hunger coiled inside me, urging me to reach for them. "I need you."

A dazed expression crossed Terran's face. "You're my fated mate, I'm yours."

I sensed a magnificent font of energy simmering inside him along with his lust. It was like a drug spiking the air. "Touch me." I grabbed his hand and brought it to my breast.

He cupped it and dragged his thumb across my nipple.

Need unfurled within me. "Kiss me."

Terran hesitated for just a moment. "I will kiss you, only you." Then he brought his mouth to mine.

"No!" Raze shouted, but it was too late.

I parted Terran's lips with my tongue and inhaled. The sweet metallic flavor of his essence gushed into me, filling me with power.

"Yes," he groaned, thrusting his tongue against mine.

"Stop, Terran!" Raze shouted, trying to yank Terran away.

I broke the kiss and reached for Raze.

Raze flinched before the full impact of my gaze hit him. Then his pupils dilated, his nostrils flared, and he swayed toward me. "I forgive you, Sydney. You are my fated mate, I'm yours."

"Yes." *He, Terran, and Jasen belong to me.* I wrapped my hands around Raze's neck, my fingers tangling in his soft black hair.

He crushed his mouth to mine and kissed me hungrily as I absorbed his smoky essence.

Soon my chest felt tight with the glut of power I'd consumed, but my body still craved what these males had previously denied me.

"Pleasure me," I whispered against Raze's lips.

Terran must have heard my plea too, because he went down on his knees before me and licked my nipple.

Shuddering with want, I gasped brokenly, "Yes, more. I want both of you."

As Terran continued licking my sensitive peaks with his hot wet mouth, Raze moved behind me and began undoing the ill-fitting uniform pants I wore.

As soon as the fabric fell to my ankles, Raze slid his hands between my legs and found my center.

I threw back my head as he circled my sweet spot. *Good. So good.*

"More!" I cried.

He pulled one of my legs free of the pants and placed it around Terran's shoulder.

The action put me off balance and I fell back against Raze's chest.

The fire elemental supported me all the while he dipped his fingers inside my wet channel.

Currents of lust spark through me with every wet slide in and out of my sensitive flesh.

Raze ground the heel of his palm against my bud at the same time Terran rasped my nipple with his teeth.

"Yes," I panted, my heart racing. "Give me more."

Terran let my nipple fall out of his mouth with a pop and kissed his way down my stomach.

As if they were communicating in some inaudible language, Raze shifted his hands to my breasts and Terran brought his mouth to my core.

The wet heat of his lips and tongue was almost too much.

Raze played with my nipples as Terran thrust his tongue inside me over and over until I shuddered and thrashed between them.

"I need... I need..." I panted, unable to speak.

The males understood.

As Raze pinched both nipples, Terran sucked hard on my bud.

Letting out a wild cry, I exploded. I came so hard and fast I shook like a doll between the wardens.

I quivered with uncontrollable spasms but Raze held me firmly upright and Terran continued his erotic kiss.

Terran licked and sucked every inch of my core, while Raze worked my nipples. When Raze bit down on my neck, they drove me to orgasm a second time.

Still Terran worked his tongue over my oversensitive flesh.

I ached for more than his tongue. Gasping for breath, I pushed the huge earth elemental away.

He fell onto the floor, a few feet from Jasen's prone body.

Twisting out of Raze's grip, I sunk down, kicked off the fabric clinging to my foot, and crawled over to Terran.

The huge male groaned as I tore at his pants, freeing his huge tattooed shaft.

The thick length throbbed in my hand, pre-cum beading the tip.

Needing to taste it, I gave it one experimental lick.

Delicious. Delighting in the earthy flavor of him, I suckled.

"Yes, enchantress." He bucked on the floor, thrusting against my lips.

A hand gathered my hair and pulled my head back.

Startled, I twisted around to see Raze standing behind me. He was nude and his long, curved shaft twitched inches from my mouth.

Unable to deny him, I fastened my mouth to Raze's manhood.

His smoky flavor was equally intoxicating.

As I moved my mouth over him, Terran made a noise of frustration.

I turned my attention back to the enormous male. Seeing

his beautiful shaft glistening with my saliva made me ache for him.

"Behind me," I ordered, positioning myself on my hands and knees with my legs apart.

Moving with incredible speed for a male his size, Terran rose and aligned his shaft at my entrance. Then he eased me open and pressed inside.

I hissed at the stinging sensation. His member was massive, and I felt as if it might rend me in two.

He paused a moment, allowing my flesh to adjust to his invasion, then he pushed in a few more inches.

Waves of pleasure-pain shot through me as he pulled out slightly and thrust in further. Chasing that sensation, I arched back.

Terran let out a rough groan and gripped my hips. I could tell he was fighting the urge to slam into me.

I rewarded his self-control by rocking back, seating him fully inside.

We both moaned.

Terran moved, slowly thrusting in and out of me.

An inferno of heat built between my legs as he increased his speed.

Raze made a noise, bringing my attention to where he stood watching us. His face drew tight with lust and the crimson around his dark irises glowed.

I arched off the floor as I beckoned the fire elemental over.

Terran grabbed my breasts as my back bowed into his chest. Never did he stop the pistoning of his hips.

As Raze approached, I grabbed onto his muscular thighs for support and brought my lips to the velvet steel of his shaft.

Raze chanted my name and thrust inside my mouth.

All at once both their energies were flowing into me,

pulsing through my pelvis, thrumming down my throat in an intoxicating rush of heat. Drunk on power and passion, I moved my mouth to the rhythm of Terran's thrusts and the three of us began to dance.

Terran thrust under me. I writhed against him and worked Raze's shaft between my lips. Then Raze thrust into my mouth, driving me back down on Terran's hard rod. Again, and again.

Our pace increased. Faster and faster.

My thighs trembled, my hips rocked frantically, and my vision blurred. Passion rose higher and higher until I didn't think I could take any more, and then I was rocketed straight to the stars in a bright burst of pulsing pleasure.

Terran bellowed and emptied into me as Raze shouted my name and filled my mouth with his heat.

Seconds or hours later, we collapsed in a sweaty heap, still connected.

Completely blissed out, I lazily suckled Raze's softening shaft and moved my hips against Terran's.

Neither male stirred.

Sharp needles dug painfully into my leg.

"That's enough, cupcake. You don't want to drain them any more than that."

"AL?"

"Yes, I'm here."

Hearing my friend's husky voice broke whatever spell I'd been under. Pushing away from my wardens, I watched in fascinated shock as the lavender and cream warg climbed its way up the bare flesh of my thigh one claw at a time.

Gritting my teeth against the pain, I looked into the creature's enormous black eyes. "Al?"

The warg nuzzled my jaw. *"Thanks for the show, baby cakes. I think I orgasmed just from being in the room."*

So thrilled and relieved she was alive, I didn't care she'd watched us. Cupping her in my hands, I stroked the soft purple fluff circling her scaly head. "I thought you died?"

She snorted. *"I died a long time ago, sweetheart. But this pretty beast acted as a host after my soul marker was destroyed."* She flicked her furry tail.

Guilt weighed on me. "I'm so sorry—"

She didn't let me finish. *"I'm not blaming you, princess. Kayla is going down. Vengeance is a bitch and it bites."* She bared her tiny fangs and hissed.

Trying to soothe her, I rested my hand against her iridescent scales. "Can you jump into another host?" *Maybe one that didn't bite.*

"I'm afraid I'm stuck here until this creature dies. Although, it's a shame you didn't drain those lovers of yours back in your prison cell. As weak as they are, I could have taken one of their bodies. Just think what I could have done with that shapeshifter's abilities." She made a chuffing sound.

A feeling of horror swept over me. I twisted around to look at all three males passed out on the floor.

Each one was pale, but their pulses beat steadily at their throats and none of them looked mummified. *That's a good sign, right?*

"Will they be okay?" They had to be. *Why does this keep happening?*

Al climbed onto my shoulder and licked my face with her forked tongue. *"Stop freaking out. They will all be fine after a nap. If they aren't, you can always heal them."*

I raised my shaking hands. "I-I can heal?"

"Based on all the power I sense swirling inside you, I'd say there are a shit ton of things you can do."

That was a frightening thought. I could barely control

Raze's power and now I'd added water and earth elemental power to the mix. We'd be lucky if I didn't burn us all to death while simultaneously triggering an earthquake and a flood.

Seeming unaware of my inner turmoil, Al continued. *"But let's start by getting dressed and getting our asses out of here."*

As I glanced at the wardens, something inside me rebelled at leaving them. Raze and Terran had called me their fated mates. *Can that be true?* If so, it explained why I felt the need to stay.

"I can't leave them, Al."

Al rolled her eyes. *"You can't get attached to what you eat. It's unnatural."*

I located my tunic and dragged it over my head. "This is different. There's a bond between us. All four of us. I think we belong together."

Al shook her snout from side to side. *"You're hopeless."*

"And you're a cynic."

"Fine, just grab that lanyard over there and put it around your neck."

I looked down at the rope necklace attached to a thin shard of stone on the floor. "This?"

She bobbed her head. *"That's the portal key. We can take it to the prison temple and leave as soon as the portal activates. It's been turning on around this time each day."*

When I didn't immediately put the lanyard on, she growled, *"Girl, don't wait until those wardens wake up and lock you away again."*

They wouldn't do that. Not after pledging themselves to me. Not after our bargain. "They said they'd give me my freedom if I found your brother."

Al stiffened. *"What now?"*

"They're trying to track him down. Apparently, he's been killing things."

"Sounds like my brother." Al's voice was tinged with bitterness. *"But that's even more reason to escape the prison now. If he finds out how powerful you are—"*

The door opened and Kayla stalked into the room. "There you are."

Curse it. The redhead was the last thing we needed right now. Just the memory of how she'd nearly vanquished Al made me gnash my teeth. "Get out of here if you know what's good for you." I didn't know how to use my new powers, but I wouldn't hesitate to trial them on her.

Kayla made a tsking sound. "Such rudeness, child of night. Remember, I saved you from that fire elemental in your prison cell earlier."

What the hell is she talking about? Kayla is the one who tried to kill me.

Kayla's normally silver-rimmed eyes were pitch black as they inspected the naked males passed out on the floor. She wrinkled her nose in distaste. "I see my whore of a sister has been influencing you." She gave Al a derisive look.

Al trembled from snout to tail.

In a moment of slow horror, I realized the female warden had been possessed by Al's brother. "Who are you?"

The warden formerly known as Kayla gave me a sweeping bow. "I am Z'syron Quago eldest son of Daagan."

"Such a daddy's boy," Al groused.

Z'syron paused as if waiting for some reaction from me, but I struggled to place his name. It sounded slightly familiar.

"They called him the Nightmare of the Realms," Al whispered into my mind.

Oh, Goddess. He was that Z'syron. The monster that, along with his notorious family, had slayed thousands and started the War of the Realms. I clenched the lanyard so tightly the rope dug into the flesh of my palm.

"What do you want with me?" *And why did he possess Crazy Eyes and save me from Scar Face?*

Kayla's face stretched into a facsimile of a smile. "I want you to be my new apprentice, child of night. I'll teach you to wield your power, and together we will exact vengeance on those who imprisoned us."

Al let out a rumbling growl. *"He wants to use you as a weapon."*

Bile climbed my throat.

"I can see you are overwhelmed by my offer." Z'syron gave me an indulgent smile and reached out to touch my face.

I shuddered.

Al lunged at his arm.

Z'syron jumped away before she could bite him. "You don't seem to favor this form. I'll choose a new host. Which do you prefer?"

I blinked in confusion.

Z'syron studied my wardens. "Fire, water, or earth?"

Al's trembling increased. *"Z'syron is going to possess one of them."*

"You said possession wasn't possible unless the spirit elemental was invited."

"Or if a host was weak of mind," she reminded me.

My stomach curdled with the realization that I'd drained my males to the point of vulnerability.

Z'syron moved closer to the wardens.

"Leave them alone!" I shouted.

But it was too late. Kayla's body fell to the floor like a discarded jacket.

A moment later, Terran's eyes snapped open. Only they weren't Terran's beautiful green-rimmed eyes. They were Z'syron's obsidian eyes.

"Yes, this host is much improved," Z'syron said in Terran's

deep voice. "I might even make it permanent." He rummaged through Kayla's pant pocket and retrieved a crystal.

Al let out a hiss of air. *"That's his soul marker. If he destroys it while in possession of Terran's body, he'll possess it until death."*

Ice water sluiced through my veins. "Get out of Terran now."

Z'syron straightened to Terran's impressive height and chuckled. "Do not presume to tell your master what to do. Come. We leave this infernal place at once."

"How can I stop him?" I asked Al.

She gave me a helpless look. *"Any ideas I have would permanently harm your earth elemental's body."*

Panic gutted me. *"There has to be something he fears. Some weakness he has."*

"None." Something flickered in Al's luminous eyes. *"Unless you can summon our grandfather."* She flashed me an image of an ancient looking male.

Z'syron marched over to the door and opened it. "I grow impatient, apprentice."

He wants me. He needs my power. Out of options, I did the only thing I could think of to save Terran.

"Take me," I blurted. "You can use my body."

Al dug her claws into my neck. *"Sydney, no!"*

I yanked her from my shoulder and set her on the table. *It's the only way.*

Z'syron stared at me with an intensity that chilled me to the bone. "Are you issuing an invitation?"

"Yes," I whispered. Then, hoping I wasn't making the worst decision of my life, I let the monster in.

TERRAN

A sudden sharp pain in my head brought me to awareness.

I coughed, trying to clear a foul taste in the back of my throat while rubbing the side of my face. It throbbed as if I had slammed it against the floor.

Did I fall out of bed again?

I opened my eyes and stared into Kayla's pale face.

The female warden's eyes were closed and her breathing shallow. The sickly-sweet odor of Spark emanating from her blue-tinted lips was so strong, I was getting a contact high.

What's she doing here?

Kayla like me was lying on the floor in one of the visitor rooms. At least she, unlike me, was dressed.

As I gingerly sat upright, I realized I was naked, and so was Raze.

My friend, looking more relaxed than I'd seen him in years, was passed out next to a shaggy-haired warden I now knew to be Jasen, the shapeshifter who'd been pretending to be Victor.

Raze had pieced together his involvement when Warden

Clover mentioned running into the Head Warden in the hallway. There was no way the Head Warden would return to the prison without alerting Raze and me. And there was no way he'd go strolling through the prison with Sydney in tow. There had to be a shapeshifter masquerading as our boss and Raze remembered a student he had who was both a high-level water-elemental and very attached to Sydney.

Fucking Jasen.

I glared at Sydney's unconscious friend, wondering what we would do with him. I was okay sharing my enchantress with Raze, but that male... No way.

But what if that meant losing her? My stomach sank. *Ah, fuck. I guess I'll have to learn to deal with Jasen.*

Sydney suddenly shouted in a language I'd never heard before. I looked over at where she stood screaming at the Head Warden's warg.

Those annoying ankle biters were always causing problems. If she wanted me to lock it up, I'd gladly do it. I'd do anything for her.

My blood warmed and my cock throbbed as I remembered what we'd been doing before I passed out.

I'd taken her... or rather she'd taken me, and it had been fucking amazing. Being with her was like nothing else I'd ever experienced. Even though I knew she'd fed off my life force, I'd gladly sign up to repeat the experience. Like right fucking now.

I eyed her shapely bare legs. Maybe she and I could get in a quickie before Raze and that other male woke.

My balls tightened. I tried to stand but found my legs too rubbery to support my weight. *Fuck. Maybe I should put the negators back on her before we go for round two.* At this rate, she'd put me in a coma.

Sydney's shouting increased in volume, making my head ache even more.

"Enchantress, stop yelling at that creature and come here." I beckoned her over.

Sydney turned her head, staring at me with eyes as black as night.

Her eyes had looked like that just before she'd ordered Raze and me to pleasure her. According to Raze, It was some kind of indicator that her power was uncontrolled. Gentling my voice, I said, "I want to kiss you."

And I did. Never had I been willing to share that intimacy with a female. But Sydney was unlike all the other females I'd been with. My gaze involuntarily drifted to Kayla's unconscious body.

Comparing Sydney with Kayla was comparing the ocean to a pond. Not only did Sydney have incredible depth and courage, she'd somehow remained sweet and positive despite the shit life had dumped on her.

Even more, my enchantress woke primal needs inside me. Even now, I felt the urge to touch, soothe, and protect her. My body ached to claim her again and again. And I somehow knew that no matter how many times we came together, it would never be enough.

Sydney was my female. My fated mate. And I prayed to the Goddess she'd accept me as her consort. I knew I wouldn't be her only one, but I was okay with that. If our last encounter was any indication, it would take Raze and me, and maybe a few more males to meet her needs. As long as I was one of her chosen, I'd be happy.

Sydney's lips curled in a snarl. "I'm afraid your little enchantress is gone, earth elemental. But you and I have a score to settle, don't we?"

What the fuck?

She pointed one hand at me. "Such a pity. I would have preferred you as a host, but then, you lack the power to do this." She shot a stream of fire straight at my chest.

Instinct had me rolling out of the way, and the flames hit Kayla.

The redheaded bitch woke with a pain-filled scream. "What's happening. I'm on fire! I'm on fire!" She clumsily tried to beat back the flames.

Sydney motioned as if she would shoot another fireball, but the warg suddenly lunged at her hand. With a shrill cry, Sydney spun around and played tug of war with the small creature intent on stealing whatever she was holding.

Sydney's curses and Kayla's screams roused Raze.

My friend reacted first by scrambling over to Kayla's side and absorbing the flames into his hands.

Kayla wept in gratitude.

Sydney shook the warg. "Give me the portal key, sister, and I'll let you continue your miserable existence."

Portal key? How did Sydney get one of those?

The warg cowered but didn't release the lanyard in its jaws.

"What in the realms is going on?" Raze shouted.

I shook my head. Sydney's behavior was confusing as fuck. "She's not acting like herself. She tried to burn me."

Kayla sobbed and gingerly touched the raw, blistering flesh visible through her smoldering uniform.

I didn't enjoy seeing anyone in pain, even crazy bitches. "We need to get Kayla to a healer."

Raze nodded. "Yes, but first we have to talk some sense into Sydney."

I had a feeling it wouldn't be easy. I pushed myself to standing and helped Raze to his feet. "Enchantress, stop abusing that warg." It disturbed me the way she violently shook the small creature.

"I will attend to you shortly." She tightened her fist around the warg's throat until it released the portal key, and then she threw the animal at the wall.

The warg let out a pain-filled cry and collapsed where it fell.

The hair on the back of my nape rose as the words Edison had uttered in the crypt came back to me. *Oh, fuck. That's not Sydney.* Somehow the Soul Eater had possessed her.

"Help me!" Kayla pleaded through her sobs.

I held my finger to my lips, warning her to be silent. Then I looked to Raze.

My friend, not realizing the danger he was in, marched over to Sydney. "That's enough, Ms. Castaway."

I waved my hands, trying to warn him.

"Finally!" the Soul Eater exclaimed as it retrieved the portal key lanyard from the floor and put it around its neck.

Raze, who'd noticed my frantic movements, went still. "What?"

Just as I was mouthing back, "Z'syron," the Soul Eater spun around.

"Trying to catch me off guard? I don't think so." The Soul Eater raised its hand and unleashed a torrent of water into Raze's face.

Sputtering, Raze fell back. "Sydney stop this."

"It's not Sydney," I shouted. "It's Z'syron." And we couldn't let the Soul Eater leave the room.

Raze's eyes went wide. "No."

"Yes," the Soul Eater said, clearly enjoying Raze's expression of horror. He shot me an imperious look. "And, for the record, my name is Z'syron Quago first son of Dagaan."

I flung my hands out, and the cement floor under the Soul Eater dropped several feet. I could have brought the ceiling down on its head, but I didn't want to hurt Sydney's body. *Is she still in there? Ah, fuck.* I hoped so.

Raze lifted his hands to unleash his power and froze. I could see him wrestling with the same fear. *How do we subdue the Soul Eater without injuring Sydney?*

We can at least trap the Soul Eater. I waved my hands, and the cement reformed around the Soul Eater's feet, locking Z'syron in place.

"Fools." The Soul Eater jerked free of the concrete. "Through this host, I have affinities to earth, water, and fire." The Soul Eater shot a fireball at me.

Raze jumped between me and the flames, his body absorbing the fire.

The Soul Eater waved his hand. One of the large stones dislodged from the wall and flew at Raze.

It was my turn to step up. I disintegrated the stone with a burst of power.

The Soul Eater let out a war cry and sent a wall of freezing water at us.

Raze pushed his hands out as he tried to turn the water to steam. "Release your claim on Sydney's body."

"Never!" the Soul Eater shouted. More water exploded from his hands with enough force to send Raze and me into the metal table. "I need more power."

I did too. The encounter with Sydney had weakened me more than I wanted to admit.

Raze's strength seemed to flag too.

Kayla let out an inopportune sob.

"Yes," the Soul Eater hissed. "You'll do." It stepped over to the female warden, all the while keeping us pinned with a powerful flow of water.

"Kayla!" I tried to fight through the blasts of water hammering my body. Despite my animosity for the redhead, she was in no position to fight off the Soul Eater.

The Soul Eater wrenched Kayla's face up and started to mash their lips together.

It will drain her!

Kayla struggled and the Soul Eater backhanded her so hard Kayla's eyes rolled back and she went motionless.

The Soul Eater brought its mouth down on Kayla's.

"No!" *We have to save her.* Frustration and rage pounded through me as I tried to rally my power.

Through the onslaught of water, I saw Jasen, the male I'd all but forgotten about, slowly stand.

Jasen's eyes were the same black color as the Soul Eater's, but he shouted, "Stop hurting them!"

When the Soul Eater ignored him, Jasen morphed into an old bearded male, stooped with age. "Let them go, you sniveling bespawler."

The Soul Eater jerked around and let out a hoarse cry.

As the old bearded male reached for the Soul Eater, Z'syron dropped Kayla and bolted from the room.

Immediately, the violent flow of water ebbed and Raze and I were free.

"Thanks, Jasen," Raze said, sloshing over to the shapeshifter.

I wouldn't go as far as thanking that asshole, but I jerked my head in acknowledgment.

Jasen morphed into the body of my enchantress. "It's me, Sydney. I'm so sorry about what happened earlier. I never wanted to hurt you guys."

What the fuck? "Is this a joke?" I sure as shit hoped this was a joke.

The new Sydney shook her head, her gaze following the water dripping down my body with more interest than I was comfortable with. "Afraid not, Handsome. When Z'syron possessed my body, he shoved me out. I'm able to possess Jasen's body because he's still unconscious." She gulped in a deep breath and said, "I'm so sorry for attacking you two earlier. My power overwhelmed me."

This was some fucked up shit. I rubbed my aching head, wanting the world to make sense again.

Raze seemed to have no trouble handling it. He ran over

and hugged her tightly. "Do not for one second apologize for our time together. I'm certain I speak for Terran when I say, it was the hottest encounter of our lives."

"Fuck, yeah," I added, trying not to stare at her naked body. *Because that isn't her body and if we had sex, I'd actually be having sex with Jasen. Right?* My head hurt.

Raze searched her face. "Sydney, do you have full access to Jasen's powers?"

"I-I think so."

"Could you try to heal Warden Skye?" Raze pointed down at Kayla's pale face.

Sydney wrinkled her nose. "She's a bitch."

Isn't that the truth.

"Sydney, please," Raze urged in a firmer voice.

"All right. What do I do?"

As Raze talked her through the textbook version of healing, Sydney knelt and lay one hand on Kayla's forehead. A second later, a stream of blue light poured into the redhead.

Slowly, the raw burns on Kayla's leg healed and her color returned. Although the female warden's eyes didn't open, her breathing deepened.

"I think she'll be okay now," Sydney announced. "Did anyone see where Al... the warg went?"

I pointed at the corner of the room, where the pitiful creature lay panting in a puddle. "It doesn't look long for the world."

Sydney let out a cry and rushed over to heal the sad, wet thing.

After a solid minute of receiving healing blue energy, the warg rolled to its feet and bounded into Sydney's arms.

Sydney caught the creature and nuzzled it. "I know. I saw that. You were so brave. It's okay. We'll stop him."

"Are you communicating with it?" Raze asked, looking as confused as I felt.

Sydney nodded. "She said, we can't let Z'syron escape. He has a portal key."

"And your body," I interjected in case she'd somehow forgotten.

"Good thing the portal is closed then," Raze said with a heavy sigh.

Sydney started to say something but was interrupted by the warg jumping to the floor.

The creature immediately started dry heaving.

"What's it doing?" I shouted over the warg's gagging noises.

The warg coughed up a crystal.

"Z'syron's soul marker!" Sydney picked up the goo covered crystal and held it up for Raze and I to see. "All we have to do is force the Soul Eater back in here."

"Right." We were going to force a thousand-year-old spirit elemental in possession of my mate's body into a tiny rock. "How in all the realms are we going to do that?"

25

SYDNEY

Under Terran's and Raze's expectant looks, words failed me. *We need a plan.*

"*Can I help?*" a familiar male voice asked.

"*Jasen!*" Turning inward, I closed my eyes and sought him out.

Jasen's presence crashed into me like an ocean wave. Strong, reckless, and never faltering, his consciousness lapped at my own. "*Syd, this wasn't what I had in mind when I pictured us sharing one body.*"

I snorted. Even unconscious he was making sex jokes. That was so Jasen. "*I'm sorry for borrowing your body without permission and for draining you earlier.*"

"*Nah. It's my fault, Violet Eyes. I should have listened to you and not taken your negators off.*"

Yes, he should have, but we were long past that.

"*Besides, you can use my body any time you like.*"

His tone was full of so much innuendo, I had to stifle a groan. "*Now is not the time.*"

"*Raze and Terran ruined our escape plans, huh?*"

"That's the least of our concerns." I quickly filled him in on what had happened since he passed out. Well, the parts involving Z'syron anyway. I didn't see the need for him to know about my threesome with Raze and Terran.

"Oh, shit!" Jasen exclaimed. *"So, the demon guy has your body, a portal key, and wants to go fuck up the realms. What are we waiting for? Let's stop him!"*

His enthusiasm momentarily burned away my anxiety. *"I love you, Jasen."*

"I love you too, Syd. I'm sorry I didn't spring you from your cell sooner. I'm sorry for—"

As I shushed his apology, I became aware of Raze and Terran shouting. Neither warden seemed happy I'd stopped responding to their questions. They would have to wait though. I needed to find out where Z'syron had gone.

"You've got to wake up now and I've got to go."

Jasen called after me, but I was already moving out of his body in an incorporeal mist. It was both exhilarating and disconcerting being invisible and floating around. Especially since I could still sense everything around me.

Raze and Terran were huddled around Jasen who had reverted to his true form.

Despite the urgency of the situation, I took a second to appreciate the three gorgeous males in the room. Jasen's blond, lanky, tan body was such a contrast to Raze's darker, more compact and muscular form. And they both were dwarfed by Terran's brawny, colorfully tattooed deliciousness.

A strange feeling of possessiveness swept over me. *Mine. They are all my mates.* I didn't want to choose between them. I didn't want to give any of them up. They were all perfect for me in their own ways.

Jasen's playfulness and zest for life forced me to lighten up and pulled me from the darkness. Raze's scholarly curiosity and confidence in my abilities pushed me to think of the world in new ways and to trust in myself more than I would otherwise. And Terran's courage to confront past emotional wounds inspired me to do the same.

Somehow, I'd fallen for each of these very different males.

It took a burst of self-control to force myself to refocus on Z'syron and move away from my wardens. With my ability to fly through walls, it took me all of two seconds to find the Soul Eater. He marched my body purposefully down the hallway toward a set of double doors.

"Hey! Inmate 18734, stop right there!" Warden Clover shouted.

Z'syron twisted around, shot a fireball straight at the female warden and kept walking.

Warden Clover was engulfed in flames so fast she didn't have a chance to summon her own power. Her dying shriek of pain echoed through the hallway.

Although I wasn't a fan of Warden Clover, the callous, impartial way Z'syron murdered her, chilled me to my soul. *I have to stop him.*

Moments later, the Soul Eater blew the double-doors open and strode into what I quickly realized was the prison temple.

The empty dome-shaped room was a less ornate version of the academy temple, with rows of concrete pews and long aisles that led down to a simple wood altar. Next to the altar was a pentagram. The affinity symbols on the wooden pedestals at each point of the pentagram were inactive, and the portal in the center was mercifully dark.

He can't escape.

Z'syron let out a roar of frustration and rushed down the aisle. After shouting something that sounded like a curse, he paced around the altar.

On his third pass, Z'syron strode over to the pedestal of

fire and ignited the flame of the snuffed candle with a flick of my finger. Then he moved to the empty dish on the pedestal of water and filled it.

He's trying to open the portal himself. Filled with panic, I flew back to the room where my males were dressing and arguing with each other.

"Where the fuck is Sydney?" Terran shouted at Jasen.

I slid into the only dormant host in the room and opened my new eyes. "I'm in Kayla's body." I slowly sat up, blinking the room into focus.

All three wardens gaped at me.

Seeming to experience none of their shock, Al bounded into my lap. *"Nice going! You're jumping hosts like a boss, baby girl."*

At least I was doing something right. Cradling Al in my arm, I stood. My breath caught at the slight tenderness in my upper thigh. Well, technically, it was Kayla's upper thigh. Although, weirdly enough I didn't sense Kayla's presence anywhere inside her body. *"Kayla is not in here. Where did she go?"*

"My brother must have devoured her soul," Al answered. *"They didn't call my family Soul Eaters for nothing."*

"Ugh! That's horrible."

Al shrugged. *"The bitch had it coming."*

"Sydney?" Terran asked, peering into my face. "Is that you?"

"Yes, Handsome." I smoothed a hand down the warden uniform shirt and pants I wore. Kayla must have taken off her duty belt and her shoes before Z'syron possessed her. I looked down at her bare feet.

Terran stumbled back, looking gobsmacked. "Unfucking believable."

"Believe it. We have to get to the temple, Z'syron is trying to open the portal." I pointed in the direction I'd come.

"He doesn't have the power to do that," Raze exclaimed.

Then an expression of uncertainty crossed his face. "Does he have the power to do that?"

I had no idea. "We can't take the chance." Aside from all the lives he would take, if Z'syron left with my body, I might never get it back. I ran toward the door, nearly tripping over the set of negators on the floor. *Yes! This is what we need.*

I scooped up the metal cuffs and shook the water off them. "We need to get these on Z'syron." Once Z'syron was stripped of his powers, or rather my powers, he'd be easier to deal with. Although I had no idea how I could kick him out of my body.

"That's easy," Al purred into my mind. *"You just uninvite him. The way you did me, back in your cell."*

But I'd been inside my body at the time. *"How do I throw him out from outside my body?"*

She gave a feline-looking shrug and licked her front claw.

My stomach sank as I remembered her brother's special abilities. *"Can he mind control us?"*

She looked up. *"No. He's limited to whatever powers you possess."*

Well that was something.

Raze strode over. "Using the negators is an excellent idea, but we should have additional support." He grabbed his radio.

"No," Terran said with a shake of his head. "Don't call in backup. We don't want some trigger-happy warden accidentally blowing a hole in Sydney's head."

I cringed. Yeah, that didn't sound great.

Raze shook water out of the black device. "I don't think the radio is working anyway."

"We can handle this ourselves." Terran took a deep breath. "You, Jetson."

"It's Jasen," Jasen and I said at the same time.

"Whatever. Can you shapeshift into that old guy that scared Z'syron again?"

Jasen gave him a blank look.

Curse it. I should have shared the image of Z'syron's grandfather with Jasen when I'd had the chance.

I started to describe the elder when Jasen interrupted me.

"I can change into something so scary the demon-guy will piss himself." Jasen gave me a cocky grin before his eyes dipped down to Kayla's chest. "Is it considered cheating if I kiss you in a different body, Syd?"

Terran smacked Jasen hard on the back of the head. "Focus, Jackson."

"It's Jasen," Jasen corrected through gritted teeth. "And you'll want to increase the intensity on those." He pointed at the negators I held.

I handed the cuffs to Jasen. "You do it."

"Okay, you take this then." Jasen handed me Z'syron's soul marker.

Feeling as if I'd just been given a bomb, I carefully slipped the crystal into Kayla's pocket. The last thing I wanted to do was break Z'syron's soul marker and lock him into my body forever.

As Jasen fiddled with the settings of the negators, Terran strode over to the door and opened it. "Our best chance of apprehending the Soul Eater is by using my favorite element."

"What's that?" I asked.

"The element of surprise."

I let out a choked laugh while Jasen rolled his eyes.

"That's lame, bro."

Terran scowled at Jasen. "You and Raze will use the main entrance and distract the Soul Eater, while Ka—Sydney and I will enter the temple using the secret entrance, sneak up on the creature, and cuff it."

"What secret entrance?" Raze asked, looking a little surprised at how Terran was taking charge.

Terran waved away his question. "Don't worry about it. Your job is to draw the Soul Eater's attention."

"We can do that," Jasen said, handing the negators back to me and kissing my cheek. "You take care of my girl."

Terran scowled. "Sydney is my—"

A sudden, invigorating burst of power flashed through the room. All four of us staggered and then righted ourselves.

"The portal! Z'syron must have opened it," Raze shouted.

No sooner did the words leave his mouth than the influx of energy was sucked away, leaving us all gulping for air.

"It closed," Jasen announced, giving me a relieved look. "He didn't have time to leave."

"We may not be so lucky next time. We have to make sure the Soul Eater doesn't open the portal again." Terran motioned Raze and Jasen out the door. "Get to the temple."

As the water and fire elemental took off running down the hallway, Terran snagged my free arm and dragged Al and me in the opposite direction.

I dug in my heels. "But the temple is that way."

"Secret entrance, remember." Terran pointed to our left.

There was the faint outline of a door in the wall. I never would have noticed it if Terran hadn't brought it to my attention.

Terran waved his hand, and the door scraped open. "Come on."

As I followed him into a dark passage, lights flickered on overhead.

"They're on sensors," Terran explained. He led me through a long corridor and then down flight of dusty stairs.

Al sunk her claws into my shoulder. *"Sydney, you can't let my brother leave in possession of your powers. He'll destroy everyone in the realms."*

"I won't let that happen," I promised, biting back a gasp of pain. *"Can you ease up on the claws though?"*

"Sorry, cupcake." Al loosened her grip. *"I'm still pissed Z'syron tried to murder me again."*

Again? Sounded like some really screwed up family dynamics. Maybe it wasn't such a bad thing that I never knew my family.

Terran stopped at a doorway at the base of the stairs. "This leads straight out to the temple altar." He gave me a worried look. "You should wait here."

"Don't be ridiculous." I was the only one who could rip Z'syron out of my body. *Assuming I could figure out how.*

"Please," Terran pleaded, his fingers tightening on my hand. "I don't want you getting hurt."

Al purred in my arms. *"Aw! I think the big guy has feelings for you."*

Ignoring her, I rose up on my toes and brushed my lips against Terran's.

He flinched.

Remembering his aversion to kissing, I started to apologize.

Surprising me, he crushed his mouth against mine and kissed me with a desperate passion that made my head spin.

"I can't lose you, enchantress," he murmured against my lips.

"This is so damn sweet, my teeth are rotting," Al interjected. She opened her snout wide enough to show us her fangs.

I lightly tapped her head. "Shush. I'm having a moment with a male I love."

A wide smile spread across Terran's face. "You love—"

A loud crash and a monstrous roar outside the door broke us apart.

It had to be Raze and Jasen. They were doing their part, now we needed to do ours.

"Stay behind me," Terran ordered, slowly opening the door.

We exited onto the first floor of the temple a few yards from the wooden altar where Z'syron stood in my body.

"That cocky fuck needs to be put down," Al growled as she crawled up my shoulder.

Z'syron's attention was on the other temple doorway where Raze stood next to a creature so monstrous, it took my breath away.

"What the fuck is that?" Terran said, pulling me down to a crouch.

The massive humanoid-insect looking thing could only be a Xenomorph from Jasen's favorite movie.

"The Alien Queen," I whispered.

"Awesome," Al said, tasting the air with her forked tongue.

Jasen flicked a long, blade-tipped tail and gnashed a double set of terrifying jaws. Then he let out a hair-raising roar and rushed toward Z'syron.

Instead of cowering in fear like any sane elemental, Z'syron merely laughed. "Is that the best you can do?" He flung out a hand.

Jasen fell to his knees, morphing from alien back to his true form. A steady stream of iridescent blue light poured from the center of Jasen's chest into Z'syron's mouth.

"He's feeding," Al said, a tremor rippling down her spine.

"How? You said we had to suck from the body..."

Terran motioned me to be quiet.

Al gave me a bleak look. *"My family—the Quagos—can feed from a distance. Z'syron had that power. You apparently have that power too."*

Stunned and sickened, I rocked back on my heels.

"Stop!" Raze shouted as he hurled a volley of fireballs at Z'syron.

Z'syron absorbed the fire with a wide smile. Then he waved his hand.

Raze's face twisted into an expression of shocked horror as he collapsed, and his life force poured into Z'syron's gaping mouth.

Oh, Goddess. He's draining both of them.

26

SYDNEY

The glowing connection between Z'syron and Jasen grew dimmer as if Jasen's life force was waning.

"We have to do something!"

Al bumped her snout against my chin in agreement.

"Stay here," Terran ordered in a hushed voice. He pulled negators from his duty belt and ran up behind Z'syron. Just before he was about to snap the cuffs around Z'syron's arm, the Soul Eater spun around.

"Join us," Z'syron hissed.

Terran flew back into the altar as if struck by lightning. Then pulses of green light surged from Terran straight into Z'syron.

"Yes!" Z'syron shouted, stretching his arms out. His body, my old body, thrummed with so much power, it glowed.

What chance did I have going up against that by myself?

Al put one claw-tipped paw on my face. *"The moment he's focused on me, you get those cuffs on him."*

"No, wait!" He'd destroy her tiny body with one wave of his hand. I tried to grab the warg, but she bounded off my shoulder and zipped across the pentagram toward her brother.

So focused on gorging himself on the wardens, Z'syron didn't take notice of Al until she chomped his bare ankle.

Z'syron shouted in pain and tried to kick her off.

Al bit down harder.

With Z'syron's concentration broken, the otherworldly connections between him and the wardens snapped.

All three wardens stumbled forward looking dazed.

Z'syron bent down and forcibly ripped Al off his leg.

This is my shot. Summoning my courage, I took a deep breath and ran at the Soul Eater.

When I was but a hairsbreadth away, he shouted, "Die, pest." Then he wrenched Al's head around.

"No!"

The sound of her small bones crunching, and the sight of Al's limp body being thrown into the center of the pentagram filled me with a rage more intense than any I'd ever experienced. Shrieking, I lunged at Z'syron, trying to snap one cuff on his wrist.

Z'syron spun around and knocked the restraints out of my hand.

I turned to go after them, but he grabbed me with a preternaturally strong grip and held my face up to his.

"Get out of my body," I screamed.

He chuckled. "It's my body now. Your power is mine. And your soul will be too." Z'syron roughly grabbed the back of my head and fused our lips together.

There was a painful tugging sensation in my chest. *He's feeding from me.*

I struggled against him, trying to remember what Al had instructed me to do. There was too much pain. An intense lethargy hit me along with the sensation that my essence was unraveling. My legs gave out. My eyelids fluttered shut. *It's over.*

Someone called my name. I couldn't tell if it was Terran, Raze, or Jasen, but it gave me one last burst of strength.

Remembering Al's words, I telepathically screamed, *"Get out, Z'syron. Your invitation is revoked."* At the same time, I barreled out of Kayla's body into my own.

I felt Z'syron's shock and denial as my spirit dislodged him and flung him out.

In a dizzying moment of disorientation, I settled back inside my own body and opened my eyes to see Kayla's face in front of mine.

Z'syron's obsidian eyes stared out at me from her face. They were filled with shock and outrage.

Before he could even consider jumping into one of my weakened mates, I yanked his soul marker from Kayla's pocket and smashed it on the floor.

"No!" Z'syron shouted as the crystal shattered.

"You're stuck in there," I informed him with a grin. The Soul Eater thought he could defeat me. *I'll show him.* A black storm of power whipped inside me, filling me with the urge to feed.

I wrenched Z'syron closer to my face. "I'll devour you."

A weak fireball hit my shoulder.

As my skin hungrily absorbed the flames, I lifted my head to see Raze stumbling toward me. *I'll also take him.*

Motion in the aisle brought my gaze to Jasen, who used a pew to push himself to standing.

And him.

And him, too. I swung my gaze at Terran. The large male rolled off the altar and onto his feet. "Let her go!" he shouted, his green-rimmed eyes flashing. He waved and a hunk of concrete broke off a pew and hurled at my head.

Dropping Z'syron, I flung my hands, disintegrating the rock and wrenching the life force out of all four of them.

Waves of intoxicating energy pulsed through me as I fed from their power. The taste was sublime. The smoky sting of fire. The cool balm of water. The rich tang of earth. The sharp ozone of air. And something else. Something dark and sweet.

Immense power crackled around me, invigorating every cell in my body. My hair flew around my head like a curtain of billowing purple silk. My skin glowed a pearlescent white. Crying out in bliss, I rose several feet off the temple floor. I was flying!

More. I need more!

I wrenched more energy from them.

The gaping darkness deep inside me shuddered in plea-sure. It'd been starving for an eternity, and it urged me to feed deeper. *Take more. Take everything.*

My mates howled in agony, but Z'syron bowed before me. "You are the true darkness, child of night. You're our legacy. You'll be our vengeance."

Oh, I'd be that and so much more.

Z'syron's eyes rolled back and he collapsed.

Still I fed. Rejoicing in the influx of power and life.

A wispy sigh sounded in my ear and I smelled licorice.

Al?

Coming to my senses, I crashed down. The moment my feet hit the floor, the soul sucking connections with the wardens snapped.

Grief and shock backhanded me as I sensed the state of my pale, motionless wardens.

They're dying.

How could I have murdered the males I loved? Hysteria choked me.

A cool breeze whipped across my face.

It had to be Al. And she was trying to tell me something. *But what?* "What do I do?" I cried.

The cool draft of air ruffled my hair before slowly dissipating.

As terror and guilt tore at me, I realized Al could have possessed any one of my mates in their weakened state. Instead she was choosing to fade away. When she left, I'd lose her insight, her friendship, and whatever she was trying to tell me right now.

I needed her.

Clenching my hands into fists, I shut my eyes and whispered, "Al, I invite you in."

Nothing happened. *Is it too late?*

My next breath was filled with her sharp, sweet, licorice flavor. I fought through the drowning sensation and then her presence was inside me.

"Reverse the flow," she shouted.

"What?"

"Push the life force back to your wardens as if you were healing them. I saw my father do it to my mother once. Just visualize it."

I lifted my hands and imagined transferring power and life back into Raze, Jasen, and Terran. As I visualized healing my mates, a long glowing connection snapped between the center of my chest and theirs.

Closing my eyes, I pushed my life force at them. I sensed them growing stronger with each breath, but I didn't know if it was reality or wishful thinking.

"That's it!" Al exclaimed. *"Look, it's working!"*

I opened my eyes to see my wardens' color and strength returning. Slowly the three males stirred and opened their eyes.

"Sydney?" Raze called out to me.

I nodded, relief making me dizzy.

"Oh, thank fuck," Terran said from the base of the altar. As he slowly stood, the connections between us faded away.

Al chortled. *"Congratulations, cupcake. You did it!"*

"We did it," I corrected.

"I guess we make a good team, huh?"

We really did. *"It's a good thing since we're stuck together until death."* My death anyway.

"Normally," Al replied. *"But given the way you threw my brother out of your body, I think you could eject my ass with no problems."*

"Really?"

"Go ahead, princess. I'm ready for the sweet hereafter."

But I wasn't ready. I needed her. *"What if you didn't go? What if you stayed?"*

"In your body?"

"Yes." It freaked me out to consider what I was offering her, but it freaked me out more to think of my life without Al in it.

"And what, we'd share your bod fifty-fifty?"

I coughed. *"No. But maybe we could arrange for a dance or two while we find you another body."*

"For real?" she squealed.

Before I could reply, Terran rushed over and crushed me against his chest. His earthy scent surrounded me, filling me with the sense of belonging.

Then Terran quickly pulled away. "How do I know this isn't some trick? Prove you are Sydney."

"I still think you're pretty," I said without tearing my gaze from his green-rimmed eyes.

Terran let out a whoop and kissed me full on the mouth. He jumped when my hand drifted between his legs.

"Al!" I yanked my hand back, my face flaming.

"Sorry," she said, not sounding sorry at all.

We would need to establish some ground rules.

"I suppose you won't let me have play time with these sexy hunks either."

Most definitely not.

Jasen flew at Terran and me, wrapping his long arms around us. "Syd, thank God you're back."

Terran pushed him away. "Wait your turn, Jameson."

"It's Jasen, big guy." Jasen pulled me out of Terran's arms and kissed me senseless.

When he finally released my lips, I rested my head against his chest so thankful and relieved to have my best friend with me.

"I thought we were best friends," Al groused.

I felt a familiar thrum of power at my back. I pulled away from Jasen to see Raze standing behind me.

Never had I seen my former professor look more disheveled. His long hair was tangled around his face and his uniform shirt hung open exposing his hairy chest.

Al approved. *"He looks like a sexy pirate."*

I couldn't tear my gaze from Raze's rippling muscles. Heat moved low in my body and my hunger flared back to life.

As the dark need clouded my mind, Al gave me a mental bitch slap. *"You just healed them, sweetheart. Give it some time before you feed."*

She's right. I blinked and the hunger dissipated.

Raze smiled at me. "You saved us all, Miss Castaway. Thank you."

I stepped away from Jasen and walked over to Raze. "I'm so sorry for attacking you. Repeatedly. You were right to fear me."

Emotion flared in the fire elemental's crimson-rimmed eyes. He reached out and cupped my chin. "I could never fear my fated mate."

"Fated mate?" I echoed incredulously.

"We're meant to be together. Can't you feel it?"

I did, but I also felt that sense of completion with Jasen and Terran too. *What did that mean?*

As if reading my mind, Raze pressed his lips against mine and said, "Terran is your fated mate too."

"So am I," declared Jasen with a fierce expression on his face.

"Pipe down, Johnson," Terran said through gritted teeth.

Jasen flipped him off. "For the last goddamn time. It's Jasen."

"We're all going to have to share," Raze said in his professor voice.

I swallowed hard. *Can I really be with three males?*

"Hell yeah, girlfriend." Al was quick to provide me with visuals that made my mouth dry and my heartbeat quicken.

I looked between the wardens. "And you are all okay with this?"

Raze and Terran nodded quickly.

Jasen reached over to grab my hand. "I may not like it. But if we are a package deal, then I'll take you however I can get you."

I interwove his fingers with mine. "Would I need to stay here, in the prison?"

Terran tensed. "You want to leave?"

Jasen rolled his eyes. "Of course she wants to leave."

"I fulfilled my end of the bargain," I reminded Terran. "The Soul Eater is trapped inside Kayla." I motioned toward Kayla's unconscious body.

The three wardens turned to stare at her.

Terran broke from the group and peered down at the redhead. "She's still alive." There was no emotion in his voice, but I wondered if he still cared for his ex.

"Kayla is gone. Z'syron... ate her soul." I didn't know how else to explain it.

Terran clenched his jaw. "Fuck." He grabbed the negators

off the floor and put them on Z'syron. "We'll keep him locked up until the Assembly decides what to do with him."

"They'll stick him back in his coffin with a new soul marker. The bastard will starve to death a second time." Al sounded not the slightest bit disturbed by her brother's fate.

I shuddered, not wanting to think about the suffering the Soul Eater would endure.

Raze cleared his throat. "Sydney, I'm not sure you leaving the prison is the best idea."

My chest grew tight. "So, you want me to go back to my cell?"

"Fuck that," Al snarled. *"As soon as that portal opens again, we're blowing this joint as hard as you blew that shapeshifter."*

"No way!" Jasen exclaimed.

"Fuck no," Terran shouted.

Raze shook his head. "Absolutely not. You can stay in my room—"

"Syd will stay with me, bro," Jasen interrupted, pulling my hand into his chest.

"She'll share my quarters," Terran boomed.

Raze put up his hand. "Sydney can stay with whoever she chooses whenever she chooses."

I couldn't resist a sarcastic, "Thanks." I yanked my hand from Jasen who looked at me with contrition in his blue-rimmed eyes.

"Syd, I didn't mean to—"

Raze interrupted Jasen, "Sydney, I am merely suggesting you remain here until we get a handle on your powers. We don't want a repeat of what happened here on a larger scale." He motioned around the temple.

My anger dissipated. *Raze is right.* As long as I lacked control of my power, I was a danger to others.

"Don't worry, sweetness, I'll help you with that," Al said in a soothing voice.

"Each of us can teach you about the powers you've... gleaned from us. Moreover, I believe the burial chamber holds the key to understanding and controlling your spirit elemental power."

A spark of excitement lit inside me. "Really?"

"Most assuredly," Raze said with a smile that weakened my knees.

"Let's save the graveyard visits for another day." Jasen slung his arm around my shoulder. "Syd needs to rest."

"I think we all do," I added, noting the fatigue in the wardens' faces. "Also, I could go for a meal that in no way resembles the horrible loaves I've had to eat."

Jasen glared at Raze and Terran who shared guilty looks.

"We're sorry about putting you in tier four and I swear we'll make it up to you," Raze said in an apologetic voice.

"You'll have the best food from now on," added Terran.

"And warm showers?" I said with a mock glare.

Terran took my free hand and kissed it. "The hottest showers you've ever had."

My breath caught as a frisson of lust curled in my belly.

"Sign mama up for that," Al said gleefully. *"This will be more fun than I've had in a thousand years."*

I didn't know about a thousand years, but it would be more fun than I'd had in my short lifetime.

Terran unceremoniously tossed the unconscious Z'syron over his shoulder as Jasen, Raze, and I started walking up the aisle.

Terran glanced behind us and paused. "We should probably get the warg carcass in case the Head Warden comes back."

Oh no! The warg! I couldn't believe I'd completely forgotten about the poor creature. "I'll get it."

"She was a good host. Maybe we could bury her in the crypt," Al suggested.

"Good idea." I broke away from the wardens and bolted back down the aisle. I'd just bent down to retrieve the warg's body in the center of the pentagram when a loud hum sounded, and a blinding light appeared all around me.

The wardens shouted my name in warning, but it was too late. The floor underneath me transformed into a swirling pool of energy that swept me away.

27

RAZE

The bone-weary fatigue I'd been experiencing evaporated when the portal opened and Sydney disappeared.

My momentary shock gave way to confusion. *Where did she go?*

"Syd!" Jasen called, charging down the aisle toward the portal.

Hellfire. The male would die if he crossed into the pentagram without a portal key.

"We have to stop him," I shouted to Terran.

My friend dumped the still unconscious Soul Eater on the floor and together we ran after Jasen.

Terran's long strides ate up the distance between him and the smaller male. He grabbed Jasen's arm before the water elemental reached the five-pointed star on the floor.

Jasen fought his grip with the same desperate panic I felt myself. "I need to go after Syd."

I caught up to the two males. "Do you have a portal key?"

Jasen shook his head. "Syd had the key around her neck…"

Thank the Elders for that. I didn't want to consider what

would have happened if the portal had opened and she hadn't been wearing the key. I reached down and pulled the portal key I always carried out of my pocket.

Jasen's eyes fixed on the lanyard. "Give it to me."

Terran yanked the male back. "Slow down, kid. We all want to go after her."

And we all could. I put the portal key lanyard around my neck. "Take my hands," I instructed the two other wardens.

Sydney could not have gone far. This portal led directly to one of the off-realm junctions. No doubt one of the portal Guardians there had already detained her. A purple-haired witch in prison garb would have immediately grabbed their attention.

Jasen grabbed my hand, but Terran hesitated.

"If you and I both go, who'll be in charge at the prison and who will ensure the Soul Eater is taken into custody?"

Trust Terran to think of the best interests of the prison at a time like this. However, it was a fair point.

"I'll stay," Terran declared. The harsh set of his jaw told me how much it cost him to make that call. "Just bring our mate back."

"Are you sure?"

"Stop this bullshit, we need to go after Syd now," Jasen exclaimed.

"That won't be necessary," an all too familiar voice announced.

I jerked my head toward the center of the pentagram where my personal nightmare appeared holding a gold-handled cane.

Father's silver robes swirled around his ankles as he stepped out of the glowing energy pool. His crimson-rimmed eyes zeroed in on me. "Ian, you look a disgrace."

I bristled at the censure in his gaze, all the while fighting the urge to button my shirt. *Screw how I look.* I wasn't the little boy who cared about pleasing him anymore.

Father moved his sharp gaze to my friend. "Lead Warden Lander. A pleasure."

Terran bowed his head.

The respectful gesture no doubt stroked my father's inflated ego and accounted for the curl of his lips.

"Do you know where Sydney is?" Jasen demanded.

Father's smile turned to a sneer. "I do, not that it is a concern of yours half-breed."

Jasen didn't react to the insult. "Everything about her is a concern of mine."

"And mine," Terran echoed, his gaze still on the floor.

"And mine," I added, mystified that my father would have any interest in my mate. "We need to bring her back here."

"The witch will not be returning." My father strode over to me. The tap of his cane on the floor brought to mind all the childhood beatings.

Forcing myself to meet his eye as he approached, I said, "Sydney belongs with us."

"Don't tell me you're smitten with the witch?"

When I didn't respond, my father threw his head back and laughed. "If she turned your head, she's far more powerful than I credited."

"Where is she?"

His tone took a hard edge. "That is Assembly business. Your business is cleaning up this mess." He motioned at the Soul Eater still lying in the aisle. "We want that thing sealed inside the burial chamber immediately."

Terran lifted his gaze. "Archwarlock Razell, can't we please see Sydney?"

Father gave the earth elemental a measured look. "No. You best forget her. I can assure you she's forgotten all about you."

Jasen bared his teeth. "What did you do to her?"

"We wiped her memory of all this." Father waved his stick around the room.

"Why?" I blurted out before I could stop myself.

Father gave me a thin-lipped smile. "That's my Ian. Always curious. Always trying to figure out the mysteries in the realms. Well this is one mystery you will not solve. Suffice to say, you've all played an integral role in this test."

"Test?" Jasen exclaimed. "This was some fucking test?"

My father ignored him. "And you all will be justly rewarded." He tapped me on the shoulder with his cane. "The Assembly is making you the new Head Warden of the prison." He cocked his head to the side as if awaiting my gratitude.

I frowned. "What happened to the previous Head Warden?"

"He's taken another appointment." Father's eyes narrowed. "Aren't you happy to be promoted? Running the Lost Soul's Penitentiary is quite a step up for a null."

I formed a ball of fire in my palm and lifted it in front of his smug face. "I'm not a null anymore."

Father blinked, clearly surprised. "This is a most welcome turn of events. You didn't lose the family legacy after all." I could see the machinations brewing in his eyes. "We can make you Headmaster at one of the academies. What about the Academy of Mystic Arts? You'll like that, won't you? Instructing young minds and reading all the dusty old books you can get your hands on."

The offer made my heart race. Becoming Headmaster had been my life-long dream. I'd be getting back what I lost and more.

Taking my stunned silence as acceptance, Father looked over at Terran. "We'll make *you* Head Warden."

Terran made a sound of surprise.

Father nodded, seeming to warm to the idea. "You'll no doubt be a credit to this place like your father before you."

Terran swayed for a moment. I feared he might fall over, but he caught himself.

Jasen crossed his arms and glared at my father. "What about me? How are you going to buy me off?"

The water elemental was right. That's exactly what the Assembly was trying to do. They wanted our cooperation and our silence. *Why? What did they want with Sydney?* It had to be very important if they were desperate enough to make us these offers.

Father wrinkled his nose and curled his upper lip as if he had a bad taste in his mouth. "You're being offered a Guardianship in San Diego. Additionally, the Assembly will allow you contact with your human family."

Jasen blinked, a dazed expression on his face. "But relationships with humans go against elemental law."

Father chuckled. "The Assembly makes the laws. We can break them." He brushed one hand down his robe and straighten his spine. "However, tragedy could just as easily befall your family if you were to refuse my offer." His warning hung heavy in the air.

Jasen paled. "I wouldn't want that."

"Then we are in accord." Father turned toward the portal. "You and Ian need to follow me."

Neither Jasen nor I moved.

"No." My love for Sydney could not be bought with reinstatements and promotions.

Something dark flashed in Father's eyes. "Warlocks, let me make something clear. The Assembly will do whatever it takes to sweep this under the rug. Whatever it takes..." There was no mistaking the threat.

Either we went along with this or we didn't live to see another day. And we had to survive, for Sydney's sake. Whatever the Assembly was planning for her couldn't be good. She needed us. Which was why I had to let go of my old dream for a new one.

I forced a smile. "Of course, Father. However, I would prefer to stay on as Deputy Warden and assist Terran in his leadership transition."

All three males gave me incredulous looks, but I dug in my heels. Not only could Terran use my help here, but the burial chamber held untold secrets. Those secrets could help Sydney learn to control her power and escape the tyrannical grip of the Assembly.

The skin around Father's eyes pinched together the way it always did when he was disappointed in me. "Power is everything, son."

No, it wasn't. It'd taken a beautiful, caring witch to teach me it was love, not power or the pursuit of knowledge, that mattered more than anything else. But my father, the warlock who'd arranged my birth via a surrogate because he abhorred romantic entanglements of any kind, would never understand that.

Biting back my sharp retort, I played along. "Perhaps when things are settled here, I could have a raincheck on the headmaster position."

Father's shoulders relaxed. "I'm sure that can be arranged. We'll be in touch." Dismissing me, Father motioned Jasen to followed him into the portal. "Come half-breed, we have dallied long enough."

Jasen gave Terran and me a defeated look. I reached out and clasped his hand. "Farewell, Mr. Carlow." While the water elemental weakly pumped my hand, I pulled him closer and whispered, "We'll formulate a plan tonight."

Jasen stumbled back, his brows knit in confusion. It would be clearer to him later when I cast the dream spell bringing the three of us and Sydney together. Then we could all figure out our next steps.

Terran caught on and gave Jasen a conspiratorial wink. However, when Jasen reached out to shake the big male's hand, Terran crossed his arms over his chest. "Fuck off, Jasen."

Jasen gave a ghost of a smile. "You finally got my name right, bro."

"Don't let it go to your head, *bro*."

My Father thumped his cane on the floor. "Half-breed!"

Jasen hurried over to his side and together they stepped through the portal.

When they'd disappeared from view, Terran slung his arm around my shoulder and hugged me.

"What's this?" I said, pushing free of his giant arms.

A flash of emotion shone in his eyes. "You didn't leave me." The tremor in his voice cut me to the quick.

"No, old friend, and your enchantress didn't either. The Assembly took her."

Terran clenched his hands into fists. "But we'll get her back."

"Or die trying," I added with a tight smile.

"Or die trying," he echoed.

❧ 28 ❧

SYDNEY

The sound of singing roused me. I inhaled the scent of lilacs as I slowly peeled my eyes open.

Caregiver Novah, dressed in her soft pink robes, sat on a wooden chair next to my cot, brushing my hair.

I did a quick scan of the wood beam ceiling and rows of cots. *Why am I in the academy infirmary? Did I get sick or something?*

"Novah?" I croaked.

Her brown eyes went wide and she dropped the brush.

It clattered on the wood floor.

Instead of picking it up, she grabbed my hand. "Sydney? Are you really awake?"

I slowly nodded, being careful not to shake my throbbing head too much. It felt as if one wrong move might crack open my skull.

Tears gathered in Novah's eyes and she kissed my forehead. "It's a miracle." She turned and shouted, "She's awake. Healer Rivers, Sydney is awake!"

The dark-haired and notoriously gruff academy healer rushed over.

As the healer listened to my pulse, I tried to reboot my mind. "What happened?" And what was that terrible moth-ball-like taste in my mouth?

Novah chewed her bottom lip. "Do you remember falling during the testing ceremony?"

"Oh, yes." My face heated. *How embarrassing.* "Is everyone talking about what happened?" Instinctively, my hand went to the necklace I was wearing. The gemstone was back in the center of my star pendant. Novah must've repaired it for me. I'd have to watch that it didn't get loose and fall out again.

Novah looked at the healer. "Do I tell her now?"

My blood pressure spiked. "Tell me what?" *Am I paralyzed or something?* I looked down at my bare feet sticking out from under the white sheet and wiggled my toes. *Nope, not paralyzed.*

The healer nodded. "It'd be best."

Novah took a deep breath. "Sydney, dear. You've been gone... You've been in a coma for the better part of two years."

My heart skipped a beat. "What?" *Two years. Did she really say two years?*

"I... we... didn't think you were ever going to come back." She let out a sob.

The healer averted her eyes. "Sydney's vitals are fine. I'll notify the headmistress."

"Thank you," Novah choked out as she left.

I squeezed Novah's hand. "I'm okay. Really. Don't cry. It's okay."

Novah tried to blink back her tears. "You're right. Every thing will be okay now." She leaned down and hugged me.

I closed my eyes, savoring the embrace. It'd been forever since I'd felt love like this.

"No, it hasn't," a strange female voice whispered inside my mind.

I jumped. "Who said that?"

Novah pulled away. "Said what, dear?"

I did another scan of the empty infirmary. "I-I thought I heard someone else talking."

Novah pursed her lips. "We'll tell the healer about it. You hit your head hard on one of the temple pedestals. She said there might be some complications, but you should make a complete recovery in time."

"Right." A fragment of a memory teased me and for a moment I saw an unfamiliar temple in my mind along with the faces of three males. I couldn't immediately place the ruggedly handsome male with close-cropped brown hair, but I recognized Professor Razell and Jasen.

I sat up. "Is Jasen here?"

"No. Sorry, dear. He's a Guardian now."

"Yes, I remember," I said in a small voice. He'd probably completely forgotten about me by now.

The husky voice in my mind scoffed. *"Fat chance. That shapeshifter is wild about you."*

I let out a cry and cradled my head in my hands. *Oh Goddess. Am I losing my mind?*

"Be quiet. I want to listen to more of the sweet lady's lies."

"Stop talking!" I ordered the voice in my head.

Mistaking my distress, Novah patted my hand. "There's no need to be upset, dear."

"Certainly not," an icy voice interjected. "This is cause for celebration."

Novah and I turned to see the headmistress sweep into the room in her dark chocolate robes.

As usual, the headmistress's silver hair was pulled back into a severe bun and her top lip curled as if she found something distasteful. Probably me.

I shivered as her frosty aura dropped the temperature of the room.

The headmistress moved to the end of my cot and studied me with the intensity of a raptor eyeing their prey. "How do you feel, child?"

Unsettled by her interest, I blurted the first thing that came to mind. "Confused."

"That's to be expected under the circumstances." She turned to Novah. "What does she recall?"

My caregiver, who'd jumped to attention when the headmistress appeared, rubbed her hands together anxiously. "N-nothing, headmistress. Just falling and hitting her head at the testing ceremony."

"Good. Very good." The headmistress swung her pale blue-rimmed eyes back to me. "Rest up, Ms. Castaway. When you feel restored, we'll start preparing you for your new assignment."

Disappointment settled inside me. "I'll be a caregiver, right?" Maybe it wouldn't be all bad. Novah seemed to enjoy her role. And I'd only need to remain at the academy until Logan and I became consorts. Assuming he hadn't taken a consort in the two years I'd been unconscious.

Before I could ask Novah about my sworn, the headmistress laughed.

"No, child. The Assembly has assigned you a Guardianship."

"What?" All the breath seemed to leave my body. "But the testing stones…" None of the stones had responded to my touch.

The headmistress smiled. "You triggered all four stones, child. Fire affinity level six, water affinity level five, earth affinity level four, and air affinity level four. You are the first omni elemental in the history of the academy and perhaps all the realms."

I gasped for breath. This couldn't be happening. I couldn't go from having no affinity to having all four affinities. *Can I?* I looked down at my hand. "Omnis don't exist."

The headmistress's smile widened. "Apparently, they do now. The Assembly is eager to make use of your abilities. So, rest up." She gave Novah a sharp look. "Keep me updated on her recovery."

Novah bowed. "Of course, headmistress."

Giving me one last appraising look, the headmistress left the room.

"Novah, is it true? Am I really an Omni?"

My caregiver didn't meet my gaze. "I don't think I've ever seen the headmistress this happy." I could hear the pain in her voice.

"But you're not happy?"

Novah blinked away her tears. "I'll miss you, dear." She forced a smile. "But Saguaro Valley is only a portal or two away. We can still visit."

"Saguaro Valley?" For some reason, the name of the place tugged at my mind.

"You've been assigned as Guardian to the temple there. I believe there's a sizable coven in the area."

"That's amazing." I'd have to learn everything I could about the place.

"I'll be your tour guide."

"Ah!" That voice again. I rubbed my temples.

Novah's forehead furrowed. "There, there, dear. I know we've thrown a lot at you. Why don't you rest some?"

"That might be a good idea." I lay back down.

Novah pulled the sheet over me, tucking me in as if I were a child. "I'll have some food waiting for you when you wake."

As my eyes fluttered closed, I mumbled, "No loaves."

"Loaves of what, dear?"

But I was already sinking into the state between wakefulness and sleep. As I tumbled further and further into the darkness of my mind, I discovered I wasn't alone.

"Who are you?" I said to the incredibly beautiful, barely clothed female.

The strange female's ruby lips quirked up. "I'm Al, your best friend and copilot. We have a lot of catching up to do, cupcake..."

Sydney's adventure continues in:
CLAIMING HER CONSORTS

A witch... Her warlocks... And some smoking hot shifters...

As a Temple Guardian, I'm charged with protecting the local coven and the portal to the other realms. Seems simple enough, right?

Wrong.

The other Guardians are too afraid of my power to let me do my duties and the thousand-year-old succubus I share my body with is only interested in getting horizontal, vertical, and diagonal with anyone we meet.

I'm ready to throw in the towel on this job and arrange for a freaking exorcism when the apocalypse hits.

Now the only thing that matters is saving the coven from annihilation. Thank the Goddess I'll have help from some sexy warlocks and shifters. If we can keep my inner succubus in check, we might be able to save the world. If we can't, death will be the least of our worries...

ABOUT THE AUTHOR

Dia wanted to be a writer from the time she could hold a pencil. A lover of paranormal romance, reverse harem, science fiction, urban fantasy, and horror, she writes action-packed stories featuring kick-butt heroines and the alpha male heroes who fall for them.

If you want to be notified when the next book in the series releases please sign up for my newsletter on my website.

https://diacole.com/

EXCERPT FROM CLAIMING HER MATES: BOOK ONE

❧ I ❧

HAVANA

"What do you want for Christmas, you naughty girl?" asked the middle-aged man leering at me. The light from the dusty chandelier reflected off the gold band on his left hand, temporarily blinding me.

He probably told his wife he was working late. Ugh. Years of playing my seductive role prevented me from curling my lip in disdain. Instead, I continued undulating to the beat of the dance music being piped into the small red velvet VIP room.

"Come on, you can tell me," the man insisted, stroking his Santa-like white beard.

I should've been coy with my answer, but the truth sprang from my lips before I could bite back the words. "Someone to share it with."

The man blinked up at me with blood-shot eyes.

Great, Vana, why don't you just kill the mood? Trying to salvage the moment, I tossed back my hip-length black hair and winked playfully. "Is that someone you?" With a practiced flick of my fingers, I slowly removed my silver-studded black top and tossed it to the man.

He tried to catch it and missed. The tiny scrap of material

slithered to the blood-red carpet as he fixed his gaze on my swaying bare breasts.

"Have you been a bad boy this year?"

"Y-yes," he stammered. His eyes glazed over as he swayed in his seat.

He must be trashed. Good. A drunk and his money are soon parted. Throwing club rules out the window, I stepped down from the small raised platform I was dancing on and approached his chair. "Then you need to be punished."

"Yes, Mistress Robin," he gasped. Unlike most of the club patrons intrigued by my dominatrix persona, this one seemed truly snared by the fantasy. For the right price, I was happy to indulge him.

I cast a furtive glance at the camera nestled at the base of the chandelier. In the past, Max, the club owner, might've skinned me alive if he'd caught me doing a little extra on the side. Now he'd only ask for a percentage.

Times were tough for everyone. Strip clubs included. Case in point, this guy managed to secure a private dance from me for a mere seventy bucks, something that would've been unheard of before the canine flu hit this past spring. But global pandemics had a way of changing things.

I leaned over the man, my nipples grazing his rumpled tweed vest. "It'll cost you."

"I have money." He reached into his olive dress pants pocket and pulled out a worn leather wallet with trembling hands. "How much?"

I arched an eyebrow. "How much do you have?"

He opened his wallet and out fluttered several receipts.

Sadly, it looked like he had only a handful of twenties, but it was better than going home broke. "That works," I purred. I wouldn't have sex with him, of course, but men like him weren't after that anyway. Years ago, my mom explained some men get off as much on pain and humiliation as they did pleasure. Ah, the joys of having a stripper mom. While other kids were learning how to ride bikes, Mom was giving me crash courses in the various ways to seduce men. Big surprise I ended up at the same club where she used to work.

The man swallowed hard, sweat dripping off him as if he was in a sauna. "Take it all." He pushed his wallet at me.

I found myself staring at a family photo. Gathered in the arms of a heavyset woman were three young children. I couldn't help glancing between the professor and the photo. *Why isn't he home with them?* Hell, if I'd had kids there's no way I wouldn't be with them right now. With a pang, I remembered the big amber eyes of the little girl I'd used to nanny for. *I miss Mira so much...*

Her father's handsome face flashed in my mind and my throat tightened. It'd been three months since Nathan shattered my heart, but the pain was still fresh. Trying to put my ex out of my mind, I flipped past the photo and found the twenties. Mentally tallying the money, I pulled out the folded bills and slid them into the top of my thigh-high stiletto boot. A genuine smile tugged at the corner of my lips, it was a better haul than I'd anticipated. "Take off your clothes, Dr. Sullivan."

He gaped at me for a moment.

I tossed his wallet back at him not bothering to explain that I'd seen his Southern Arizona University ID badge inside. "I said, take off your clothes. Now."

He jumped to his feet. "Yes, Mistress Robin." He gazed up at me adoringly.

My five-foot-ten height plus my seven-inch stilettos ensured I towered over nearly everyone I encountered, including the professor.

He fumbled with the top buttons of his oxford shirt before realizing he needed to remove his vest first.

"Fold your clothes and place them over there," I

instructed, pointing at the side table that in better days held ice buckets filled with Cristal. Now a bottle of drugstore champagne swam in a plastic tub of melted ice.

He practically tore off his vest and shirt. As he unbuckled his belt, he turned to face me. "I've never done this before."

I made a noncommittal noise. *Right. That's what they all say.* Finally noticing his bare torso, I inhaled sharply. *What the hell?* Black veins covered the man's flabby arms and a portion of his silver-haired chest. I'd seen some strange-looking tattoos over the years, but nothing like that. Unable to help myself, I asked, "What's going on there?"

The man looked down and paled. "My God. Those weren't there this morning." He gave me a frantic look as if I had the answers.

I backed up a step studying his bloodshot eyes, pale skin, and sweaty face with new eyes. *He's not just drunk.* "You're sick." And that meant I needed to get as far away from him as possible. I'd never heard of the canine flu causing dark veins like that, but you don't mess around with a bug that killed a quarter of the world's population.

He raised his hands. "I'm not. I just got the canine flu vaccine yesterday," he said, mentioning the coveted shots the CDC had just rolled out. "I-I don't feel so good." His knees buckled, and he fell back into his chair.

Shit. "I'll get help." *Max will know what to do.* I turned to grab the curtain.

"No. My wife. She can't find out…" he gasped sliding to the floor.

Damn. If the guy passed out in my VIP room, I'd never hear the end of it from the other girls. Especially Jess. That nasty redhead would love to get one over on me. She'd been downright venomous since I reported one of her stupid pranks to Max. *Who the hell coats the stage steps with baby oil? Seriously.* I'd taken a nasty fall and probably fractured my spine, not that I could afford to get my aching back looked at by a doctor.

"Please, don't call Sharon," the professor wheezed bringing my focus back to him.

"No one will call your wife. Just relax. I'll be right back." I bent down, retrieved my top and tied it back on.

He nodded, flashing me a relieved look.

I blinked. *Are more of his veins darkening?* Shuddering, I pushed through the heavy velvet curtain door and rushed down a long hallway back into the main club. Immediately I was assaulted by the smell of liquor, cigarette smoke, and the twang of the latest hit country single. On the stage, the new girl, Jade, twirled around the pole in a cowboy hat and crotchless chaps. *Poor girl,* I thought with a stab of sympathy. Max had wanted me to cover Jess's country set after she was a no-show for the second time this week, but I'd talked him into having the new girl do it. Good experience and all. Seeing her dance to a sea of empty tables filled me with guilt. No one even watched. Sly, one of the regulars, was already passed out and the group of dark-haired men sitting in the back of the club ignored her.

As if feeling my gaze, one of the heavily tattooed men looked up at me. He gave me a once-over and flashed me a dazzling set of gold teeth. The long-haired man sitting next to him followed his friend's gaze and leered at me with a predatory intensity that made me glad for the knife hidden in my boot. A girl couldn't be too careful these days.

I bit back a shiver of fear as the long-haired man beckoned me over. Their gang, the Calaveras, was one of the deadliest in Arizona and I needed their kind of attention like I needed an engineering degree. Ignoring the men and their menacing vibe, I scanned the rest of the near empty club for Max.

He was at the bar, eyes glued to the television along with

Donna, the cocktail waitress, and Justin, the gray-haired bartender who looked like he'd been a defensive lineman back in the day. I'd always wondered why he had a television at his bar. *I mean who comes to a strip club to watch TV?*

Donna looked up as I approached. "Honey, you need to see this. There's some freaky shit going down." She ran a hand through her bleach blond hair, knocking aside the felt Santa hat she was wearing.

I shook my head. "Tell me about it. I got a guy covered in black veins about to pass out in the VIP room."

"What?" Max jerked his bald head up so fast his jowls shook.

"We might need to call an ambulance." I waited for Max to make an obscene joke, but instead a panicked expression crossed his face.

"You said his veins were black?"

I nodded.

Donna let out a gasp. "The news reporter said to watch out for people with dark veins. Some folks are having bad reactions to the canine flu vaccine. They're getting sick and..." she lowered her voice, "turning into cannibals."

I gave her an incredulous look. "What?"

"See for yourself." She waved at the television hanging above a tower of colorful liquor bottles.

On the screen a flustered news reporter was babbling. "Reports of violent behavior in some of the recently vaccinated are coming in from all across the country."

The program cut to a clip of dazed-looking people in hospital gowns attacking a young man on the street. The jerky footage must've been taken on someone's cell phone. Whoever was holding the phone kept repeating, "Holy shit," over and over while the crowd literally tore the screaming man to pieces.

My stomach churned as I watched the deranged crowd

gulp down handfuls of the man's flesh. "That's horrible. I can't believe they showed that on television."

Donna shook her head. "It's not just happening here. It's happening all over the world. They rushed the flu vaccine to market without doing the proper tests and now it's turning people into monsters. Oh, God. And just an hour ago I was cursing the fact that they didn't have the vaccine available for Gavin." She let out a sob at the mention of her son who'd died of the flu earlier in the year.

"Don't cry, muffin," Max said in a gruff voice. He slung one beefy arm around Donna's thin shoulder and gave me a hard look. "Get that sick guy out of here. Now." He used his don't-argue-with-me voice.

That tone hadn't worked on me since I'd been ten. "But Max—"

He interrupted me. "I'll call him a cab. You get him in it. We're closing early tonight. Donna, go get Sly up. I'll tell Mr. Diaz and his men that they need to leave." He looked over at the dark-haired men in back and shuddered. "Let's hope they don't kill me," he muttered under his breath as he headed over to their table.

I'd take the sick professor over throwing deadly gang members out of the club any day. As I turned to walk back to the VIP area, Donna called my name softly.

I spun around to see that the older woman wore an anxious expression on her face.

She smoothed an invisible wrinkle from her short black skirt. "Honey, I'm sorry but Max and I won't be able to make your Christmas Eve dinner."

"Oh," I said, trying not to let my disappointment show. *You and everyone else.* "That's too bad."

"We're sorry to miss it, it's just that with everything going on..." She waved weakly at the television set. "And it's our first Christmas without Gavin." Her voice hitched.

"I understand." I reached over and hugged her. I missed that kid something fierce. Pushing the memory of the mischievous little boy out of my mind before I started tearing up too, I looked over at Justin. "You and Sam are still coming, right?"

The big guy shook his head. "Sorry, sweetheart. Sam just wants to do a family thing this year." He gave me an apologetic smile.

Family thing. Right. "Well, more turkey for me," I said, hiding my misery with a smile. "Have a good night."

Donna and Justin waved as I headed back toward the professor. My chest tightened. Bad enough that the anniversary of my mother's death was Christmas Eve. Now I'd have to endure it alone.

The wail of country music faded as I moved past the stage and through the long, deserted hallway. I stopped at the closed velvet curtain to the room where I'd left the professor. A low moaning sound came from inside. "Dr. Sullivan?" I reached out to pull open the curtain and hesitated. I'd never realized how far from the main club this area was. *What if the professor is sick like the people on TV? What if he attacks me?*

HAVANA

A large hand clamped down on my shoulder.

A shriek lodged in my throat as I spun around and came face-to-face with two tall, muscular men.

The shorter man, if you could call a man over six feet short, offered me a dazzling, panty-dropping smile. "Sorry to startle you, love."

The man's sexy English accent paired with tousled blond hair and ocean-blue eyes had me returning his smile and flipping back my hair. "No harm, no foul. How can I help you?"

The other man stepped forward. His six-foot-four height put me at eye level with the black eye patch over his right eye. The patch combined with his five o'clock shadow and collar-length hair gave him a definite bad-boy vibe that made my blood hum.

"We're here for you," tall dark and handsome said in a deep voice.

Holy hotness. I'll stay after hours for these guys. I licked my lips feeling my hormones wake for the first time in months. "If you want to step into a room—" I gestured to the open rooms down the hall "—I'll be right there."

Tall dark and handsome frowned. "You misunderstand. Havana, you need to come with us right now."

The sound of my real name had me staring at the two men in shocked silence for half a second. "Do I know you?" *Have I danced for them before? No.* I'd definitely remember men this good-looking.

The clean-shaven blond, who looked like a *GQ* model, shook his head. He wore khakis and a blue polo shirt under his jacket, which matched the stunning hue of his eyes perfectly. "I'm Mason Wheeler and he's Gabriel Perez."

I looked over at the dark-haired man whose black clothing and golden complexion almost made me mistake him for one of the Calaveras. But there was no way I would've missed his eye patch and smoldering good looks among the gang members.

Why are they here for me? There was only one plausible explanation. "Are you guys cops?"

The two men exchanged a look.

Fucking A. And I didn't think my night could get any worse. My stomach sank and my mind raced as I tried to think of a reason the cops would want to talk to me. "Is this about the Strip Club Killer?" My throat tightened as I remembered how close I'd come to joining his victims.

"No," Gabriel said.

Okay. Then what? "Look, I pay my taxes." Maybe I didn't always report every tip, but enough.

Mason's sinfully full lips quirked up. "This isn't about your taxes."

Damn, these were the sexiest cops I'd ever seen. I almost wanted them to arrest me. *Maybe this is about the internet stuff?* I folded my arms over my chest. "Last time I checked being a cam girl wasn't illegal and—"

Gabriel cleared his throat interrupting me. "Enough. We're running out of time." He stepped forward and stared into my eyes. "Ms. James, come with us now." His voice rang with a strange tone.

Rubbing my temple where my head suddenly ached, I said, "Don't I have a right to an attorney and a phone call?"

Gabriel's mouth fell open as if I'd shocked him.

"Mistress Robin," the professor wheezed from the VIP room. "I think I need to see a doctor."

Gabriel stepped by me, slid open the curtain, and cursed. "It's one of the infected."

I peered around his muscular shoulder and found the professor slumped on the floor with his shirt in his lap. There were even more dark veins running across his chest. "Can you get your shirt on, Dr. Sullivan?" I asked with a calmness I didn't feel. "Max is calling you a cab. You can take it straight to the hospital. We can call an ambulance if you want…"

"No. A cab is fine. Thank you." The professor slowly pulled on his shirt with shaking hands. In that moment, he looked old and frail.

Feeling sorry for the man, I reached into the top of my boot and pulled out his money. "You can have this back since we didn't—"

"Move away from him," Gabriel said, grabbing my arm. "He's infected with the virus."

"The virus?" I echoed. *Is he talking about the canine flu?*

"Keep the money," the professor said with a wan smile. "It can be a holiday advance. I'll come back and collect my… punishment when I'm feeling better."

"Thank you," I replied, not knowing what else to say.

Gabriel tugged my elbow. "Come on. This way." He pulled me toward the main part of the club.

I caught a whiff of his scent—smoke and leather. The dark masculine smell made my insides tighten.

Mason fell into step beside us. "We're parked out front."

Sandwiched between the two hot men, my knees weakened. *Maybe I can ask them to handcuff me?* I quickly bitch slapped my libido. *Get a grip, Vana.* It figured the first men I'd be attracted to since my breakup with Nathan would be cops wanting to question me.

We'd almost passed the side stairs to the dressing room when I remembered my things. I stopped short, dragging Gabriel back a step. "I need to change." No way was I going to walk into a police station in my dance outfit. Besides, I didn't want to leave the rest of my money here where it could grow legs and walk out of my locker before my next shift.

Mason let go of my arm. "Okay."

Gabriel frowned. "We don't have time—"

"Couldn't we spare her a minute?" Mason asked, inter-rupting the taller man.

I beamed at the blond, deciding I liked him more than his gruff partner.

Gabriel gritted his teeth and nodded. "Just one minute."

Relieved, I rushed up the stairs. When the men tried to follow me, I held out my hand to stop them. "You can't come back here." Max was the only guy allowed in the dressing room and it was only because he barreled his way in like a bull whenever he felt like it.

"Hurry," Gabriel ordered, looking down at his watch.

Wondering what crawled up his butt and died, I headed backstage and made a beeline for the empty dressing room.

It wasn't much, just a row of vanity mirrors and a bank of lockers. I went straight to my locker and pulled out the duffel bag that held my purse, makeup, toiletries, spare dance outfits, the wad of ones I'd milked out of the professor earlier in the night, and most important, the bottle of pain pills my back would soon be begging for. I quickly chewed the pills and dry swallowed down their bitter taste.

After throwing a skintight black dress over my skimpy dance outfit, I shrugged into my long charcoal wool jacket.

My aching feet pleaded with me to ditch my boots, but I'd neglected to bring other shoes.

My cell rang as I was closing my locker door. I answered it to the shriek of my roommate, Sydney.

"I can't believe you talked me into this, Vana!"

"What?" I drew a blank for a moment before remembering she was covering a private party for me. "Are you at that bachelor's party?"

"I'm hiding in a freaking stranger's closet wearing nothing but a thong and some pasties."

I couldn't help laughing. "There are worse ways of making two hundred bucks."

"You know how I hate dark, cramped spaces. I owe you big-time for this."

"Yeah, like twenty percent," I reminded her. Thinking of how little I'd made tonight, I sighed. *Serves me right for ditching that job in favor of Max's request to work late tonight.* Family before work, I would've reminded myself if he and Donna hadn't just bowed out of the one event I asked them to attend all year.

"It smells like mothballs in here," Sydney said, returning my focus to our phone call. "This has to be the worst night ever."

"At least you don't have two cops waiting to take you down to the station."

She gasped. "What? Why?"

"I don't know."

"Crap, girl. Are you in trouble? Do you need me to blow this gig? I could—"

"No, you stay in that closet," I said with a tight laugh. "You need the money. *We* need the money. Besides, they aren't arresting me." *At least right now.* I looked down at my bag, unzipped it, and reluctantly put the pain pills back in my locker. Back pain or no back pain, I couldn't afford to get busted with illegal meds. "And they're the hottest cops you've ever seen."

"Hot enough to make you forget about that asshole Nathan?"

Not this again. I rolled my eyes already anticipating the lecture.

Syd took a deep breath. "I know he was rich as Midas and gorgeous as hell, but Nathan was also a cheating son of a bitch. It's been three months since you two broke up. Time to get back in the saddle."

"Right," I said, agreeing to end the conversation. There was no point in me trying to explain heartbreak to someone who'd never been in love.

"You need to promise me you'll give the next guy who goes after you a chance."

"And what if the next guy is Phil?"

She laughed. "Okay, obviously not our pervy neighbor. But you know what I mean."

Knowing she could be as tenacious as a Gila monster when she set her mind to something, I sighed. "I promise. Look, I've got to go, but I'll text you when I figure out what's going on."

"Okay. I'm heading right to the airport for my red-eye after this, but I'll call you as soon as I land."

"Have a safe flight," I said feeling a stab of envy that she had parents and siblings to share the holidays with. It seemed everyone had a family, but me.

Jade walked through the dressing room door just as I hung up the phone. "Heading out?" she asked with a sniff. Her heavily kohled eyes swam with tears.

Now, she's definitely having a worse night than us. "Are you okay?" I didn't know much about the green-haired woman other than she'd started last night.

She pressed her trembling lips together and shook her head.

Damn. I'd been there before. Setting down my bag, I walked over to her side and put my hand on her shoulder. "It's not always like this you know. There are good nights and bad nights." *Just more bad nights lately.* "Things will pick up after the holidays." *I hope.*

Her expression crumbled. "I didn't make jack tonight."

Anxiety ate at me as I glanced at the empty doorway. I'd already made the cops wait far longer than a minute. Torn between the need to comfort the girl and the need not to piss off the officers who might hold my fate in their hands, I chewed my lower lip.

Jade let out a loud sob.

Screw it. The cops can wait. I led Jade to the nearest swivel chair. She sat, her chest heaving. "I'm sorry. I'm such a mess." She swiped a hand across her face, smearing her makeup. "I never thought it'd come to this. Me taking off my clothes for money. And when I finally get desperate enough to do it, I don't make a fucking cent." Tears trekked down her face. She was an ugly-crier, something that made me like her even more.

"It'll be okay," I said squeezing her shoulder. Desperation drove a lot of girls to dancing. Me included.

Jade let out a heavy sigh. "I thought for sure I'd make some good money. I'm so broke I can't even pay the sitter."

"You have kids?" I asked, grabbing a tissue from the counter and handing it to her.

She gave me a watery smile. "Payton just turned two."

My chest tightened. I was a sucker for little ones. Forbidding me from seeing Mira had to be one of the cruelest things Nathan could have done after breaking up with me.

I gave Jade a once-over. She was pretty in that girl-next-door kind of way. With the right makeup and outfit she'd kill it. "Look, how about I give you some pointers tomorrow night?"

Her raccoon eyes widened as she studied my face. "Seriously?"

"Until then, take this." I fished out two twenties and gave them to her.

Her eyes widened and then narrowed. "For real?" Like most of us, she'd probably been kicked around by life to the point she had a hard time believing that anyone would do something nice for no reason.

"Yeah, consider it a welcome-to-the-club present. I was new once too, and I barely made anything my first night," I said, lying. "I'm Havana, by the way." I held out my hand to her.

She shook it. "Melody."

"Nice to meet you, Melody. Now don't waste any more tears on this shithole. Go home and enjoy your baby."

She smiled for the first time. "I will."

I walked back over to my bag and slung the strap over my shoulder. As I walked through the doorway, I stopped and said, "Hey, if you and Payton aren't doing anything Christmas Eve you're welcome to come to my place. I cook a mean turkey with all the sides."

She blinked up at me. "Thanks, but we're going to my sister's."

Of course. It was destined to be me and me alone this Christmas. "Well, I'd better not keep those cops waiting any longer. See you tomorrow assuming they don't throw me in jail."

She blinked. "You mean the pirate-looking guy and the hot blond that came in a little while ago?"

"Yeah."

"They aren't cops."

I whirled around. "What do you mean?"

She dabbed her eye with the tissue. "My stepdad was a sergeant with SVPD before he died. If there is one thing I know, it's law enforcement and those guys aren't it. Not by a long shot."

My stomach dropped to the floor as I looked toward the side stairs. *If Mason and Gabriel weren't cops, who were they? And what did they want with me?*

DID YOU ENJOY THIS PREVIEW OF CLAIMING HER MATES: BOOK ONE?

You can find it available here: http://mybook.to/ClaimingHerMates

Please don't forget to leave a review if you enjoyed this work!

Thank you for reading!